my daughter's wedding

GRETEL KILLEEN

my daughter's wedding

hachette
AUSTRALIA

hachette
AUSTRALIA

Published in Australia and New Zealand in 2021
by Hachette Australia
(an imprint of Hachette Australia Pty Limited)
Level 17, 207 Kent Street, Sydney NSW 2000
www.hachette.com.au

10 9 8 7 6 5 4 3 2 1

A catalogue record for this
book is available from the
National Library of Australia

ISBN: 9780 7336 4488 7

Cover design by Christabella Designs
Cover image by Gretel Killeen
Typeset in Baskerville by Kirby Jones
Printed and bound in Australia by McPherson's Printing Group

The paper this book is printed on is certified against the
Forest Stewardship Council® Standards. McPherson's Printing
Group holds FSC® chain of custody certification SA-COC-005379.
FSC® promotes environmentally responsible, socially beneficial
and economically viable management of the world's forests.

For the greatest loves of my life

In my Apartment

March 23
My Living Room
1.07 AM

Dear Diary,

Hello, do you remember me? My name is Nora Fawn.

You were given to me when I was a twenty-six-year-old mum of four-year-old Joy and a brand new baby called Hope. You might not recognise me nowadays. I looked much prettier then. Ageing makes us all look like we've melted.

I was married in those days too. To Leonard. We lived in the burbs, in a solid brick house with a bindi-pocked lawn that was more stimulating to walk on than the suburb was to live in. I secretly wanted to be an artist.

I found an injured bird on that lawn once. I used to love finding injured birds. I liked talking to them and singing to them and protecting them until they healed. Well, usually the birds healed. But that bird I found on the lawn didn't. Leonard threw it out with our dinner scraps when I fell asleep reading to our Joy. The next morning he told me he'd thrown the bird out after it died. But I knew that wasn't true. I remembered I'd heard it calling when I woke in the night. It must have been calling from inside the bin. I still feel bad that I ignored it, but in my defence, in my half-awake daze, I thought the chirping was Leonard trying to seduce me.

Anyway, you probably never saw that lawn or that house, Dear Diary, because shortly after my friend Thilma gifted you to me, you got lost in the hospital laundry pile full of bloodied towels and pads and surgical gowns and then brought home in a plastic bag, with just a smudge of transparent red mucus on your top right-hand corner. After that my mother hid you in the garage in case the sight of you made me too sad. Turns out she was right. I found you in a bucket several years later and you did make me sad, but I still moved you safely to my Treasure Box.

Thilma, my independently wealthy/unemployed bird's-nest-haired friend, made you herself. So basically you're two exercise books sticky-taped together, with pink tissue paper stuck on the cover, and the words 'Baby's First Diary' written in dripping blue glitter-glue on the front. Thilma is one of those people who believes that anyone can be creative, and at the same time completely disproves it.

I love Thilma but I find it hard to show it. I find it hard to show my love for my other best friend, Soula, too. In fact I don't express my love for anyone very well. I had a therapist once who told me that I resent both loving and being loved because it makes me feel vulnerable. This comment also made me feel vulnerable, so I stopped going to the therapist. I can't afford to have strangers tell me my faults. I have children, that's their job.

When Hope was born, Soula, a 'semi-professional' bikini line waxer, gave my newborn daughter a voucher for 'a day of pampering' at the local beauty spa. I remember my mother,

Daphne, said, 'What a stupid present to give to a sick baby,' and then re-gifted the voucher to herself.

Anyway. I'm sorry I haven't written in you before this moment, Dear Diary. I guess I've just been very busy for the past twenty-five years.

These days I'm a fifty-ish-year-old single mother of two adult daughters, Hope is aged twenty-five and Joy is twenty-nine. In dim lighting I still look like my twenty-nine-year-old self, but just a really, really tired version of her. Yes, I look like a younger me who's been completely deflated of air, energy, spirit, soul and optimism and yet I somehow weigh the same, if not more. But even if I do weigh exactly the same, the weight has relocated from my face and my boobs to my bum. But not in a Kim Kardashian hourglass way, more like a reticulated python who's swallowed a hippo, which is currently stuck in its colon.

I guess I should probably thank God that nowadays I'm invisible. When I was young I wasn't particularly good looking, marginally above average apparently – my eldest brother's best friend gave me a six out of ten, but now I'm probably a five, if not less. My hair is wiry and styled in a 'just stuck a fork in a power socket' bob. I dye my hair once a month and in between, when the grey roots come through, I colour them in with a Sharpie.

I'd do anything for someone to pay me attention now. Or just show some sign that they can see me at all – you know, in an elevator or a supermarket or when I'm crossing the street, just so I don't get run over.

Not only has my face sagged with time but my boobs have also slid, drooped, flopped in a bizarre imitation of my attitude to life.

Come to think of it my neck has sagged as well, as have both my knees, the top of my arms and the arches in my feet. Oh, and my eyesight is also going. This makes me feel vulnerable, foolish and old, like I'm living way past my use-by date. I'm at the stage now where I can't even see what I'm writing in a text message, so ever crafty Thilma suggested I write my message in longhand, take a photo, and then text that.

Soula and Thilma say your fifties are the best time of life because you really don't give a fuck about anything. Neither of them actually needs to verbalise their belief in this philosophy because you can tell straight away just by looking at them. Soula, who is my best friend from school, dresses as if she's auditioning for the part of 'slutty cougar' on *The Jerry Springer Show*. And Thilma, who we found in our taxi in the late 1980s, is in her early sixties and dresses like a dreamcatcher.

Soula and Thilma don't speak as kindly of my dress sense. I think I dress for comfort. Thilma says I dress like a walnut.

Soula says I dress like I want to repel men. And you know what? She's kind of right. But this has nothing to do with avoiding sex; I just don't want to get my heart smashed again. My heart is already like an old worn vase that's been broken so many times it's more craft glue than ceramic. I fear that even one more very slight jolt will cause it to crash from the mantle and only be remembered as that unsightly stain that can't be removed from the carpet.

So, anyway, I'm no longer young, nor brave, nor good looking and I no longer live in the barren burbs. Instead, I live in the inner city now. I've lived here for many years, working as an executive assistant to a fabulously successful contemporary artist called

Eduardo, who dresses like a pimp from the seventies and whose most famous work is a self-portrait sculpture in which his head is a prune that looks more like a testicle. To be fair, it's actually pretty accurate.

Contemporary art, as it turns out, is the easiest industry in which to be fabulously successful if you have no real talent. It also helps if you have an internationally famous opera-singing father, a WBD clientele (Wealthy But Dumb), and the name Eduardo (which makes people think you're both Italian and artistic even though you're actually named after your mother's favourite vibrator).

Anyway it's really quite amazing I found you, Dear Diary. I was looking for my second daughter's birth certificate and there you were, still in my Treasure Box along with all the things I've kept from the day Hope was born – my hospital wristband, her hospital wristband, and some photos of her father looking like he was the one on pain-killing drugs.

I'm sorry for neglecting you for all these years, Dear Diary. If you'd been given to me after the birth of my first daughter, Joy, who was born 'perfect', then I would have started writing in you straight away. I would have celebrated with you and filled you, and perhaps many more diaries, with heartfelt poems of my dreams for her future mingled with assorted glued keepsakes: her first fingernail clipping, a locket of her hair and the 'parking fine' four-year-old perfect Joy gave to herself (after realising she'd inadvertently left her scooter in the driveway).

But you were given to me to celebrate my *second* daughter's birth and, as it turned out, her arrival was not a celebration. Hope was born three months early in Aisle 9 at our local Woolies under circumstances that were so humiliating I've been forced to shop at Coles ever since.

Hope was also born with lung problems that left her on the brink of death for the first six months of her life. I was with her at the hospital, throughout that six months, night and day. I woke and slept sitting upright in a chair next to the humidicrib, with my hand poked through a hole in its hard plastic side. I stroked Hope's tiny tummy and talked to her and sang to her and protected her, just like she was an injured baby bird.

I told her all my secrets too. I wonder if she remembers them. I wonder if that's why she's so angry with me now. Yes, Hope's been angry with me for a long time. She's avoided all contact with me for four years. But I don't know why.

What does she have to be angry about?

When Hope was a baby Leonard, my husband, only 'popped' in to the hospital to tell me I 'should get some rest', and I've *never* been angry about that. In fact years later he told me he couldn't stay for longer or visit more often because 'that horrible place wasn't easy to cope with' and no one paid him any attention once he got there so 'it really wasn't worth the effort'. And I'm not even still angry about *that*!

My mother with her two best friends, Vera and Babs, looked after little Joy night and day so she wouldn't be neglected while I was at the hospital. And neither Joy nor my mother nor my mother's friends have *ever* been angry about that.

So what is Hope angry about? And why is she angry with *me*?

I used to wonder what Leonard was doing when he'd finished work for the day, yet wasn't with us at the hospital, and wasn't helping Mum with Joy. This question was answered when he moved out on the day I brought Hope home. He said he'd waited until then 'out of respect for the situation' and then he moved in with some woman that afternoon. I guess she must have been what he was 'doing'. She had a big apartment and no children and an uncanny understanding of family law and business structures that allowed Leonard to take me to the cleaners when he divorced me. Coincidentally he left her too, as soon as our divorce came through.

We've never actually talked about that. But I guess that's why I haven't written in you, Dear Diary. I've been too busy swallowing life's hippos *and* all the elephants in the room.

So why am I writing in you now? I will explain, but I just need to lie down for a minute first. It's been a very big night and it's been extra exhausting trying to write coherently while I'm still a bit drunk.

5 hours later
6.41 AM

Dear Diary,

OK, I'm sober now and I'm lying on the lower level of the kitchen. Other people might call it the floor.

All is quiet, save for the gentle throbbing in my head and my menopausal fridge that sometimes just hums loudly for no apparent reason and then goes quiet as soon as I call the repairman.

If I look up and tilt my head (without touching the dead little cockroach I just spotted squished in a nook under the relatively new cupboards, which cost far too much in comparison to everything else in the entire universe since the dawn of time …) Yes, if I force my eyes both upwards and around, then toward the kitchen window, I can see the city skyline bathed in the brilliance of a full moon. Its brightness hurts my bloodshot eyes. Could someone turn the moon down please?

I'm alone in my apartment now. Everyone ended up at my place last night, but they've all gone home now. They were unsure whether to commiserate or celebrate over the news that after four years Hope had finally called me. So they all got pissed as newts and left just after midnight.

My mother arrived first. She thinks she knows everything there is to know about life because she's given birth to a lot of children, though clearly she knows nothing about contraception. She also knows nothing about when she's not invited. Which was last night. Nonetheless, she arrived first.

Actually, if truth be told, she was already at my house when Hope rang. She'd 'dropped in' for a Double Wine, i.e. a whine with a wine. My mother regularly comes to my place for a Double Wine because her nursing home, Happy Days, no longer lets its residents drink even a drop of alcohol on the premises. So Mum starts every Double Wine whingeing about that. She conveniently forgets that the reason why no one at Happy Days is permitted to drink is because of the sexual harassment case that was brought against both Mum and Happy Days, by Santa after last year's Christmas party.

My mother says Happy Days should be sued for false advertising because there is 'nothing happy about it'. I'm actually surprised my mother hasn't started legal proceedings herself, because she comes from a line of very litigious women. Legend has it that Mum's Aunt

Cynthia once tried to sue herself after she hit a golf ball so badly the ball wacked her in her own head.

Anyway, Mum also says Happy Days 'is a bloody – excuse the French – shithole.' But the truth is Mum's nursing home is actually very comfortable. The food is beige, but the staff are kind. In fact, there are only two problems with the Happy Days Nursing Home: 1. It's too close to my place, and 2. It's too close to my place.

I don't want to sound mean. I love my mother, but our relationship works better in theory than in practice. What does that mean? Well, I often feel like I could kill my mother but the eulogy I'll give at her funeral will be fantastic.

I don't know why this is so but I suspect she feels the same about me. Thilma says she felt this way about her mum too, but now that she's dead she misses her terribly. Soula says I should be grateful that I have a mum at all.

My ex-husband, Leonard, says that my mother and I are very similar. I think that is a rude thing to say.

In her will Mum's bequeathed me our ancestors' chamber pot, because she says it reminds her of me.

6.43 AM

Anyway, as soon as the phone started ringing last night, Mum groaned. Mum makes this groaning sound every time a phone rings. Sorry, I should correct that. Mum makes this sound every time *my* phone rings. She groans as though whoever's ringing is no doubt calling for an insignificant reason and in the process interrupting the sanctity, profundity and import of the much more

9

significant activity that we're partaking in. (Which, may I point out, at the time the phone rang last night, was discussing whether it's possible that people really do have sex with horses and also if carrots have souls.) It's worth noting, too, that when any of my seven brothers is visiting and *his* phone rings, Mum makes a completely different sound; a 'Sssssshh!' sound that demands we all respect the fact that the caller is probably God wanting my brother's advice.

So, when my phone rang last night, Mum of course immediately groaned in her Pavlovian way. But when she realised the caller was Hope, Mum quickly hushed and held her breath like an excited little girl watching a magic trick.

Before that moment it hadn't occurred to me that, for the past four years, Mum has been missing Hope too. But of course she has. She thinks my daughters are hers. In fact, with the help of her pals Vera and Babs, Mum actually raised my daughters better than her own. So, in a totally instinctive gesture, that was possibly more practical than kind, I held the phone between the two of us and shared this precious call with my mum.

When the call ended, Mum stared at me long and silently, with a schadenfreude grin and 'I told you so' eyes, until I uttered the single syllable.

'What?'

'Oh nothing, Nora.'

'What?'

'Well,' said Mum. 'It's just that being a mother of a son is like passing a camel through the eye of a needle and then looking after it for the rest of your life. But being a mother of a daughter is like giving birth to a boa constrictor and never knowing, for the rest of your life, if it's trying to crush you or give you a hug.'

I really should have expected nothing less than such remarkable unwisdom from the mother who raised her children on adages like 'people in glass houses shouldn't run around in the nude' and 'a bird in the hand probably has avian lice'. Mum's big on demotivational quotations. When I found out at the ultrasound that my second baby was to be a girl, Mum said, 'Having one daughter is like having a hobby, having a second daughter is a full-time shit of a job that you can never quit'. Whether or not this is true, it isn't a thoughtful thing to say, because I too am a second daughter. Allegedly.

I say 'allegedly' because, until recently, I'd never heard of the existence or otherwise of some other first daughter. This doesn't necessarily make it untrue, however, because Mum has always had a somewhat flexible relationship with the truth.

Growing up with Mum's tales of heroic ancestors, fictitious lovers and falsified statistics re the nutritional value of burnt chops and why it's a good thing if your shoes are too small, has of course affected me. The upside is that anything can seem possible in a fantastic world without the limitation of, um, facts. The downside is I tend to believe anything that suits me. I also tend to exaggerate. Once on a plane I told the man next to me that I'd been bitten by a shark in Tahiti. I hadn't of course. I've never been there. I just said it to spice up the conversation.

Over the years Mum's fibbed, exaggerated and fabricated a lot but lately I've begun to suspect that she's doing it because she's forgotten the truth.

So Mum's announcement, two months ago, that she had a daughter before me, really wasn't surprising. Since then Mum's changed the story of my alleged sister's birth *and* death according to her audience, her sugar level and the weather. In fact the only consistency in the whole story is that she loves the 'other daughter' more than me. And you know what, I understand. Sometimes I like myself so little that I like my non-existent sister more than I like me too.

But anyway, yes, *I* have two daughters. The eldest, Joy, is as I said, 'perfect'. She was even conceived during the only time I enjoyed sex with my husband (and hadn't yet started using the missionary position to check the ceiling for cobwebs).

Joy is tallish and remains slender. Though she always says she eats as much as she likes, she doesn't actually like to eat too much. Her hair is glossy light brown and long and straight and never, ever frizzes. Joy's hair is tame, just like Joy. Her voice is pleasant, her laugh is polite, and if you met her you'd describe her as 'nice'.

After Joy I had a late miscarriage and lost my twin boys. My girls don't know about that. My mum does, and Leonard does and Soula and Hope and Eduardo do too. But we don't ever talk about it, we prefer to discuss subjects like 'would you rather be a cockroach or a snail'.

And then came Hope. She was an accident. She's not at all like Joy. Hope's shape is rounder. She loves to talk and laughs like a tuba. Her skin is fair and freckled. Her rust-coloured mop is thick, curly and wild. If you were to meet my dear beautiful Hope you couldn't describe her with one word. Though when I finally brought Hope home from the hospital at six months of age, her father nicknamed her 'Hopeless', just before he left us.

I shared a bed with both my daughters for the first two years after Leonard left. Leonard, as I mentioned, had taken all my savings, so the semi-detached house that we could afford to live in was a much-loved two-bedroom dilapidated dump. Truth be told it didn't really have a second bedroom. In retrospect it didn't really have a first. But even if we'd had a mansion with a million bedrooms I would have wanted Hope to sleep next to me. I needed to hear her little breaths in the night, I needed to see her little chest rising. If I'd lost Hope I don't think I could have lived. For those two years Joy slept beside me like an angelic log, while Hope slept in the shape of a starfish and farted and giggled through the night.

Hope spoke early, when she was one and a half. Her very first sentence was 'ope lub bum'. In contrast, perfectly perfect Joy didn't speak until she was nearly four. She later explained that this delay was because she was waiting until she had something constructive to add to the conversation. So Joy's first sentence was, 'Can I offer you a glass of wine?'

When Hope was four she held my face in her little hands and said, 'Will you marry me?'

But on the cusp of adolescence, Hope suddenly stopped speaking to me. Her last words were 'You know from the side you look like Grandma.' And after that instead of rolling chats and laughter Hope just rolled her eyes at me.

I learnt of her decision to stop speaking via a note she wrote on the bathroom mirror using my favourite and only expensive lipstick. It was a long note that used up all the mirror space, part of the tiled wall, and all of my lipstick. There was no particular feud with Hope at the time. No more than the usual mother–daughter nipping. Nothing stands out. I did ask her to empty the dishwasher, so maybe that was it? And besides, Hope couldn't control herself and did end up speaking to me. She was such a little chatterbox, her vow of silence really only lasted a little over an hour.

But the disappearance when Hope was just about to turn twenty? Well that lasted. There was no fight, I know of no catalyst. One morning she rose early as usual, went to work at the local café and simply didn't come home. I rang her work. I rang all her friends. And I rang the police to report her missing even though I knew Hope had planned her departure because she'd taken all of her favourite clothes with her, along with my favourite suitcase.

I rang Hope's phone a thousand times. But she never answered my calls. Over the last four years I kept trying and have rung at least two thousand times more. Sometimes I've hidden my number when I ring to trick her into answering. But then the minute I speak Hope always hangs up.

During those four years I lost my little pal's companionship and gained the shame of my failure as a mum. I have been very sad ever since. And I've also been very scared.

I know she's OK. Joy tells me she is. Joy and Hope send each other little videos. Very occasionally Joy tells me about them, not with relish but with dread, knowing that her contact with Hope is a double-edged sword reassuring me on one hand and wound-salting on the other.

So, anyway, for four long, heart-aching years I've heard nothing directly from Hope. She fills my dreams when I sleep at night, and in the daytime I often think I see her: sometimes in the street, sometimes in the mirror, sometimes when I'm shopping at Coles. Often when I hear a child call out 'Mum!' I turn, thinking that it's Hope calling for me.

I worry about her safety. I worry about her health. I worry that she won't be able to afford the medication for her lungs. I worry that she isn't taking it. I worry that Hope is a sucker to every no-hoper male in town because her dad has been a no-hoper in her life, and the hole that's left in her heart might be the shape that only a no-hoper can fill.

I don't know how to explain the ache of Hope's silent absence. I do shit yoga and distracted meditation to ease it. I also eat a lot. I very occasionally go on a date, and if it's too boring I'll have sex with the bloke just so we don't have to talk.

I also drink more now. My friends, Soula and Thilma, worry a lot about my drinking and often invite me out to discuss it, over drinks.

I love Thilma and Soula. I point out when they do stupid things and they both just laugh and laugh. And they point out when I'm stupid too, like when I'm clearly not mentally present because I'm thinking of Hope.

Anyway, the phone conversation last night wasn't long. Hope was brief and to the point, 'I'm coming home, I'm getting married in one week and, as the mother of the bride, I expect you to help.' And then she added, 'I know it's rushed. Don't ask me any questions. You won't understand.' And hung up.

Ah yes, I cannot tell you how this call confused the cockles of my heart. I was delighted to hear from Hope, thrilled to be in her thoughts, reassured to know she is OK, happy to hear she is in love, fearful she is about to make a huge mistake with this rushed marriage and offended by the belittling assumption that I would not understand love, that I have never been in love, never aspired to be in love, never succeeded or even failed at love! In summary, that I am simply loveless.

Oh, I have to go now. I can hear a loud banging sound. The apartment is either being broken into or my heart is trying to finally come home.

7.03 AM

Dear Diary,

I'm back. The banging sound was Soula knocking at the door, escorted by the new concierge. The concierge didn't actually know that Soula is my friend, but he found her in the elevator and knew to bring her to my place because last night a clearly drunk, yet forward-thinking, Thilma stuck a post-it note on Soula's forehead that read, 'If found please return to Apt 707'. All praise to Thilma for this forethought, even if it did make Soula look a bit like a lost raffle-ticket prize.

Anyway Soula wasn't at the door for long. She just needed me to help her book an Uber. She'd unfortunately misplaced her glasses again and couldn't read the details on the app because she'd made the font on her phone so enormous that only one letter fitted on the screen at a time.

So Soula's gone now and I'm alone again; with only my thoughts, my fears, my hangover and you, Dear Diary.

So, where was I? Oh yes. I was telling you about last night. Well, with Mum already at my place, Soula was the first to actually enter my apartment after the phone call last night. Though to be fair she was already in the building too. For the past two months she says she's been giving a blow job to the concierge every Tuesday in the hope she'll finally accrue enough Blow Job Credits to be allowed to park in this building when she visits. I tell Soula that the building already provides free visitor parking, but she doesn't want to listen.

I also don't believe that Soula really is giving blow jobs to the concierge. I think it's a story she tells to make herself sound special. I wish she knew she already is.

I think Soula is looking for love. And I also think there's no way Soula could give a blow job – her lips are so enormously collagened that her mouth is kind of stuck open in the shape of a quail egg.

Oh. Yes, now I see that could be a good thing.

Blow jobs are clearly not my area of expertise. The last time I gave one I had a blocked nose, and of course nearly died of suffocation.

Anyway, the good news is that Hope rang on a Tuesday night so Soula was in the building, and coincidentally already on her way to my apartment, because she's made it a habit to pop in after 'blowing the concierge'. To be honest, I find this routine kind of awkward, though I should be used to Soula's behaviour by now. I mean, Soula is one of those women who men send dick pics to. And she's also one of those women who shares the dick pics with her girlfriends. I've often thought that if I were to meet any of Soula's boyfriends I'd only recognise them if they dropped their pants. In fact, maybe I *have* met them and just didn't realise.

Anyway, Thilma arrived about five minutes after Soula, because Soula rang her and said, 'Oh my Gawd, come to Nora's, I'm not fucking joking you.'

And my eldest daughter, perfect Joy, arrived moments after that, purely by coincidence. She was heading to her apartment where she lives alone. It's just around the corner from me and also conveniently located near Joy's public service job where she works as an auditor.

Joy said that on her way home last night she 'just felt like' giving me a hug. Joy says delightfully perfect things like this a lot but I never feel comfortable when she does. Maybe that's because 'I just feel like giving you a hug' is exactly what my brothers used to say before they hid dead prawns in my pockets.

I should cross that last bit out. Joy would hate to be likened to my brothers. Joy is sensitive about how much I love her. In fact Joy is sensitive about everything when it comes to our relationship. No mother has a favourite child. But I know Joy thinks she's not mine. Perhaps because Hope's health dictated that Joy received less attention. Perhaps because Joy thinks she looks like Leonard which is weird because Leonard looks like a potato.

Sometimes I find myself insensitive to Joy's sensitivity. Thilma says it's because I'm so obsessed with my own. But after last night I can completely understand if Joy's currently in more pain than usual. I know she's loved having me to herself for the past four years, so I can imagine – actually what am I talking about, I don't need to imagine at all. Joy was so obviously discombobulated at the news of Hope's phone call that her behaviour became unnaturally wild and irrational, causing her to do uncharacteristic illogical things like ring her father for emotional support.

Actually, to be fair, Leonard has become more compassionate and less 'all about Leonard' with his recent marriage to Booby, his Bosnokian wife. Booby is her real Bosnokistan name and yes, she does have big Bosnockers. Booby's brave and tough and has no idea how fabulous she is so she overcompensates with abundant gifts of food that always look like stewed shoe.

Booby herself can look like either Jessica Rabbit or Mrs Doubtfire. It depends on the light. But, no matter what the light, she always looks like she loves Leonard.

I don't still love Leonard but I increasingly tolerate him. I think part of me believes that if I forgive and make amends with Leonard then the world might forgive me and bring Hope back.

Anyway, Leonard and Booby arrived, and the final guest to arrive last night was my boss, Eduardo, specially attired in a hot pink velvet onesie tucked into matching velveteen cowboy boots. He lives in an apartment that's one removed from mine. Well actually it's not 'an' apartment per se. We call it The North West Wing and it consists of five apartments all joined together, with walls removed and 'pizazz' added in the form of his genitalia-oriented art (no it's not a genre) and elaborately patterned psychedelic wallpaper 'feature walls' that are identical to the carpet.

Eduardo also owns the apartment between The North West Wing and mine, apartment 708, which we call the Buffer Zone. The Buffer Zone is filled with all the creations that don't fit in The North West Wing. Eduardo bought it to serve as a kind of demilitarised zone to protect himself from all of the female comings and goings of my place. He arrived at my place last night asking us to keep the noise down, as usual. And then hung out with us all night … as usual.

So everyone was here, and everyone screamed 'What?!' when I told them that Hope had rung and wanted my help with her wedding.

'But who's she marrying?' Thilma asked.

'A guy called Aspen,' my mother blurted with a gusto fuelled by savvy blanc.

'And?' said Joy.

'Well,' continued my mother, finishing her wine, standing on the coffee table and falling onto the couch with the satisfied grin of an Olympic gymnast who'd just completed a perfect 10. 'The conversation between Hope and Nora went like this. Hi Mum, it's me. I'm just ringing to tell you that I'm getting married. Oh darling I'm so happy for you. Hello? Hello? Hello? Are you there, darling? I'm so happy for you. And then Hope said, Oh for God's sake, Mum, it doesn't matter how happy *you* are, this is not about you! And then Nora said, OK, yes, yes, you're right, are *you* happy? Of course I am, said Hope, I'm getting married! Yes, yes, of course you are, yay! What do you mean "yay"? said Hope. And Nora said, I mean hoorah, isn't that fabulous! And Hope said, I think you and I both know that isn't what you meant. And Nora said, Isn't it? And Hope said, I have to go I don't want to talk anymore. And Nora said, Oh OK, do you mind if I ask you one question before you go? And Hope said, What? And Nora said, Could you tell me anything about who it is you're marrying? And Hope said, I don't know why you want to know about this person, because it's not like you've bothered to get to know any of my previous partners. And then she hung up.'

While most of this reiteration is surprisingly accurate, considering the emotion and adrenaline that were pumping at the time of the incident, plus the fact that Mum was retelling it pissed. But the last bit, the bit about me not ever 'bothering' to get to know Hope's partners, is absolutely not true. I mean it's true it was said. But it's not true that it was true, because even before Hope disappeared I have *always* wanted to get to know Hope's partners but was forbidden on the grounds I was 'too embarrassing'. And besides this I did in fact meet several! I met one when he fell from our drainpipe, and one when I caught him stealing my jewellery and one at a friend's funeral where Hope's 'boyfriend' was delivering the sermon.

I needed to nip this 'I've never bothered to get to know Hope's partners' fib in the bud and and get the truth inserted into the family almanac – because like all families ours has to be careful that any slight deviation, more interesting than the truth, does not become fact simply through repetition.

So I seized the proverbial talking stick from my mother. 'Actually I said I would like to get to know more about the man you'll be marrying because you're going to spend the rest of your lives together. And Hope said, Yes, Mum, Aspen and *I* are spending the rest of our lives together. Not you. And I said, OK, well thank you for asking me to help with the wedding. And Hope said, Well to be honest it's the least you could do after all that you've done.'

'And then?' asked Joy, interrupting me in a tone that some might consider to be curious and others might assess as suppressed jealousy verging on hysterical.

'And then she hung up,' I said sadly. And that's when Joy grabbed her phone from the 'made by Thilma' little felt pouch that always hangs around Joy's neck and began tapping furiously while muttering, 'Maybe there's evidence of Aspen on Facebook.'

'Any sign?' Soula asked after waiting an agonised second.

'No,' replied Joy, shaking her head in disbelief. 'I've found a photo of her first puppy, her first car, her first older man, her first younger man, her first guru, an African love, a Jewish love, a Muslim love, a Buddhist love, a tall love, a short love and the first person she loved who had a job. There are Alfonsos, Pierres, Omars, Nikolais, Bruces, Garys, Waynes, Christophes, and even a Whopper Burger – but there are no shots of anyone called Aspen.'

It was at that point that my mother who, for no apparent reason, suddenly became remarkably broadminded, perhaps in the way that a flyscreen door is accidentally blown open by the wind, only to be slammed shut by that very same gust. 'You do realise that the name Aspen could also be the name of a woman.'

'Oh, that's arousing,' said Eduardo.

'I think,' chimed Booby in her deep mellifluous voice, 'That ignore you gender preference should, what matters our daughter Hope hoppy is.'

'"Our daughter?"' I bristled territorially at the mere thought, then recovered and joined the others as we all paused to process the dual carriage notions of whether Booby had totally mastered the art of speaking English backwards, and why Eduardo was such a dick.

Our thoughts were interrupted by dear perfect Joy. 'Well, I think you should ignore the entire wedding, Mum. I think the whole thing is a minefield and a trap. Don't fall for it. This is the kind of thing psychopaths plan before they murder you. And besides, who the hell is going to pay for it?'

Thilma then dragged me to the corner of the room and, whispering over a schooner of emergency Pinot Grigio, the preferred medication of the middle-aged femme, suggested I find a believable way to be unavailable for the next week, 'You know, like a car accident or amnesia. You can't stop the wedding per se but you also cannot go! You are being set up to fail! You'll have to pay for everything, it'll rain on the day, the food will be off, the grog will dry up, Hope will think she looks fat, your mother will be there, so will your seven or eight siblings who, by the way, all hate you, and someone will steal the wishing-well cash, and that someone will possibly be Soula. There'll probably be a fight, the fiancé's parents will be there, and they'll be crooks or communists or members of some sort of weird cult 'cause Hope will be desperate to make a point about something that none of us has ever understood and, nightmare of nightmares, you'll have to book me as the celebrant because I'm your friend. And because I'm your friend I'll feel obliged to do it – even though we both know I'm a shit celebrant.'

'Isn't it possible,' I asked, 'that Hope is reaching out to me to build a bridge so that we can walk over it together?'

'Yes,' Thilma said, 'and it's also possible she's building a bridge so the two of you can jump off it.'

Soula, who'd surreptitiously joined the conversation by offering us hors d'oeuvres from a plate that was empty, then whispered, 'For heaven's sake, Thilma, I have seen a vision of the future and you are being ridiculous.'

Soula is a self-confessed unreliable psychic – and the chance that her psychic visions will be wrong is pretty much the only reliable thing about them. Over time this has meant that her visions are now really only pronounced once they've actually happened. But last night she went out on a limb and said, 'I have seen a vision and no one is going to kill *themselves*.'

'Oh,' I replied. 'Thank you, Soula, that's a huge relief.'

'Well, not really,' Soula said, 'I do have a strong sense of "tragic death" around these nuptials but, I don't know if it's a person or just the outfit you'll be wearing.'

As profound, eye-opening and prescient as this may have been – though not as eye-opening as the time a date told me that he liked passionfruits stuck up his bum – it was not at this moment that I decided to keep a diary, Dear Diary.

So, when was it, you may ask.

Well we all sat and drank for hours and hours and I decided to keep a diary just *after* the final drunk guest had left – after drunk Mum had been collected and taken 'home' by the nursing home charity bus (which she calls 'the hearse'); after drunk Joy had finished playing Bach using the recorder Thilma carries in her hand-woven backpack at all times ('just in case of emergencies'); after my drunk ex-husband and his drunk Booby left (armed with more food and crockery than they actually arrived with); after drunk Thilma had departed to realign her chakras by weaving a love blanket out of oxygen; after drunk Soula had left to pass out in the spare room (i.e. the elevator); and after I'd rolled my faux Italian piss-head boss, Eduardo, down the hall to The North West Wing that he bought after his famous opera-singing father dropped dead while having sex with Eduardo's girlfriend, and Eduardo's mother subsequently killed herself.

Yes, it was after all that, when I was looking for Hope's birth certificate in preparation for registering her wedding, that I found you, Dear Diary. And it was then that I decided to quietly start writing in you over the forthcoming wedding week as evidence of how perfectly I've behaved should anything untoward come to pass and anyone/everyone try to blame me.

7.17 AM

Actually, that's not quite true. The real reason why I want to record things, Dear Diary? I want to discover what I'm doing wrong, so I can make things right with Hope.

But I have to go now. Hope has just texted. Her plane homeward bound is about to take off from wherever she is and she wants me to pick her up from the airport.

AT THE AIRPORT

11.32 AM
The Arrival Areas
It's still March 23

Dear Diary,

I'm at the airport now. It took me a little longer than I expected to leave my apartment building because, in the chaos of my excitement and mortal fear of missing Hope's arrival, I neglected to raise the garage door and drove into it. So, I borrowed Eduardo's car, which is the kind of toy vintage convertible sports car that screams 'I have a small penis and no friends.' It's also a manual which I don't know how to drive, so I had to putt-putt the whole way here with the car stuck in first gear. Thanks to the backdraft of a front-end loader on the freeway, the drive here only took forty-five minutes, but parking took me three hours.

First I had to find a space in the airport car park. The nine-level concrete car park is owned by a private company. They charge according to the length of your stay and the time starts as soon as you enter and accept a ticket from the eager machine. It's therefore in the car park owner's interest to make sure it takes everyone a long time to find a space. But the truth is I really only drove around looking for a space for a little over two hours. The rest of the time was spent trying to perfectly reverse park.

This reach for 'the perfect park', Dear Diary, is a classic sign that I'm feeling out of control in every other element of my life. When Leonard left us all those years ago we had no money, we had no home, I had no job, my baby was ill, my four-year-old was, well, a four-year-old, so all up our lives were in complete 24/7 chaos – but the one thing I really obsessed about was that the toothpaste was always neatly, neatly squeezed from the bottom of the tube.

Soula says that I want to be a toothpaste tube. Thilma says I am one. And one thing we all agree on is that Thilma's opinion is worth more than mine and Soula's put together because Thilma did an online psychology course. Well, not the whole course, just the first free trial session one morning during the newsbreaks on the home-shopping channel, but nonetheless she calls herself a psychologist. Soula also calls Thilma a psychologist because it makes Soula feel smarter to have a friend who's 'involved in mentalness'.

Anyway, I finally found the perfect parking space and then took another age trying to park in it, perfectly, obsessively; equidistant from the cars on either side, the front of the space and the back. My pursuit of precision could have gone on much longer had steam not started rising from under the bonnet.

But I'm inside the airport now! And I'm trying not to cry. Don't worry, Dear Diary. I'm not crying because I'm sad. I'm crying because airports always make me cry. Is it the aura of love, loss, reunion, hope, change and possibility? Or is it the fact the airport décor is so homogeneous, the air-con is turned up too high, the coffee tastes like crap and everyone is so badly dressed? I don't know, but I'm crying. Not an elegant, glistening solo tear kind of cry, more a snotty, snorting, red-nosed, red-eyed cry that makes me look like I have myxomatosis.

If this were a movie, and I was crying more delightfully, and I was thirty years younger and more attractive than I actually was when I was thirty years younger, then at this point some handsome bloke would appear by my side and offer me a hanky and then we'd probably get married and have blonde children.

But I'm fifty-ish and the only attention I've received here so far is a massive 'beep' from the man who's driving the sit-on floor polishing machine and wants me to get out of the way. I refused, of course, in either an act of defiance or a desperate need for attention, and he didn't detour, possibly also in an act of defiance or a desperate need for attention, and as a result he polished the top of my left shoe, which is now very shiny indeed.

Between you and me, Dear Diary, I'll probably end up marrying that floor shining guy. But in the meantime I haven't a clue where to sit. There are four arrival areas at this airport and the one you normally wait at is determined by the airline you're waiting for. So, because I don't know the airline that Hope is travelling on, nor where she's coming from, I don't know where to wait. As a result, I've spent the last however long sitting, standing, walking, running, from arrival area to arrival area, staring at the incoming flights board and then running to the next one to stare at it.

I'm pretty sure if I keep this up then Security's going to arrest me and there's no way Hope will accept 'imprisonment' as an excuse if I'm not here when she lands.

12.57 PM

Dear Diary,

I'm still in the Arrivals Area at the airport. I just woke up. I sat down at EXIT B for only a minute and fell asleep for half an hour. While I was asleep I dreamt that I couldn't get to sleep, so now I'm awake again but completely exhausted.

Normally I love a daytime snooze. Well, I say normally, but I mean I have loved them since about the age of fifty. Before that I used to feel guilty if I slept in past 6 am. It's a legacy of the 'work ethic' based faith my domineering mother invented, wherein if you find yourself doing anything vaguely enjoyable, you can be confident you'll end up in hell.

Nowadays I snooze at will. Sometimes even when I don't intend to, for example, when I'm on a date.

But back to me sleeping at the airport. I was woken by my phone vibrating. I was terrified it might be a fuming Hope, furious that I hadn't been at the right exit. But instead it was Joy.

'Mummy?' she said. 'I'm at your house. It looks like a bomb's gone off and you were nowhere to be found. So I cleaned the mess in its entirety for fear you were buried underneath it.'

'I'm getting a colonoscopy,' I fibbed, just as an announcement declared the arrival of an Abu Dhabi flight at rear EXIT A.

'Why are you at the airport, Mum?' Joy asked with a distinct vocal key change.

'Um … Hope texted and told me to meet her here.'

'Well according to my assumptions, based on the time of Hope's last call to me and the discernible languages spoken in the general hubbub in the background, Hope was calling from

29

somewhere in Asia, so you're at least five hours early. Why is that, Mother?'

'The traffic wasn't as bad as I anticipated.'

'Mum!'

'Hope didn't actually tell me the arrival time,' I confessed.

'What? So you just went all the way out there to wait for however long it took?'

'Yes, it's a natural thing for a loving mother to do. You know, to go to any length that's required in order to safely pick up her child.'

'Really, Mother, is it? Because I remember once you completely forgot to pick *me* up.'

'Joy, I can't believe you're still going on about that. It was twenty-six years ago.'

'Yes, Mum, it was twenty-six years ago and that is my point exactly. I was three years old and you forgot to pick me up from daycare.'

'Do you have another point, Joy?' I asked, somewhat keen to move on.

'Yes, I do, Mum,' Joy said, apparently thrilled to bits that I'd asked. 'My other point is this, Mother – I think we both know that "love" is not your motivating emotion when it comes to Hope.'

'What?'

'You're motivated by fear.'

'Yes, I agree – fear that something bad will happen to her on the flight, fear that her medication won't work …'

'And?'

'… fear that Hope will feel unloved if I'm not there when she arrives and she'll catch the first plane out again.'

'Wrong!' said Joy with the confidence of a judge's gavel.

'Really?' I squirmed.

'Your primary fear,' Joy explained patiently, 'is that you have to be beyond reproach when it comes to Hope because you're terrified that she'll stop loving you if you aren't. You're not scared of *my* love for you stopping, because you know it never will. So Hope's love is more valuable to you for the very reason that it shouldn't be: because its fleeting, unreliable nature makes it more rare and precious.'

I couldn't believe Joy was being so harsh and blunt and cruel. But you know what? She was right.

But I have to stop writing now. Because I'm crying again.

IN THE AIRPORT CAR PARK

2.14 PM
Still March 23

Dear Diary,

I'm still at the airport but now I'm back in the car park, sitting in the car. I came out here because I thought I may as well drive to work as wait at the airport for the next nine hours or so. But then I read the conditions on the parking ticket and realised that the hourly rate decreases the longer you stay and it would be more cost effective for me to remain parked here basically forever than to leave, get paid for working half a day, and then buy a new parking ticket when I return early this evening.

So now I'm going to ring Eduardo and let him know I'm not coming to work today.

That should take only a moment, unless of course he's in one of his 'Italian speaking moods'. He thinks speaking Italian enhances his aura as an artist and I agree it kind of did when we first met. But then I studied Italian in order to understand him and discovered that his poetic Italian utterances are actually phrases like 'Fish, where is the table'.

About 2 hours later

Dear Diary,

I'm still sitting in the car. I was nervous about ringing Eduardo so I spent two hours listening to a self-help motivational podcast made by the same nude YouTube guy who in 1983 gave Thilma one-on-one emotional support to help her deal with the trauma of inheriting her parents' fortune. Then, after that, I rang Eduardo, my boss and one time apathetic lover. (Oh yes, I forgot to mention the lover bit, Dear Diary, but in my defence the sex really was only one time and it was totally forgettable, even while we were doing it.)

His response to me not coming to work loosely translated to 'cow, spoon fuck off'.

Yes, I know, Dear Diary. What woman would allow a man to speak to her like that? Well, turns out I would. For two reasons: 1. Because I have *no* self-esteem, and 2. Because I realise that this kind of emotional blurt by Eduardo should be recognised as an expression of pain from a man who is the unfortunate product of the two worst influences any man can inherit: a famous father and no talent.

As always however, the thought of being fired by Eduardo was initially thrilling. Suddenly I could see myself unshackled from this caveman and his paleolithic sensibilities, unleashed from a boss who, when we first met twenty-one and a half years ago, told me that a lesbian is a small type of bird.

So there I was, reclining in his sports car bucket seat, ready to luxuriate in the fantasy of finding a job where I'm not referred to as Turd Head, when I accidentally set off the car alarm and came to my senses; reminded in sense-surround that I'm a woman over fifty who has no training or skills and who's only recently mastered sending a fax. I can't do budgets, I can't balance bank statements, I can't do online banking and I can't do spreadsheets, because they make me feel sad.

I'm basically only a potential employee to someone who doesn't actually need an employee and yet is willing to pay the substantial wage that I randomly made up when Eduardo originally asked me to write down what I'd like to receive, and I wrote a bigger wage than I'd intended because I'd always wanted to earn 'a six-figure sum', but didn't know if 'six-figure' included the zeroes after the decimal point, and so added extra zeroes just in case.

Anyway, I'm going to do what I usually do when Eduardo fires me, which is nothing. I won't go to work today, and I'll just act like I haven't been fired whenever I do go back.

But I have to stop writing now because Hope's just texted to say she's landed. This is hours earlier than Joy calculated so I pray for Joy's sake that Hope purposely misled her in order to surprise, because if dear perfect Joy made a mistake, she will never forgive herself.

BACK IN MY APARTMENT

8.57 PM
It's still March 23

Dear Diary,

I'm sitting in the chair in my living room that you could see the harbour view from if you stood on the chair and they demolished the building next door.

Hope is in the bathroom. A lot and yet not much has happened in the past couple of hours. I greeted Hope at the airport arrival gate (EXIT C). I ran toward her and as we hugged she whispered in my ear, 'You're late.'

I looked around for Aspen. He was nowhere to be seen. I wanted to ask where he was. And why hadn't he come too. Or was he already here? And where has Hope been? Where did she meet Aspen? When will *we* meet him? Has Hope missed me as much as I've missed her? But as we sat in the car I told Hope that I'd missed her. And Hope said nothing at all.

I told her she looked beautiful, she told me I looked tired, we paid for the parking, I commented on how exorbitant airport parking is, she said well if I didn't think she was worth $183 I didn't have to pick her up because she and her three suitcases could have walked the seventeen kilometres to my place. And then she said, 'But now that the $183 is spent, you should feel free to deduct it from my inheritance.'

Hope is staying in her old room, next to mine. Her first emotion on entering the room was outrage that I hadn't 'left it the way it was'. Apparently, according to American cop shows and heartbreaking chick flicks, this is what a mother does when her daughter disappears; she leaves the room as an untouched shrine to the memory of her child. But that's assuming the child has tidied their room before disappearing. Chances of which are bloody nil. And had I left the room 'untouched' I would have been arrested by the department of sanitation because Hope's room, at the time of her disappearance, looked like a compost bin and a washing basket had moved in together and then exploded.

Anyway, Hope's in the bathroom now. When she's finished in there I've been ordered to sit down with her and complete 'Number Zero' on her Wedding Do-List. 'Number Zero' is apparently 'Write a Wedding Do-List'.

I'm a little scared, because I know that when Hope says 'Let's write a Do-List' Hope means that *she* will write a 'Do-List' and I will watch her while maintaining an expression that suggests emotional support, and no sign whatsoever of horror. Since Hope went to the loo I've been practising my expression using the selfie mode on my phone.

At first I looked like a half-opened clam, but I think I've pretty well nailed a good face now so I'm trying to hold that facial pose.

I'm proud to say I look both serious, yet fun-loving, which will be entirely inappropriate if Hope comes back, after all this time in the loo, and announces that she's constipated.

2 minutes later

I wonder why Hope's taking so long in the bathroom.

5 minutes later

Hope's still in the bathroom. I'm beginning to worry that she isn't feeling well. She continues to take medication for her lungs every day. Maybe she's been affected by the air conditioning on the flight.

1 minute later

Oh my God, maybe Hope's pregnant!

8 minutes later

Hope finally came out of the bathroom. And now she's gone to her bedroom to get her laptop so we can write The Do-List.

When she came out of the bathroom I delicately asked if she was feeling ill, perhaps a little nauseous? And Hope moaned, 'I knew you'd think I look fat.'

Turns out she took a long time in the bathroom because she was 'just feng shui-ing it,' i.e. throwing out all the things in my bathroom cabinet that in her eyes are either economically or environmentally unsound, uncool or ugly. Lucky I wasn't in there or she might have thrown me out, too.

I plan to retrieve all my things later and hide them somewhere that Hope will never go near, e.g. the laundry basket.

11 PM
I'm still in the living room
It's still March 23

Dear Diary,

I'm so exhausted I can barely write. Where should I begin? Probably where I left off. OK, so in the hours that have passed since I last wrote, Hope emerged from her room with her laptop. She then sat on the stiff, yet strangely comforting, poop brown floral couch that we inherited from my mother, and said, 'Can I ask you a question, Mum?'

And I thought, 'Oh my God. Is it possible? We're going to have *that* conversation, solve our differences and resume our once perfect mother–daughter love?'

Yes, I hoped that Hope's question could be the tip of the end of the piece of wool that unravels the home-knitted straitjacket of our relationship; a question about something, anything, to do with our bond. But instead Hope asked, 'What, in your opinion, should I write on The Do-List?' and I felt the jacket tighten. You see, I know from experience in the trenches, Dear Diary, that whenever a daughter asks for 'your opinion', she's not in fact wanting *'your* opinion' at all, and just wants you to agree with hers. This agreeing thing is difficult for a mother to navigate at the best of times, but made even more difficult when your daughter hasn't yet divulged what her opinion actually is.

In this situation a mother has only three possible courses of action if she wishes to survive. The first is to say, 'Well, you're always very good at this type of thing, what do you think?' The second is to run, run, run far away and never come back, and the third is to fake a heart attack. I suggest the first option. The third is not credible unless you've completed at least two years of professional acting training, and the second can be expensive as it requires the purchase of a new identity from underworld criminals and at least rudimentary plastic surgery.

The upshot is I took my own advice and chose the first option. It worked brilliantly and within five minutes Hope had completed, and was reading to me, the first draft of The Do-List.

'1. Choose a venue (cheap but amazing)
2. Plan a budget (is 'crowdfunding' inappropriate? Is there a way to make entire wedding tax deductible? e.g. as a charity fundraiser for ourselves)
3. Catering (or should it be bring a plate?)
4. Photographer, make-up trials, flowers (can Thilma weave them?)
5. Cake ('testing, etc' – gluten free, sugar free, wheat or just uninvite guests with any permutation of a food intolerance?)
6. Write vows, plan honeymoon, dress fittings (lose three kilos each day)
7. Find something old (does Grandma count?)

8. Find something blue and borrowed (has Mum got anything that isn't crap?)
9. Discuss Mum, Grandma, Thilma, Soula, Dad and Booby's roles at the wedding (i.e. permitted conversation topics, permitted dress codes, e.g. no kaftans, fascinators or 'comfortable' shoes)
10. Organise bridal gift registry (bit naff? Is cash a better option? Yes, obviously)
15. Meet the in-laws (is this necessary?)
16. Hen's night (no penis decorations – too depressing)
17. Find celebrant, not Thilma, is it too late to elope?
18. Discuss carbon footprint of wedding (and whether it's OK to care more about my wedding than the environment?)
19. Miscellaneous; the guest list, bridal shower, choosing the bridal party, wedding rehearsal, preparation of conversational cards to avoid awkward silences, actual wedding day run-through, post-wedding return/exchange of all shit presents (try to get refund not credit).'

After reading the list out loud, Hope then handed it to me.

'Here, Mum,' she said. 'Can you check we haven't left anything out?'

Despite my lack of professional acting training I made a mighty effort to look like I was reading The Do-List. But the mere holding of it triggered an asthma attack. So, in order not to make it all about me, I pretended that my breathlessness was due to wedding excitement.

'Wow,' I wheezed.

'Wow?' groaned Hope, immediately arching like a scorpion ready to strike, 'I knew you wouldn't think it was any good. Nothing I do is ever good enough for you!'

'What are you talking about?' I said. 'I've always thought everything you do and are is amazing. All your life I've praised you and nurtured you. Why on earth do you feel like you aren't good enough?'

There was a very long pause, until Hope spat, 'Because Dad left as soon as I was born. And you didn't try to stop him.'

I couldn't speak. And Hope said nothing more. We both sat there for minutes, me with my eyes downcast to avoid Hope. She staring at me like a cat watching a turd in a trap. And then Hope spoke, all of a sudden, as if the storm had blown out to sea, 'So tell me, Mum, what do you think of The Do-List?'

'Well,' I whimpered, 'it seems very comprehensive. I mean amazingly comprehensive and …'

'Yes …?'

'And, well, at rough count it looks like we'll have about thirty major tasks per day, which is about four tasks per minute if fitted into the average work day. So with the wedding in just seven days we'll be quite busy.'

'Six days, Mum. Today's nearly over.'

'Oh right, well, even busier then, so I'll probably have to leave my job after all. But well done, it's good to know everything that's ahead.'

'Oh, Mum?'

'Yes.'

'There's one more thing I need to add to the list. It's "visit a relationship counsellor".'

'Oh, that's an excellent idea,' I said, thrilled to bits the spotlight had been averted from me and I could now unclench my heart and my butthole. 'A relationship counsellor is a brilliant idea. That will be fabulous for you and Aspen.'

'No, Mum, a relationship counsellor for you and me.'

'What?'

'So we can clear our past and move forward.'

'Good idea,' I said, thrilled to bits, 'we could do it with Thilma.'

'OMG, Mum, we are *not* going to do therapy with Thilma!'

'Why not? She's cheap and she loves us.'

'She's insane and self-serving. Don't you remember the time she told you that your hair needed a trim and then glued your hair cuttings to a bathing cap and sold it to a bald man as a wig?'

'You're misconstruing her actions. Thilma just loves helping people.'

'Mum, don't you see?' Hope gasped, exasperated. 'That is precisely the issue. Thilma likes being needed. So it's not in her interest to make things better, if she did then she wouldn't be needed!' Having finished her spray, Hope yawned and said, 'I'm starving.'

'Would you like to go somewhere local to get some dinner?' I asked. 'Toscinos or Tummy Hub?'

I waited with apprehension, as though I'd invited Hope on a date. 'I'd like to,' she said, but I can't.'

I wanted to ask if she wasn't feeling well or if she had other plans, but instead I bit the bullet, braced myself and tentatively asked, 'Have I said or done something to offend you, Hope?'

And Hope said, 'Yes, you've done a million things to offend me, Mum, but right now I just can't go to Toscinos because it's run by a hipster who I once made out with.'

'Are you sure it was him?' I asked chattily. 'I mean all hipsters do look alike.' We laughed.

It's a funny thing the mother–daughter thing. Fighting like hostile foes one minute, laughing like best friends the next.

'Well,' I replied. 'How about we make some nice toast and we can look forward to eating out again, should I ever move to a different suburb.'

After this Hope asked if I wanted to sit on the couch with her to eat the toast and watch our *Chitty Chitty Bang Bang* video. Yes, it's an actual cassette video, the one we used to watch when she and Joy were little and we'd snuggle on the couch in our pyjamas. And I tell you, Dear Diary, when Hope asked me this, my heart sprayed glitter and fireworks. But I stifled my joy for fear it would suffocate Hope and busied myself instead with finding the old video cassettes (from my Treasure Box) and the old video player, and the remote control, and a double adaptor and an extension cord, and when I came back I found Hope on the couch fast asleep gently farting and giggling.

Hope woke just as I'd finished setting everything up.

'So,' she yawned, 'just to confirm, you did read the whole Do-List and you're happy with everything, including the last point?'

'Oh,' I replied, 'which one was that?'

'Well, I didn't actually write it down. But if I had it would have said, "Ask Mum if she'll be paying for the wedding". You know, because traditionally the bride's family pays.'

'Traditionally the father pays.'

'Do you really want to go down this path, Mum, because you know my father can't pay,' threatened Hope.

'No, I don't want to go down it at all. I wish the path didn't exist. But I would like to know, just innocently, curiously, why do you just accept your father's failings and not mine?'

Hope took a deep breath and feigned patience as she said, 'I accept my father the way he is because I cannot change him or our relationship. But I would very much like *our* relationship to change.'

'By making an effort together?' I dared to ask.

'No,' Hope replied, 'just you. And I thought you could start by paying for the wedding.'

'But, darling, I can't pay,' I replied, not sure if the conversation was now over or continuing, so I kind of sat and stood and then sat again.

'Why can't you pay?' Hope demanded. 'You earn a good wage and you live with the abundance of a monk.'

'I use my money to pay for Grandma to live at Happy Days.'

'Really? Do you, is that the truth? Because Grandma said she pays for it with her money.'

'Grandma also says she invented the wheel. Do you honestly think she's a reliable source of information?'

'Well, OK, if you're telling the truth, I'll ask Grandma to pay for the wedding, and it can be deducted from your inheritance when she dies.'

'Um, OK,' I said, despite knowing full well that my only inheritance would be the chamber pot. 'So do you still want to watch *Chitty Chitty Bang Bang*?'

'Nah,' said Hope, 'I'm really tired.'

'Um,' I mumbled as an afterthought, as I began to dismantle the video player in order to hide my tear-welling eyes. 'Isn't it more normal nowadays for the couple to share the cost of the wedding?'

'Aspen never talks about his family's jobs, income or assets. I can only assume they have none.'

11.37 PM
Still in my apartment

Dear Diary,

It's dark outside. The city is glowing with the night's lights. Hope is asleep and in between her farts and giggles I can hear a dog barking in the distance and the horn of a departing cruise ship on the harbour. I can also hear the TV from the neighbour on my right. He's watching football. The neighbour on my left is either having sex or expelling a gallstone. I heard him when I went into my bedroom to get my pyjamas because his bedroom and my bedroom share a non-soundproof wall. If he is having sex, I hope he's enjoying himself, and that he does it very quickly. If he's expelling a gallstone I really hope he doesn't die because he's truly an excellent neighbour; good at recycling his garbage and always polite in the elevator.

Anyway. I've been looking through my Treasure Box again while Hope sleeps. My search for *Chitty Chitty Bang Bang* has made me wonder if there are clues to fixing our relationship in here.

It's odd what a mother finds precious and keeps. Well, I can't speak on behalf of all mothers. My mother, for example, didn't keep anything of any of her eight, possibly nine, children. She says there were too many of us to keep all our 'crap' and it was crap enough just living with each other. But I've kept a lot of my children's things. I've kept them in my Treasure Box.

Hope, Joy and I made all three of our Treasure Boxes when the girls were very, very little. We sat down at the kitchen table one Easter, and instead of flying to Bali or Fiji for an exotic four-day holiday like everyone else in our city, we made containers for our treasures using old cardboard fruit boxes with another box as the lid. Thilma and Soula came over to help us make them. Well, to be more specific, Thilma and Soula dropped in drunk after attending a session of Tranny Bingo at the local pub. They needed to sober up before driving home so Thilma took over supervising the craft activity while Soula put a placemat on her head, declared the 'retrospective psychic is now in session' and told us what had happened in our lives by asking us what had happened in our lives and then saying, 'Yes, that is correct.'

Like the girls' Treasure Boxes, the lid of mine is decorated with shells and stickers, an uncooked pasta bracelet and stick drawings made of actual sticks, and then covered with that adhesive plastic that we used to cover our school books with – and always adhered to ourselves in the process.

There are so many things stored in this box. Who was I keeping them for? For my daughters? For me? For whoever will chuck them out, armed with rubber gloves and big garbage bags, when I die? I wonder why I kept these things. I wonder if I imagined how long I'd keep them for. I wonder if I imagined I'd throw them out myself one day because they'd lose value with time. Well, as it turns out, quite the opposite has happened. As I search through the box tonight I realise that every item has become more precious over the years, because they all remind me of happy times. But they also remind me that happiness has passed. And nothing makes you sadder than that.

I started to collect treasures when my girls were very little. I thought I'd been even-handed but now, as I sort the contents into a Joy Pile and a Hope Pile, I see I've kept a lot more memories of Hope. There actually isn't a Joy Pile at all. I wonder why that is. I suspect because Joy has removed all evidence of every cute/special/delightful thing she's ever done because she doesn't think any of it is good enough.

I've just realised there also isn't a Me Pile. I've kept some of the landscapes I've painted but they're rolled up and shoved right at the back of the cupboard.

Anyway, the first thing I put in my Hope Pile is a tooth in a little plastic bag. Inside the bag was a note written by Hope: *Dear Easter Bunny, please give Mummy a slug.* (The writing is a bit messy, I'm hoping it's meant to say 'hug'.)

Next for the pile was the scab that fell from Hope's knee when she was four and she kept because it looked like a heart.

And now I've found the tiny doll pyjamas that dear little underweight Hope was wearing when I brought her home from hospital, a photo of us with the proud nursing team that kept her alive, and a card from my mother addressed to Hope. Inside the card is a message welcoming Hope into the world, and there's also a cheque made out to Hope for the sum of thirty dollars.

Thirty dollars!

The sum total of *all* the cash or cheques that my mother has ever given me in my entire life adds up to less than $10.35. In fact the only time she's ever gifted me anything of value was when she gave me a UOME on the night of my twenty-first birthday. (In case you don't know, Dear Diary, a UOME is like an IOU but the other way around.) It was an invoice for everything she'd spent on raising me, including the cost of school textbooks and tampons.

So, yes, I found my mum's card to Hope and the cheque in my Treasure Box and I also found the dead bee Hope took to kindy for 'show and tell' and told the class was our 'family pet'.

And I found a note that read *Please excuse Hope for her absence this morning as she was feeling ill.* At the end of the note was my signature, clearly forged by Hope.

The box also contained records of a million hospital visits and medical reports that spanned the twenty years before Hope left, and the photo I took of that note that Hope scrawled on the bathroom mirror.

And finally, at the bottom of the box, I found a completely blank piece of paper, which I'd put in the box four years ago to represent the note that Hope never gave me the day she disappeared.

Still in my apartment
11.54 PM

Dear Diary,

Hope has gone to her room to sleep in her bed instead of the couch where she first nodded off and I'm now outside her closed bedroom door, preparing to sleep on the hallway floor. My bed would be warmer and much more comfortable, but I want to be near Hope. I'd like to lie on Hope's bed with her, like we did when she was little, but if I did that now I'm pretty sure that Hope would call Police Rescue.

So I'm lying out here, on the floor outside Hope's door, because I want to be as close to her as I can and I want to physically apprehend her should she decide to disappear again. Basically I'm being a bollard.

The floorboards hurt my hips and my neck and my arms and my legs and my bum and my back and my front and my bones and pretty much all of my internal organs. But even if I were lying on broken glass and sharpened nails and being eaten by rodents with chainsaw teeth, this position could not possibly hurt me as much as every part of me hurt when Hope disappeared. It hurt us all; me, Joy and Mum, Soula and Thilma.

As I write I'm on the cusp of thinking Hope was selfish and cruel to leave without warning. But maybe Hope was hurting, and that's why she left.

I wish my bosoms were a little bit saggier, because then I could use them as pillows.

32 seconds later

Oh, turns out they are saggy enough after all.

In Vietnamese Gloria's OK Glam on the Go

Dear Diary,

I've relocated to *Vietnamese Gloria's OK Glam on The Go,* No, I'm not being racist, that's the name of the 'boutique'. It's branded as such with a flickering fluoro light on the building's outside, though a few of the vowels have blown.

I came here pretty well immediately after I woke up. To my surprise I slept through the night for the first time in years, despite sleeping fully dressed (including shoes) and reposing on the hard wood floor as though I were on display in a coffin.

In fact, I not only slept, but I actually slept in. I felt ashamed about this when I woke up, like I'd failed yet again as a mother, because good mothers don't sleep in. In fact, a perfect mother probably shouldn't sleep at all.

It's been said that a mother is only as happy as her unhappiest child. I know this to be true. When a woman becomes a mother she loses all emotional independence. And this can never be changed. The umbilical cord is never cut. The scissors just make it invisible.

When you give birth, your babies leave your body, but are always part of you. Their pain and fears and hopes and disappointments become yours. When a mother is cold she warms her children; when she's hungry she feeds them. When a mother is tired she bathes the children and reads them a story and falls asleep in their beds and then wakes with a start and gets out of bed to make tomorrow's school lunches, iron the school uniforms, do the washing up, clean the kitchen, walk the family dog and then go to bed, to lie awake and worry about her children's retirement plans.

As I drove alone in my car one day after dropping my children at school, I remember thinking that if I were hit by a passing car – not badly, just a nudge – then I might be admitted to hospital, and for that short time have a legitimate, unquestioned, unchallenged opportunity to climb off the mother rollercoaster for a moment as I recovered in the public hospital ward. But then I realised I didn't have time for such indulgence, because I had to go to work all day, then pick the kids up, then take them to sports practice or guitar lessons or a pal's place to play and then do the grocery shopping, and then pick the kids up again, then help with their homework and negotiate their fights, and then cook dinner and then make a polar bear out of an old tennis sock for six-year-old Hope's 'show and tell – with a focus on the environment'.

I remember both Hope and Joy were incredibly impressed with my ability to make a polar bear, much more than by the dinner I'd cooked. I remember they both sat on our long dining table and watched me at work. And I remember that when I finished, Hope presented me with an invisible medal that she'd 'made' for 'the absolute bestest mum ever'.

I don't remember when it all began to go sour. I am so desperate to know. Was it when Hope was twelve and had started high school, and I forbade her from staying at her friend's house because she'd been wheezing with asthma all day and I feared it might lead to pneumonia again? I remember she was furious. Is that why she's so fired up with anger now? Or did it start years earlier, when I accidentally cut her hair like a coconut?

Anyway, where was I? Oh yes, trying to understand how I'd slept in. Well, when I woke I rang Thilma to ask her opinion.

'Do you want my personal or my professional opinion?' said Thilma in her croaky morning, 'I used to smoke heaps of pot', voice.

'What's the difference?' I asked.

'Twenty-five dollars.'

'Well, I'd like your personal opinion please.'

'My personal opinion is I think you should talk to a professional about this.'

'And what's your professional opinion?'

'I have two professional opinions, actually.'

'Will that cost me fifty dollars?'

'Yes, it will.'

'What about mates' rates?'

'I can't offer you mates' rates, that would be unprofessional.'

'OK, then what if I only want *one* of your professional opinions?'

'Do you want my professional opinion on whether you should just take one of my professional opinions?'

'No, actually forget it, I think I want to speak to Soula and get her opinion, because she won't charge me a cent for what you were going to charge me fifty bucks for. And she always gives me your opinion anyway.'

'Sorry, it's seventy-five bucks now.'

'Why?'

'I'm charging twenty-five for this chat. And by the way …'

'Yes?'

'I'll tell you this for free. You slept in because you're happy.'

And you know what? She was right. I did feel happy-ish. I'm suspicious, I don't want the evil eye, but between you and me, Dear Diary, with Hope coming home I feel like the missing piece of my soul has finally returned to me, or at least can be sighted through the window.

It was at this point, after speaking to Thilma, as I tried to stand, like a newborn giraffe, and realising that sleeping on the hard floor had caused me to lose feeling in every part of my body except my heart, that I noticed a message on the hallway mirror. The message was written in a tiny weeny script with my favourite and only expensive lipstick. You can imagine, I was terrified to read it.

Hi Mum,

I've gone to the gym to get in peak physical condition for the dress try-outs today. I didn't wake you to see if you wanted to come with me because you were sleeping and also because I wasn't sure if the gym still has a restraining order on you, after that terrible time your treadmill got stuck on full speed and you ran the equivalent of

halfway to Africa before anyone had the wherewithal to use their leg
warmers to lasso you off.

Anyway, after the gym Joy and I are going for the dress fitting,
so meet us at Vietnamese Gloria's OK Glam on The Go, corner of
Abbott and High Streets at 10 am! In case you're wondering, yes,
this was the plan that we agreed on last night. (I just forgot to tell
you about it.)

So, I am now in *Vietnamese Gloria's OK Glam on The Go*. It's not
actually a boutique. It's an 'outlet' on a main road just near where
I live. The road is lined with once thriving shops now boarded shut
so it looks exactly like the beginning of the end of the world. I
really hope this isn't a metaphor.

I arrived about six minutes late and was told by the girl at the
front desk, who was dressed somewhat like a bridal bouquet, that
'the young ladies are already in the dressing room trying on the
first "gown". Please wait for them in *Le Show Off Room* because the
dressing room is also the toilet so there isn't a lot of space.'

The place feels familiar to me. Though I've never actually been
here before, I have seen it advertised many times on late night
television. The ad, as I recall, proclaims an 'immediately available
wide selection of frocks and gowns in all shapes and sizes and all
for one price – cheap!' Interestingly the ad doesn't focus on, nor
even mention, the words quality or style. Oh, but it does mention
that for a minimum extra charge you can return the frocks 'severely
stained'.

And yes, it is an outlet, a huge, cold factory space with rows
and rows and rows of assorted dresses, tiaras, feather boas, heels

and fascinators. I have to admit it's the perfect place to find a last-minute wedding dress, though I imagine the target market is usually low-end escorts suddenly being asked to work somewhere 'dressy', like a mobster's wake at *Knobs and Knockers*.

I'm actually all alone at the moment in *Le Show Off Room*. It's an annex that I think used to be a caravan until someone welded it to the 'outlet' exterior. So now it's the room where relatives and loved ones sit and wait while their bride-to-be, grieving widow or social-climbing ladies of the night parade their dress selection in return for opinions, approval and donations toward the frock rental.

The room has 'wall to wall' mirrors on all the walls, and the ceiling. I suspect the impact of this is intended to be 'magnificence' but it's actually really depressing to see yourself from every angle and yet be physically incapable of sucking all your blubber bits in at exactly the same time. When I first saw a glimpse of my reflection in here I thought I was ageing brilliantly. But then I realised I didn't have my glasses on.

Admittedly I raced here, my clothing unchanged from last night, my makeup accidentally 'goth' and my hair like windblown fairy floss, so I'm not looking my best. Even the greeting from a complete stranger, the girl at the front desk, was, 'Oh my God, you look terrible. Do you want me to call an ambulance?'

I feel like I've been sitting here for quite a long time waiting for Hope to appear in her first outfit. Other than writing in you, Dear Diary, and contemplating how gross my body is and how I should have slept with more people when my shape was less like flowing lava, I'm worrying why Hope is taking so long. Hope is usually incredibly quick when it comes to trying on clothes. She just throws the garment on and doesn't bother primping and preening because she thinks she 'looks like shit in everything'.

I have a few ideas as to why she's taking so long this time. The most optimistic is that the choice has overwhelmed her. The most negative, and therefore probably the most realistic, is that nothing fits. The absolute worst situation I can imagine is that Joy is in there also trying on dresses and they all look fabulous on her.

3 minutes later

Dear Diary,

I've decided to constructively prepare for Hope's appearance by Googling 'phrases to avoid at your daughter's wedding dress fitting for fear they may be misinterpreted'.

30 seconds later

So I Googled and it appears it's best if I say nothing at all; no questions, no answers, no facial expressions and no breathing in or out as any breathing whatsoever can also be misinterpreted as frustration, exasperation, shock and/or disgust.

I remember reading once about a woman who learnt to breathe through her ears. I remember thinking, 'What a nut! Why would anyone do that?' But now I'm beginning to understand why. She was obviously the mother of daughters.

10.52 AM

Dear Diary,

I'm still sitting here in *Le Show Off Room*. Just next door is *Le Fitting Room*. I can hear the goings-on inside and I can feel what I think is an anxiety attack coming on. Oh dear, this isn't good. Luckily there's a bottle of calming 'champagne' on the small table beside me. A note attached to the bottle says, '*Vietnamese Gloria's OK Glam on The Go* offers up to six glasses of bubbly for renting bridal parties'. That seems fair. Six glasses should be just enough to calm me.

AT THE LOCAL POLICE STATION

3.33 PM
Still March 24

Dear Diary,

Well the fitting didn't go to plan. I'm writing from our cell at the local police station. The cell isn't underground like in the movies. It's essentially the police station foyer.

Hope and Joy are here with me. We've been here for hours. Despite their presence I'm able to keep writing in you, Dear Diary, because I told the girls I'm making notes for the wedding.

I don't like lying to my girls, but if I were to ask Joy or Hope what they were writing in a circumstance like this there's no way in the world they'd tell me the truth. These days Hope wouldn't tell me the truth if I asked her what the weather's like outside.

My daughters both fiercely protect the privacy of *their* lives and yet feed on mine like it's a buffet. At their discretion they go through my toiletries, my wardrobe and my handbag. I remember once trying to search delicately through Hope's bedroom drawers for my tweezers and getting sprung by a mouse-trap she'd set in there to catch me.

The officer in charge here at the police station is wearing several badges, including one that says, *Officer Wittle*. Officer

Wittle said he wouldn't normally let someone make notes while arrested, but he whispered that he was willing to do me this favour because we used to date. To be honest, I think 'doing me a favour' should involve Hope, Joy and I being released. But I didn't want to make a fuss about things, in case the officer realised, amidst the fluff of the fuss, that he and I never dated at all. Or did we?

I mean he seems somewhat dull and is not very attractive. So maybe we did. Plus he's overweight, which increases the probability, because overweight blokes make me look slimmer.

'Did you really date him, Mum?' Joy whispered. I didn't answer. But only because I couldn't tell if in Joy's eyes dating Wittle made me more or less pathetic.

'He looks too unfit,' Joy continued, 'you know, to have long and lasting sex.'

'Actually, Joy,' I said, regretfully attempting to choose this bizarrely inappropriate moment to connect with my daughters as woman to women. 'Old people like me don't want enduring sex. We want it over and done with as quickly as possible so we can get on with more important things before we die.'

'What can be more important than intimacy?' said Joy.

'Bingo?' said Hope deftly, with just two syllables, swatting the conversation like a bug.

'Well,' I persevered out of a mixed combo of pride, stubbornness and stupidity, 'to be honest most women my age don't want sex, because it's all too difficult.'

'How difficult can it be?' quipped Hope. 'Even single-cell amoeba have sex.'

'Well,' I replied. 'Older human women have to use their imaginations to orgasm during intercourse, and when we get older it's often impossible to remember what it was that you were imagining.'

When I finished this monologue, even I felt a bit yuk.

The officer's hair is grey, and not in a silver fox way, more like a school cleaner's damp and listless floor mop. And he also has a beard that's not cool like George Clooney's 'three day growth', but unkempt like Rip Van Winkle. And he has a moustache that looks like a ferret is trying to burrow sideways up his nostrils. I know some people could find this kind of hot, and there would definitely be an internet porn category titled 'Fat Rip Van Winkles with Ferrets' but I don't know, it just doesn't turn me on. Yet, I find myself wanting to stare at him. I have to force myself to look away. He looks like he's trying to hide his identity from himself. And I can relate to that.

'Well?' said Joy. 'Is it possible you dated him during The Void?' This was a period that lasted for about three years after Hope disappeared. It was fuelled by my low self-esteem, lack of self-will and a perhaps subconscious desire to kill myself by being bored to death by people who, for example, think 'Bali is nice because it's so European.'

'Maybe you dated him and just forgot,' continued Joy. 'I mean Soula says she was once married to a really boring guy, but she can't remember who. Maybe when we get out of here, you could call Thilma and ask her if she recalls if you ever dated a policeman.' This is a typically practical suggestion from Joy and based on the fact that everyone knows that Thilma has a much better 'memory' of my life than I do because she records our therapy sessions.

I remember that when Soula found out about the recordings she said I shouldn't let Thilma make them because she might try to blackmail me one day. This, of course, was shocking to hear and it troubled me; wondering what Soula knew about Thilma that I didn't, and wondering whether to dump Thilma as one of my trusted friends. Dumping Thilma would of course be a big decision that would leave Soula as my only best mate, so I asked Soula why on earth she thought that Thilma would ever try to blackmail me. And Soula replied, 'Um. Because I would.'

Anyway. Hope, Joy and I have been here at the police station since we were arrested at around 11.03 am (Eastern Standard Time). I'm sitting on a plastic chair. Hope and Joy are sitting cross-legged on the floor. Having my own chair makes me look regal but it makes me feel like I'm not part of the gang. I'd really like to join the girls on the floor, but my body's still aching from my sleep last night and I actually physically can't get down there.

Mum is seated in the foyer, but on the 'innocent good people side'. She's on a cushioned bench and is currently staring at me with a face that could sink a thousand ships. As none of us has any cash to spare, Mum's been rung to bail us out and has turned up with a cheque. We're currently waiting for her cheque to be deposited so that we can all get out of here ASAP and go and suffer together in some completely new environment.

I should point out that the cheque depositing process might take a while, not because the bank is denying authorisation, but because the guy in charge of payments here at the police station is about twenty years old, and entirely of the internet banking generation, so has therefore not only never seen a cheque before but he's also never heard of one. In fact, when my mother handed her cheque to him he waved it in the air and said, 'Is this a joke? A rectangular piece of paper with a name and numbers and a scribbled signature? You expect me to accept this as money?' And when he said this I'm pretty sure the rest of us thought, 'That is actually quite a good point. How the hell did we ever run homes, businesses and indeed entire economies on the exchange of these scraps of paper?' But we did.

We also used to smoke on planes and drive drunk, and eat gluten, and kids would make their own firecrackers to blow up in the neighbour's letterbox and lose an eye or hearing or both and then everyone would tease them every single day until they finally left school and continued to suffer from the open wounds of that bullying until they died somewhere alone of an overdose. And a girl I knew had a dad with polio in an iron lung and a cousin of mine was conscripted to fight the Viet Cong and he was a pacifist and he was shot and died, and my friend's mother was made homeless because she had no rights in a divorce that her husband wanted because he hadn't found her sexy since he saw her give birth. And we still call those 'the good old days'.

In 'the good old days' we'd wake up in the morning and our mothers would say, 'Go out and play and don't come back till dinner time'. Of course young people nowadays think, 'OMG, the world must have been really safe then.' But we just thought our parents didn't love us.

I don't know if my dad ever loved my mum. I don't know if he loved me. On my seventh birthday Dad got hit by a car. In the hospital, before he died, he said he'd just been going to the shop to buy me a birthday cake. But really he was leaving Mum; he had a suitcase with him, full of all his clothes, and also half the money from the safe. When Mum found out she said to him, 'Wow, it must have been an expensive cake.'

Dad died eight days later. Mum told me not to tell anyone about the suitcase. She told me to just talk about the cake.

I think Mum thinks of love like a cake – a cake with a finite number of slices. And when I was born after seven boys who each took a slice, Mum assumed there were no slices left for her, not even a sliver, and whether that was true or not she then reduced her appetite for love.

I've always thought that's why Mum didn't love me – because she resented me for taking the last sliver. I wonder now if I was wrong. I remember as a teenager I once shouted, 'You don't love me!' after she forbade me from wearing lipstick to the school dance. And Mum replied, 'What do you mean? Of course I love you. I can't help it. I'm your mother!' At the time I thought her response was completely pathetic and proved that she didn't love me at all. But now, after the past four years without Hope, I wonder if maybe she was telling the truth.

Anyway, for now Hope, Joy and myself are sitting in our 'cell' and the woman who's pressing charges against us is sitting next to Mum, on the 'innocent good people' side, where she obviously doesn't belong. She hasn't been charged with anything and Wittle's told her she's free to go. But she insists she wants to stay and make sure that we all 'burn in hell'.

The woman is Gloria from *Vietnamese Gloria's OK Glam on The Go*. The charges she's pressing are assault and theft. When we arrived here Hope, Joy and I tried to reciprocate the assault charge but apparently Gloria's mean facial expressions, though unsettling, don't officially qualify as assault. Personally I think the theft charges against us will probably stick because both Hope and Joy are still wearing the wedding dresses Gloria's accused them of stealing. Gloria, meanwhile, is wearing a leopard skin jumpsuit and, in an interesting approach to accessories, has matched her boots to her teased blonde big hair. So from behind she looks like a yeti.

Joy looks like a princess in the dress she's 'stolen'. Hope looks like she needs a smaller size. I've told them both they look 'perfect'. Gloria told them they both look fat. Mum said we should charge Gloria with public nuisance for being 'such a rude cow'.

I didn't want to ask Mum for bail so I guess the question here is why. And the answer is because reaching out for help from her, for any reason whatsoever, whether it's 'Could you please show me how to plant a geranium cutting' or 'I'm giving birth in Aisle 9, could you please call an ambulance', simply reinforces the narrative that Mum's relentlessly bombarded me with all my life: that I'm full of potential but a massive disappointment, like a racehorse that hops.

In Mum's defence, all seven of my loving brothers agree that I'm being ridiculous about Mum having this 'full of potential but massive disappointment' narrative and kindly and respectfully say that I 'have made the whole load of shit up'. But what would they know? Mum raised her sons very differently to the way she raised her daughter (or daughters, whichever it may be). I think Mum raised her sons as deities to worship while she raised me as her nemesis. And my brothers' response to *this* thought of mine? Well, their kind, respectful and unanimous considered summation is that I'm 'being a fuckwit'.

We rang Eduardo to ask for bail first but he didn't answer because he was visiting his tailor getting measured for the gold lamé suit he wants to wear to Hope's wedding. So I left a panicked message with probably far more detailed information than can possibly be absorbed by a man who's most famous painting is a dot. In retrospect I should have just asked Eduardo to call back, but then again, in retrospect I should have run away from home and joined the Foreign Legion as soon as I could carry a backpack (perhaps at the age of about three). So then we rang Thilma, but she didn't answer either so I wrote her a message, took a photo and sent it as a text. 'Please call, we need cash' to which she replied, half an hour later, 'I hear ya, don't we all.'

'Mum,' said Joy moments after I received Thilma's text, 'we really need to get out of here so we can get on with the wedding plans.'

'I know,' I replied. 'But our only chance now is to call my mother.'

'We could ask Soula?' said Joy optimistically.

'No,' I replied, shaking my head. 'Soula lent all her cash to a Nigerian banker she met on the internet.'

'Well then I think we should call Grandma,' said Hope with loud determination. 'Because even if she says no, and is offended we've asked, she'll be even more offended should she ever find out that we didn't ask her at all.'

And that's when Officer Wittle said, 'I agree. I'll call your mother, and ask for bail. It'll be good to chat again after all this time.'

'What?!' gasped Hope and Joy aghast as I maintained my silence and Wittle rang my mother with the phone on loudspeaker.

'Hello, I'm the Supervising Officer at City West Police Station.'

'Really,' said Mum, 'and what are you wearing?'

'Ah, the regulation uniform, ma'am.'

'Well,' said my mother, 'I think you should know this is the worst phone sex I've ever had.' And then she hung up.

So Wittle called Mum back and said, 'I think it might make things easier if I recount the situation to you.'

'Yes,' said my mother, 'I'd appreciate dealing with a professional. Especially when I'm paying by the minute.'

'Well,' said Wittle, ignoring my mother as though he were a daughter, 'I refer to an incident earlier today at Vietnamese Gloria's OK Glam on The Go. According to my aggregation of the Witness Incident Reports it would appear that your granddaughters, Joy and Hope, and your daughter, Nora, attended a fitting at Vietnamese Gloria's. During the fitting Nora got drunk and when she saw the price tag on Hope's chosen wedding dress and Joy's chosen bridesmaid ensemble, she allegedly proclaimed, "There are a billion dresses here. No one will notice if two go missing. I insist we do a runner!" So off they all ran, but when they got to the front door, Nora fell to the ground after tripping on what is alternately described, depending on whose account you rely on, as either "Gloria's stupid foot" or "absolutely fucking nothing", and that's when Vietnamese Gloria called the police. So, in summary, three members of your family have been arrested.'

'Yes,' said my mother, 'so what's the problem?'

'Well,' replied the officer, 'I'm ringing you about getting bail money for your daughter and granddaughters.'

'Thank you,' said Mum. 'I'm more than happy to, as I no longer donate to the Guide Dogs Society.'

'Would you like me to come and pick you up so we can arrange it?' asked Wittle.

'No, thank you,' said Mum. 'I may be old, but I can still run faster than a leopard.'

And it was at this point that the officer covered the phone and said, 'Bloody hell, she's changed. My memory of Daphne is as a kind, quick-thinking and generous woman.'

'She still is,' said Joy, with both surprise and dismay. 'But unfortunately being around my mother always brings out the worst in her.'

(What? Why is my mother's behaviour my fault? In fact, while we're on the subject, why is everyone's behaviour my fault? When Leonard left us I distinctly remember my mother saying, 'Oh my God, Nora, what did *you* do?' And I still feel overwhelming guilt because I gave birth to 'a sickly child'. But I refuse to accept responsibility for my mother. Why doesn't she do what any normal woman would do and blame things on *her* mother instead?)

So then we waited for Mum to arrive. Wittle passed the time playing the drum solo from 'Eye of the Tiger' on his desktop with two biros while Vietnamese Gloria did a slow, improvised interpretive dance that looked like a caterpillar struggling to emerge from a cocoon only to become a tiny middle-aged woman dressed like a yeti. And Hope read, in slam poetry style, all the graffiti on our cell wall – for example, 'Freedom sucks (my dick, my dick)'.

And Joy? Well Joy videoed herself braiding Hope's hair into a pointy mop and posted the videos on social media, #beingkind and #nonits. Then she took a photo of Wittle telling her it was forbidden to post on social media while under arrest and attached the hashtag, #myrealdad? Then she posted another shot showing herself teaching Wittle how to follow her on Instagram #olddoglearnsnewtricks and finally a photo of herself looking earnest and kind as she talked to Wittle about who knows what, but the hashtags she used were #goodnews #possibledeadwife and #mymothersdesperate.

To be honest I thought Joy went way overboard with that post, but she was seemingly oblivious, and looking at Wittle in the police station's harsh fluorescent light it was hard to tell if he was hurting or if that cat's bum expression was just his old age resting face. I wondered whether Wittle would like a quiet and perhaps emotional chat with someone of his own generation who understands love and the grunt and grit of life rather than receiving hashtag solace from someone who thinks 'profound loss' is a nail polish colour.

But as I looked again at Officer Wittle I pulled myself together and began to get angry. 'Of course he doesn't want to talk about his emotions,' I thought. 'Not because he's a policeman, nor because his neglected facial hair may be a sign post for the condition of his heart, but because he is a man of a certain generation, my generation, and those men are totally emotionally repressed. They can tell you about their gout or their tinea, or the intricate detail of a footy game they watched in 1982, or a huge poo they did that didn't flush down the toilet. But their emotions? No way. A white man of my generation has a pathological resistance to revealing his feelings. The contents of his heart are his most guarded treasure;

despite the fact that he likes to act like there's nothing inside it anyway.

I remember I didn't know how to break up with a guy of my generation once, so I told him I loved him and he was out the door like a shot.

And I remember a guy who broke up with me by taking me out to dinner and wearing a T-shirt that said 'Single'.

After watching Wittle for a while I then watched my two daughters. Despite being born of the same father, from the same womb and raised by the same mother, my daughters are so different. Joy arrived on time. The labour was calm. I remember imagining whales singing in harmony as I gently released her into the world. No drugs, no stitches, the entire labour took exactly eight hours, and when she was born she was perfect with skin of such a magical mysterious purity we wanted to call her Pearl. But we called her Joy instead because Leonard thought that the bill would be reduced if we named our daughter after the obstetrician's mother.

Things were very different when Hope was born. I remember it all not so clearly – the fluoro supermarket lights, the wonky-wheeled shopping trolley, the playing of Christmas carols on the supermarket audio system even though it was only October, my waters breaking and the shop cleaner looking at me with disgust then flamboyantly placing a 'Caution: slippery' sign on the lino floor beside me.

I leant over the shopping trolley in pain. I called Mum. She told me to pull myself together because 'they were probably fake contractions', but nonetheless she called an ambulance and was at the hospital when Hope and I arrived, hiding her terror behind curt rudeness to the staff.

It was a short labour. It was too short, too rushed. It hurt so much, like Hope wasn't being delivered. Like Hope was being severed. The store manager delivered Hope and six weeks later, at the company's Christmas party, he was rewarded with an 'Employee of the Month' certificate.

I had no painkillers. Hope arrived at the same time as the ambulance. I was somewhat delirious; I remember looking at her, and thinking how absolutely beautiful she was and how she would match my favourite shoes, because both Hope and my shoes were blue.

They didn't place her on my chest, like they did with Joy. Instead they took her far away from me and spoke in whispered monotones. I presume they did this to keep me calm but their conversation was so unnaturally measured that they made me panic.

My baby was rushed to hospital. I trailed behind in a separate ambulance, like I was the placenta. I nearly died that day, too. But my life was secondary to that of my daughter's and thus it has been ever since.

My husband turned up at the hospital. Then of course he went away from our lives as I told you. But he was a good man.

Actually I don't know why I said that. I should say that he *seemed* like a good man when all was going well. But when things turned to shit, so did he.

Leonard and I first met at the United Nations building in the city. I know that sounds impressive, like we had a shared interest in saving the world. But I was just lost on the way to the rooftop bar and discovered some time later that Leonard was only in the building because he wanted to use the toilet. We got stuck in the lift together. After three hours waiting for help, sharing oxygen and such a confined space, it seemed only polite to arrange to catch up again. I'd just broken up with the love of my life. Actually I was dumped. My heart had a hole in it. The love was leaking out. Leonard was a plug. A few months later I asked him to marry me.

I can see a little of his character in Joy's eyes. Actually I don't know why I wrote that either. Because Joy doesn't have Leonard's character at all. In fact, I wonder if she was accidentally swapped in the maternity ward because Joy is good and kind and selfless and, except for the manageable hair, she is absolutely nothing like Leonard *or* me. On the other hand, Hope's eyes reveal a character that is impatient, impulsive and naive. Hope looks a lot like me.

As I watched the girls I could feel Wittle watching me. I was conscious I looked like a troll. I was uncomfortable. I'm not used to a man staring at me nowadays. Well, certainly not with that look on his face. I don't mean to be rude but it was a bit like a gorilla that's seeing its first butterfly (for the purpose of clarity, in this metaphor I'm the butterfly).

I decided not to stare back and instead adopted the demeanour of a woman of mystery. Basically I just didn't speak for a while. And in response Officer Wittle said, 'Don't worry, Nors, it'll all be over soon.'

'Nors?' said Joy after picking up this comment with her bat-like supersonic hearing. 'Did he just affectionately call you Nors?'

'Yes,' said Hope, as she'd heard it too. 'And that suggests he does know you.'

Thankfully, it was at that moment that Eduardo, Thilma and Soula arrived having presumably finally listened to my phone message.

'*Comme si dice freedomo?*' ('How do you call the freedom?') Eduardo trumpeted in his faux Italian whilst waving his wallet to suggest his question had something to do with payment of our bail.

'*Dieci mille dollare*,' the officer replied.

'Ten million fucking dollars?' Eduardo shrieked.

'No, ten thousand dollars,' said Officer Wittle. '*Mille* means one thousand in Italian.'

In response Eduardo refused to pay the bail on the grounds that ten thousand dollars was a demeaningly low sexist sum that didn't show respect for the value of us as either women or criminals.

At this point my mother entered. When I asked how she got here she replied, 'I rolled.'

'Good afternoon, Mrs Fawn,' said Wittle. And Mum took one look at him and gasped at me, 'Oh my God, Nora, it's him!'

Despite the fact that Mum's face was so close that I could smell the powder congealed in her pores I pretended I couldn't hear her.

'Look who it is, Nora,' my mother persevered. 'You must remember who he is.'

'A date?' said Joy, itchy with excitement.

'A lover?' asked Hope as though about to dry retch.

I held my breath and prayed for Mum's silence but turns out she's more powerful than God.

'A lover?' said Mum. 'Don't be so disgusting. This man is Nora's dead father.'

Then Mum wrote out the cheque, and as I said, we're now waiting for the young officer to return from the bank and tell us the cheque has been deposited.

4.17 PM

Dear Diary,

Officer Wittle has just prepared the bail papers for us to go home, and Joy and Hope are removing the wedding gowns, and covering themselves precariously in transparent official issue 'emergency ponchos' emblazoned with the words 'POLICE'.

'The trick I learnt in the seventies,' said Thilma as she offered her assistance, 'is to make sure the P and the E cover your nipples. And to not give a damn about your front bottom or butt crack.'

They don't look great, but are a better option for the girls than the alternative outfits Thilma's constructed for them using an assortment of the stapled STD pamphlets and some disposable coffee cups she found in the recycling. Meanwhile I folded the dresses and handed them back to Vietnamese Gloria.

'These dresses are filthy,' Gloria said, shaking her head as she unfolded the dresses and ran her fingers and eyes over the fabric.

'Well, that's your fault, the chase down the road, the grubby police cell …' I said.

'I can't accept them,' she snapped.

'Why?' I said. 'Aren't severe stains your specialty?'

'If you buy the dresses I'll drop the charges,' she said.

'How much?' I asked.

'Four thousand dollars for each dress,' she said.

'But they're stained,' I moaned as I rummaged through my purse, 'and I only have fifty-six dollars.'

'Sold,' Gloria said as she grabbed the cash, and left – running, for no apparent reason.

So now all I need to do is get the cheque back from the bank so we can use that money to finance the wedding. Easy, all problems solved.

6 minutes later

I just asked the junior police guy to go to the bank and get the cheque back. But he said, 'Sorry, madam, no can do. While depositing a cheque just takes a moment it apparently takes up to a week to cancel.'

Ah, just like the good old days.

BACK IN MY APARTMENT

It's still March 24
11.41 PM

Dear Diary,

It's night-time now and I'm once again in my living room, alone. I'm lying on the poop-brown floral couch. Mum's staying the night in Hope's room, and Joy has decided not to go home to her own apartment, and is sleeping with Hope in my bed instead. They've acted like this sleeping arrangement is completely spontaneous, but I suspect it's all been planned to keep me as far from their whispers as possible. I may be getting paranoid.

I can't sleep. It's the end of day two of wedding prep week and still absolutely nothing has been prepped!

When we got back to my apartment, dear sensitive Thilma detected my trauma and tried to ease it by telling me to sniff her armpit.

'I'm wearing lavender deodorant,' she said, 'it works as a brilliant calming agent.' I didn't have the heart or the stamina or the breath, after taking one heady sniff, to tell Thilma that it doesn't work as a deodorant.

And I didn't have the heart to tell the truth when Joy said, 'Oh Mummy, don't stress. I'm happy to take over the normal mother role and do all the wedding planning.'

I wanted to say, 'No, Joy, you cannot. You're a control freak and nuptials are intrinsically chaotic. As much as you'd like to take over the planning you're deluded to think you can. And the only deluded people allowed near a wedding are the bride and groom.'

But I did not speak. I said nothing at all. And just like that, Joy took over, and I saw the entire wedding go pear-shaped, when only moments before it had just been a lemon.

11.45 PM

I'm standing on the couch now, with my head stuck out my living room window, as I try to take up smoking.

I feel a little sick because Joy has, without proper authority, not only appointed herself Grand Wedding Poobah, but nominated my mother as the wedding caterer. So Mum decided to start trialling some 'exciting new recipes' in my kitchen and now I feel a bit like I want to faint and vomit.

To be fair to Mum, my queasiness is partially my fault as I'm the one who told her to try some 'exciting new recipes' for the wedding. You know, other than her usual fare of fish fingers, lamb fritters (with the lamb left out 'for budgetary reasons') and deconstructed tuna casserole (in which every single ingredient is poured out of a can, except for the tuna which is put back in the can after 'flavouring is complete').

And I'd like to be clear, Dear Diary, that my suggestion of

'exciting new recipes' could have worked if Mum had actually followed 'the new recipes' rather than do her usual thing of 'substitute vital ingredients with passion'; for example replacing a fish fillet with a flattened artichoke.

Mum said she can't stop herself being creative in the kitchen because 'fact is' she has an artist's spirit and was also raised during The Great Depression. Neither of these 'facts' is true. The most artistic thing my mother has ever done was regularly send me to school with half my hair plaited and the other half in a bunch, because she was 'distracted by something far more important' i.e. her hangover. So the only child I know who went through a great depression was me. (And that lasted till I left home.)

So the upshot is I've survived tonight's taste test and Mum survived the cooking, despite the fact she was wearing a totally flammable outfit. ('I can't believe you don't have any aprons, Nora, who doesn't have aprons? No, I can't possibly improvise with your tea towels, please pass me a synthetic bath mat instead.')

Fingers crossed Aspen's family won't need to eat even a morsel of this food. Fingers crossed they belong to a cult and subsist solely on air.

Perhaps I should try to stop worrying for a while. I have to go to sleep soon because tomorrow's going to be busy. Joy, as I said, has taken control of the wedding and, as much as Hope is a better organiser and much more creative, not to mention the fact that it is *her* wedding, Hope has silently deferred to Joy in a simple reflection of the relationship those two have always had; Joy power walking down the footpath as fast as she could while determinedly encouraging little wheezing Hope to catch up.

Anyway, Joy's organising has already begun. Earlier tonight she split us all into groups, which she calls 'teams', and gave each of us a task. Due to limited numbers our teams are small. Thilma and Soula are The Source a Venue Team, Eduardo and my mother are The Experiment With Taste Team, Leonard and Booby are The Venue Decoration Team and Joy and Hope are Team Guest List. I'm the only member of my 'team', Team Mum, and my task is 'not to interfere'.

Actually, I shouldn't belittle my role in all this because I have also been given a second task and that is to 'try not to be annoying'.

Thankfully I studied six weeks of law when I was at uni. Well, it wasn't actually classed as the subject 'law', it was more watching Judge Judy from the couch while I stayed home from my Art lectures to recover from glandular fever. Nonetheless I learnt that 'don't interfere' and 'try not to be annoying' are really subjective terms that wouldn't hold water if we ever took the case to court. But moving on, beyond the legal complexities of the situation, how do *I* really feel about being ousted from the core wedding planning club? I feel conflicted, I feel abandoned. I feel foolish, I feel obsolete, I feel yet again like I'm a failure.

Thilma sensed my pain, wrote something on her hand, then showed me. It said, 'I am grateful, I surrender.' But I'm not grateful. I had children in order to be a family. Not to be an outsider. I wanted to explain this to Thilma and Soula but their understanding of my perspective as a mother is complicated by the fact that they both love Hope and Joy, perhaps a little more than they love me, and they both consider themselves to have been as influential in my daughters' upbringing as I was – because Soula did things like teach the girls how to forge my signature and Thilma taught them how to knit their own underpants.

I've never had anyone to share my mother trials with. During Hope's teenage years, I did try to share my agony with my mum. Over three bottles of Riesling and three bowls of hot chips two years ago I described the impact of Hope's withdrawal of communication, her dismissiveness, deprivation of physical contact, her diminution of my self-esteem. And in response my mother said, 'Nora. It will pass.' I was furious at the time with the triviality of her reply. But now, I'm hoping that what she said is true. That would make me happy.

I used to yearn to be happy all the time. Now I just yearn to not be sad. I'm old enough now to wonder if happiness is just a momentary emotional flare that doesn't reflect either the road that's travelled or travails yet to come. In between the blurts of happy are the hurt of the life that happens. And the more life you lead, the more hurt that has happened, and the more skilled you get at not falling for the happiness, not being seduced into thinking that nirvana will arrive, not believing that you have finally landed at the top of the mountain where you will stay for all eternity with a magnificent view of existence, just because you're giggling right now. Instead you begin to realise that the good times go and new hard times come.

And the problem with getting older is you get wiser and you can start to see how a story will play out before it's even begun. Which I guess is why I have an uncanny discomfort regarding Hope's urgent marriage to Aspen.

2 minutes later

Hope and Joy just called out for me to 'Ssssshhhhh!' Apparently I've been writing too loudly.

11.47 PM

Dear Diary,

I'm lying on the poop-brown floral couch now. I'm trying to sleep but I can hear giggling. I suspect Mum has snuck into my bed with Hope and Joy and they're all laughing about me. I feel like storming in to confront them, bursting into tears and demanding they include me. I'd even be happy to join them in laughing at me – if it meant I'd be included.

11.49 PM

I just stormed into my bedroom. To my shock Mum wasn't there with the girls. In fact Mum was nowhere to be seen. I even looked under the bed. I didn't say anything and pretended I was looking for my hairbrush.

11.52 and a half PM

I just went into Hope's bedroom to look for Mum. I'd assumed I'd find her sound asleep alone in Hope's bed. But she wasn't there. Now I'm wondering whether Mum got sick of being kept awake by the giggling and has implemented one of her passive aggressive moves whereby she pretends that she doesn't want anyone to make a fuss, but then does something like quietly disappear in the night and cause an absolute freaking fuss.

Mum has always done this kind of thing. Even when she dies she says she doesn't want to 'make a fuss' and just wants to be cremated in a cardboard box. Yes, it all sounds humble and modest to be burnt in a cardboard box, but you can bet your bottom dollar that Mum will pre-arrange to have fireworks planted inside it.

11.55 and three quarters PM

I just rang Happy Days and the nurse on night duty said Mum isn't there and hasn't been seen since the afternoon. I asked her if it had occurred to anyone to call the police to organise a search party and the night nurse said, 'No, that would be an invasion of your mother's privacy.' But as she said it I got the distinct impression that the nurse doesn't actually want to find Mum. Perhaps Happy Days is happier without her.

I completely understand this sentiment but nonetheless found it very rude. I mean, it's one thing for me to be unkind about my mother, but it's an entirely different unacceptable kettle of fish for anyone else to be unkind about her.

12.03 AM
March 25

Dear Diary,

I just rang Eduardo to see if Mum's at his place. It's possible; they hang out together sometimes. In fact they often spend hours competing at backgammon (which is interesting, because neither of them knows how to play).

Eduardo didn't answer his phone. I'm not surprised. He never answers it after 8 pm because he likes to give the impression he's out partying.

I'm now going to ring Mum's mobile. I'd assumed up to this point that Mum wouldn't have it switched on because she's the kind of old lady who turns her mobile phone off so that she can save the battery for an emergency – which is exactly a moment like now.

12.04 AM

My call has gone straight to message. Mum's phone is not turned on.

I'm going to go to the bathroom to splash my face and hopefully wake myself up. Maybe this has all just been an unpleasant dream with a low budget and badly dressed cast.

12.38 AM

I found Mum on the bathroom floor. Now we're all waiting for the ambulance.

She's conscious, but she has a big bleeding gash on the back of her head. When I asked her what happened she said, 'Nothing'. Oh, and she called me Lilly.

Lilly was the name of Mum's greatest childhood love, a white-maned, dappled brown pony.

INSIDE CITY CENTRAL HOSPITAL

Ward 3
5.30 AM
March 25

Dear Diary,

I'm sitting next to Mum. She's in Bed 23 in the geriatric ward at City Central Hospital. It's meant to be a special ward for people who are elderly and suffering from old people's illnesses. But a lot of the people here just seem to be insane and some of them aren't old at all.

Mum's room is cold. The floor is shiny linoleum. In another stage of life this would have been the perfect dance floor, but now it's just a safety hazard. The walls are glowing white, the air is filled with the incessant beeps of plastic and metal machines with glowing screens. The beds are hard, as are the sheets. The blanket is thin and unloving. There's not a touch of humanness in this room, and that includes the humans.

Hope is sleeping, seated but with her head resting on Mum's bed. Joy has climbed onto the bed and is sleeping next to Mum. Mum is sharing the room with three other patients, two women and one man. I'm disgusted there's a man in the room. I feel violated on behalf of all the women. I don't know why. The man isn't talking or even awake. But he's snoring in that entitled way that adult men do, oblivious to the fact that their blessed sleep is causing others tortured sleeplessness.

Having said that, I should point out that at the moment all the patients *are* asleep. I'm the only one here who isn't. The chair I'm sitting in pretends to be a relaxing armchair but the pale olive thick square vinyl cushions that cover its seat and back somehow make the chair more hostile and uncomfortable than if the cushions weren't here at all. I haven't slept a wink. Never mind, you know what they say, sleep is for the weak, the lazy and the dead. Although I doubt they say it much in this ward, it would be way too inappropriate.

I wish there wasn't a man in this room, snoring, sleeping, awake or dead. Mum's had a tough time with men and love and life.

And she told everyone about it while we sat in the Emergency waiting room when we first arrived at the hospital. Yes, she told the young, the old, the weak, the carers and the cleaners about her challenging childhood. Some of which was definitely true and some of which was stolen from Anne Frank and Oliver Twist. I think she said all this so they'd understand she's had a life of suffering and therefore let her jump the queue. And on this occasion it really was irrelevant whether or not the story was true. She's been alive a very long time, of course my mum has suffered. That's what living is.

But not surprisingly, the fellow invalids in the waiting area with whom Mum shared this tale – the car accident victims, those with the flu, a man who somehow broke both his arms *and* shot himself in the stomach? Well, they didn't actually have the power to help Mum jump the queue. And I also doubt they had the inclination.

Thing is, we weren't meant to be in the waiting area at all. An ambulance was supposed to have rushed to my place after I called Triple Zero at 12.18 am. But the ambulance still hadn't arrived forty-five minutes later.

We waited for forty-seven and a half minutes for the ambulance to arrive. The girls wanted to stop waiting after just one minute and find our own way to the hospital. I made us stay because I didn't want to not be there when the ambulance people finally arrived, not after they'd undoubtedly made such an effort to turn up.

'Such an effort! What are you talking about?' said Joy. 'They're so late it's almost rude. Honestly, you're the one who always told us that punctuality is the ultimate sign of respect.'

'I don't know that this is really quite the same situation as a dinner party,' I replied.

'I agree with Mum,' said Hope, for the first time since she was eleven years old. 'Right here, right now, we face the very real possibility that Grandma is about to drop dead.'

'If you don't mind me poking my two bob's worth in here,' interrupted my mother (aka Grandma), 'I don't feel like I'm about to drop dead.'

'And if you don't mind *me* saying,' said Joy bossily, 'you are the last person who'd know if you're about to die. You've hit your head and you're probably concussed, plus Hope suspects you already have some low-level form of dementia.'

'I don't mean to be rude, Joy,' I simpered in genuine fear that the butterfly wings of my utterances might cause a tsunami in the land of Hope and Joy, 'but do you think *you* might be being rude in suggesting that Grandma has dementia?'

'No, Mum,' interrupted Hope, 'I don't think Joy is being rude, but I do think *you're* being naive. Has it not occurred to you that all the whimsical, fey and annoying things Grandma currently says and does are not in fact because she's a total fuckwit but because she's slowly losing her marbles?'

'Actually, Hope,' interrupted my mother, 'I'd rather think that I'm just a total fuckwit.'

'No, Grandma,' said Joy, 'I will not allow you to think so badly of yourself when there's a perfectly good explanation at hand, and that is that you're simply going mad.'

In the entire fifty-one years I've spent forensically scrutinising my mother's visage – its cracks and crevices, its spots and lines, her nose a little wide at the tip, her eyes a little too green and now underhung with bags that look like fading hammocks in the sun – I have never ever seen my mother look like she did at that moment. Her usual condescending countenance had evaporated and been replaced with utter fear.

I was overwhelmed by an urge to protect her. It was a strange contrast to previous urges I'd had to push her in front of an oncoming train.

'Um, Hope, once again I don't mean to be rude,' I said, 'but I think you might find you're making a very big call in declaring Grandma nuts when you've only been back with us for forty-eight hours.'

'I beg to differ, Mother,' Hope replied. 'Forty-eight hours is the perfect amount of time to notice such things because I'm seeing you all with fresh eyes, not blithely ignoring or seeing past or even through you, like you all seem to do. Oh yes, I've noticed Grandma's odd little tricks to hide the memory loss, the reduced participation in conversation in case she says something wrong, the loud and confident answering of the questions she does know the answer to, the agile deflection or dismissal of the questions she's unsure of, the feigned distraction when she doesn't understand what the hell we're talking about. To be honest, Mum, it's so damn obvious I'm completely shocked that you didn't notice.'

'*I* noticed,' said Joy, 'but it wasn't my place to say. I mean Grandma is Mum's mum after all.'

Ah yes, that'd be right, now even Grandma's undiagnosed dementia is my fault.

And then a profound grief struck me. It was a wave of tiramisu sadness with a base of spongy moist grief from the past covered with layer upon layer of assorted flavour grievances from the present, topped with the dark brown crumbly bitter sprinkle of all the misery still to come. And it was that layer, the dark brown layer that I had no choice but to surrender to, that flooded me with loss. I've been waiting half a century for Mum's vision of me to clear, for Mum to stop seeing me as a baby, a child, a daughter, and the thief of the last slice of Dad's love cake and instead to finally, actually see me for who I am. But now it seems that just as the countdown for Mum's final years begins, she's not going to see me as an extraordinary woman but instead as a pony called Lilly.

Oh my God. This isn't what I thought would happen to her. I thought she'd soldier on for decades like generations before her. My mum's mum and dad lived to the age of one hundred and three. They were deeply miserable but nonetheless we always held them up as exemplars of our family's superhuman genes. And even if

Mum's body had grown frail I thought that her mind would keep her going as a kind of 'fuck you' to the world.

Anyway, it was just after Hope accused Mum of having dementia that Mum decided to prove she had 'all her marbles' by reciting the most confronting and complex intellectual challenge of her recent years: the weekly menu selection at Happy Days.

'Monday breakfast, toast with or without one egg or two, poached, scrambled or fried, with or without porridge, with or without sugar or artificial sweetener, with or without full cream milk or skim milk, with or without a fruit juice, orange or apple, with or without a small tub of yogurt, with or without the added treat for those without teeth of having the whole meal put in a blender and served up as one small smoothie.'

I felt a compulsion to cheer Mum on, though if I were Mum, clinging to life and mind, that menu is the first thing I'd forget. But the one good thing about Mum's menu recitation was it made me join the girls in thinking it was time for us to drive Mum to the hospital.

We snuck into Eduardo's apartment to steal his car keys. As we entered Eduardo's Palazzo di Vomito, which is decorated somewhat like *Game of Thrones* meets *Hooters*, I caught a glimpse of Eduardo asleep on his bed. I'd like to say he looked innocent and vulnerable, relaxed and sweet like a baby. But the truth is he looked like a shelled boiled egg that had been rolled in pubic hair.

Anyway, we found the car keys in Eduardo's favourite Chanel bumbag. We then borrowed his thirteen thousand dollar Herman Miller desk chair, sat Mum in it and rolled her to the underground car park as Mum opined, 'This is the bloody worst jacuzzi ever.'

Once we got to the sports car I rolled back the convertible roof and we delicately levered Mum into the front seat using a technique I learnt as a child while watching my father tip compost from a wheelbarrow. Then I drove us to the hospital as Joy backseat drove from the front passenger seat, with Mum on her lap, and Hope squished behind me intermittently screaming at shadows in the night, 'Get out of the fucking way.'

I know it all sounds somewhat reckless, but it actually went surprisingly well for the first ten metres. Then we turned our first corner, zipped onto a main road, two policemen on motorbikes began to follow us and I made the assumption that this official escort gave us permission to drive even faster. In retrospect, I was wrong, because they approached me as soon as we arrived at the hospital.

Luckily, or annoyingly, or quite possibly both, my mother intervened before the police had even dehelmeted, let alone uttered a word. And of course Joy videoed the interaction. #DaphnerulesOK!

'I'd think twice before arresting my daughter if I were you,' Mum said with Joy's face lit flatteringly in the corner of the frame, 'I'd think twice because my daughter had a long-term relationship with your boss and it was asexual.'

'She means a sexual one,' I chipped in, preferring the notion, fictitious or otherwise, that I had performed sexual relations with their boss rather than the idea that I wasn't a sexual person, even though in reality I am currently not actually having much sex and therefore I guess that I identify as MANPH (Middle-Aged Non-Practising Heterosexual.)

'She means,' I blathered, so alarmingly flustered that even Hope looked increasingly worried about me. 'She means that

I had a sexual relationship with your boss, which I didn't. I mean, I don't think I did, but I could have, because let's face it, not all sex is memorable, so maybe I did, I mean he says we had a relationship, so I guess that means we had sex, but then of course lots of people have different definitions of sex, I mean I personally think that penetration of the vagina is required for the term "had sex" to be used in reference to a heterosexual couple, but others consider kissing to be sex, which it obviously isn't. But my friend Soula doesn't think a blow job is sex, but then the US congress did in the case of Entire Global Opinion versus Clinton. So I guess what I'm saying is you could ask him, your boss, not Clinton of course, yes, you could ask your boss for validation of my mother's allegation, which you're probably not going to do, I mean because he's your boss and also because the idea of two middle-aged people bumping their fat wobbly bits together is kind of, well, completely revolting and best avoided. So maybe don't ask him, and maybe just take my word for it, that the situation between myself and your boss is, um, complicated. And do let him know that, if it will help me not to be arrested, then I will have sex with him, unless of course that's considered to be some sort of bribery, or attempted assault, which of course it isn't, because I'm not actually suggesting sex to him as a reward for benefits because sex with me is more like a punishment because I'm not very good at it.'

'Which one of you fell and hit your head?' asked the shortest cop while raising his helmet visor to reveal himself to be a she. None of us replied. The policewoman continued, 'Let me repeat myself, and let you know in the process, that if you do not answer my question you will all be arrested for obstructing the course of justice. So which one of you fell and hit your head?'

'She did,' said Mum, Hope and Joy as they all pointed at me.

'Well, it's unsafe to drive in a condition like that, but it's not actually an offence,' said the policewoman. 'So let this be a warning.'

Let this be a warning. A warning! A warning about what? A warning not to let your mother fall in the bathroom, a warning to remember who you've had sex with, a warning about life in general. Caution: Life Ahead?

And it was then that the other policeperson approached, removed his/her helmet and revealed himself to be the one and only Officer Wittle, 'So you agree that we did have a relationship?' he said.

'I must object,' interrupted Hope, suggesting in one fell swoop that whatever she's been up to over the past four years it's either involved studying law, being arrested or watching too many cop shows on TV, 'at this point my mother can neither confirm nor deny anything without her lawyer present.'

'No problem,' said the officer, 'I'm happy to wait. I've only just moved to the city and this precinct but your mother seems to be in trouble with the law quite regularly so I'm sure we'll meet again.'

And with that he shook my hand. Not the way some men do, with either the limpness of a dead fish or firmness of an erect penis, but instead like, I don't know, a hand shaking a hand, like equals. Then Joy took a photo of herself with the two police. And my mother, with discernible droplets of blood dribbling down her neck, photobombed the shot while making what she thought was the universal sign for peace but is in fact the universal sign for cunnilingus. And then the police people left.

5.57 AM

I'm still in Ward 3, sitting beside Mum in Bed 23. And as soul destroying as this room may be with Mum's future lying like snapshots in the beds around me, it's a relief to finally be out of the commotion of the Emergency waiting room.

It's possible, after our public 'run-in with the cops' that people in Emergency thought we were cool, cooler at least than the man who kept telling everyone that he's a 'wife-loving husband' and has no idea how he managed to get part of a vacuum cleaner stuck up his bum. But even our coolness didn't progress us in the waiting list, so we rang Eduardo, the most well-connected human we know, to ask if he could pull a few strings.

'Hi, Eduardo, it's me.'

'Hello, my darling.'

'Sorry, Eduardo, this is not your darling, this is Nora, your assistant. Are you looking in the mirror at the moment, because you seem to be talking to yourself.'

'Oh yes, thank you, Nora. That is exactly what's happened.' And then he hung up.

By now Mum's head had completely stopped bleeding, because Joy had bandaged it with the tampon and emergency Hollywood tape that she also carries in her felt phone pouch.

'Oh my God,' Mum said in a somehow booming sotto voce as she looked at the couple sitting right next to her in the Emergency waiting room. They were drinking Coke and eating cold fries. 'You'd think if you were as fat as those two you wouldn't stuff your face in public.'

'Mum, sssssh! They can hear you,' I whispered.

'Good,' she bellowed.

I mentioned to Mum that she was really in no position to judge others because she herself had been overweight until very recently when Happy Days was struck by a diarrhoea epidemic.

'Yes, it's true I was fat so I'm in the perfect position to judge and suggest that what they both need is a good bout of gastro. Maybe if we sit here long enough, they'll catch it. Those foreigners over there look like they have germs. Maybe they'll be kind enough to give everyone gastro, now that we've been kind enough to give them access to our public health care system. Why don't you go over there and ask them, Nora? And maybe you could try catching gastro too. You could afford to shed a few kilos.'

When we finally reached the top of the patient queue we were attended by a young nurse whom none of us trusted, because he was too good looking. But we were more than happy to follow and perve at his butt as he led us to Mum's ward.

In the two hours that followed several other young male nurses asked for a list of Mum's current medications, a description of her daily diet and exercise routine and whether she smokes and drinks, to which Mum flirtatiously replied, 'Well that depends on the occasion.' Then they left, presumably to file complaints for sexual harassment, but perhaps also to organise tests for Mum's blood pressure, possible urine infection and an MRI to determine if she actually has a brain. We were told that the test results would take a day or so and be back 'definitely in about twenty-four hours or maybe longer or less'.

Oh, Hope and Joy have just woken up and asked for my credit card because they're heading to the café. It's made me realise how hungry I am. I'm looking forward to what they'll bring back. I've told them I'll grab this moment in their absence to try and catch a quick sleep.

6.13 AM

Joy and Hope have just returned. They did a massive coffee and toasted sandwich run for the entire ward and nearby nursing staff, for which they received tremendous acclaim, and I received the receipt. They didn't bring me anything at all to eat or drink. 'Why would we?' said Hope and Joy. 'You said you were going to have a sleep.'

Oh, I also received the receipt for the three enormous silver balloons they bought from the gift shop, which were apparently bought as gifts for each of us to give Mum. The balloons have printed messages on them: *Get Well Soon* and *We Love You*. The third balloon, the last one in the hospital gift shop, the one I'm apparently giving Mum, is emblazoned with the heart-warming message, *Congratulations, it's a boy!*

7.03 AM

The girls have left again to 'get some fresh air' so I gave the *Congratulations, it's a boy!* balloon to the bloke in the corner bed and he responded with the non traditional thank you, 'Wanna pat my weener nursie?'

7.17 AM

The girls have now returned from doing whatever they were doing in the 'fresh air'. Hope was probably plotting some sort of mum mutiny or coup. But now a doctor dripping with interns is approaching Mum's bed. So I'd better stop writing.

7.33 AM

The doctor and his posse have just left.

When the doctor arrived he ostentatiously scrutinised the chart at the end of Mum's bed, even though at this stage it has nothing written on it. Then he cleared his throat like a majestic frog. 'The test results are in,' he said as the herd of interns nodded. 'So would you like to hear the good news or the bad news first?'

What? I couldn't speak for Hope, Joy or Mum, because they'd kill me, but I was completely stunned by the doctor apparently treating Mum's crisis like the final question in a TV game show. If we chose the correct box we'd win a new fridge stuffed with plane tickets, fur coats and a million dollars. And if we chose the wrong one Mum would die?

Ludicrous. Yet Hope, Joy, Mum and I all dutifully responded to the doctor's request. Joy said she'd like to hear the good news first (of course), Hope said she'd like to hear the bad news first (of course) and Mum said she'd like to hear the 'bood' news first, which I assume means she wanted to hear the good and the bad news at exactly the same time. The final decision was left to me and I said I'd like to hear whichever the doctor thought to be the most significant. Apparently this was the correct answer.

'Well,' said the doctor pompously, 'our diagnosis and course of treatment is predicated on the obvious fact that your mother has dementia.'

'No, no, no, he's lying,' panicked Mum from the bed. 'Nora, Nors, demand a recount!'

The doctor smiled condescendingly then turned his back on my mother to continue. There was a flurry of movement as Hope, Joy, myself and the doctor's flock all scuffled to reposition ourselves so we were once again facing him.

'The good news,' said the doctor robotically with not a semblance of good news about him, 'the good news is that Bed 23 appears to have simply slipped in the bathroom.' The flock nodded knowingly. 'But the bad news is this is possibly not the first time she's fallen.'

'I told you,' hissed Hope.

'What do you mean you "told me"?' I said using no voice at all and just the squinting of my eyes.

'You know what I mean,' Hope replied with the mere pursing of her upper lip.

'These kinds of incidents are often not picked up by the family or carers around them,' the doctor continued. 'They frequently happen in the dead of night, when the patient is all alone and frightened.' I looked at Hope, she was nodding; I looked at Mum, she'd nodded off. I looked at Joy, she was making notes in her phone, transcribing the monologue like it was a dictation. Her commitment gave my mind permission to wander.

It wasn't that I didn't care about the doctor's information. I mean of course I cared. I want to know how my mum is, what her future looks like and, as a consequence, what my future looks like as well. My mother's health will impact not only on my heart, but my sanity, my lifestyle *and* my wallet because even though I have seven living siblings, they're all male, so the responsibility for Mum will land squarely on me, not because she mothered me more but because I am a woman. And it will therefore be roundly assumed that I'll look after her health – even if it kills me.

In my mental meanderings, as I imagined myself playing the part of the injured James Caan in the movie *Misery* while my mother played the sadistic nurse, I heard someone cough. Then I heard the kind of 'a-hum' some people emit when they're trying to get someone's attention and are too pathetic to say, 'Excuse me, can I have your attention?' It made me wonder why people don't just say what they mean. It's like people who tap a champagne glass with their spoon to quieten fellow guests at a reception. Why do they think that passively aggressively hitting a glass is less aggressively aggressive than simply saying, 'Excuse me, may I have your attention please?'

'Excuse me, may I have your attention please?' It was the doctor and he was talking to me. 'Sorry, could you repeat that?' I asked, as Joy continued to take dictation and wrote 'excuse me may I have your attention please.'

'I said,' said the doctor, 'do you recall your mother being vague with information?'

'Yes, always,' I replied.

'Can you tell me when you first noticed this?'

'When I was about two years old.'

'Have you been in any way aware of changes in your mother's behaviour?'

'No,' I replied, 'I haven't.'

'I see,' he said with a pout that clearly implied his series of questions and my corresponding answers had taught him more about my shit relationship with my mother than anything at all about my mother's health.

'So, tell me this,' he continued, as though I'd give a better answer if he gave me an easier question. 'Has your mother ever complained about her health?' And suddenly my emotional dial flew from shame, because I hadn't noticed my mother's decline, to outrage because this vainglorious little smart-arse was not only passing judgement on me, but on my mother, and he clearly, most ignorantly, had no idea of the kind of woman he was talking about.

My mother is a woman of her time, born between the world wars, in the aftermath of the Great Depression, raised to *never* complain, to be strong, silent and resilient in confronting life's challenges and to take tremendous pride in the fact that she was never, ever, ever sick! The last thing in the world a woman of my mother's generation of oppressed female battlers would ever do is comment on her own health, let alone *complain* about it. Sure, they'll tell you all about someone *else's* health, bloody ad infinitum; they'll even give a prognosis and possible EDACOP (Estimated Date and Cause of Passing), but they would never, ever, *ever* tell the truth about their own health. Especially not now they're growing old!

There is no way in the world Mum will tell me that she's ill. One, because she doesn't want to accept that her time on earth is nearing its end (because that means asking herself, 'Did I waste this life?'). And two, because she's terrified that both myself and the national healthcare system are champing at the bit to abandon her in some nightmarish high care *One Flew Over the Cuckoo's Nest* asylum-like institution, not dissimilar ironically to the way she perceives her current life at Happy Days.

So I replied, 'No, she's never complained about her health', and the doctor left with his buzz of interns forming a fat dull swarm behind him.

Still in Ward 3
10.05 AM

Dear Diary,

I've just woken. The girls aren't here. The ward is quiet and empty of staff. Maybe it's morning-tea time for the nurses. Or maybe it's shift changeover time. Or maybe the nurses have all run away.

Mum's watching parliament on her TV and telling the room she once slept with a prime minister. I asked her if she was feeling all right and without turning to look at me she replied, 'Yes, I am perfectly fine. Why on earth do you ask?'

'Because we're in a hospital,' I said, as I leant forward and my chair made that vinyl armchair cushion deflating noise of releasing air and sounded like I had chronic gas.

'Oh my God, Nora, will you never learn?' Mum said. 'You can't judge a book by its cover.'

'What are you talking about?' I said, standing and leaning in close, 'You're the one who taught me to *always* judge books by their covers, because it saves so much time.'

'Honestly, Nora, you didn't really believe that. Next thing you'll tell me you followed all my other advice.'

'Of course I did. You're my mother. Of course I followed your advice. Well, at least up until the age of about twelve when you told me that you make your bum look smaller by extending the crack with an eyebrow pencil.'

'I was joking,' said my mother, shaking her head with exasperation.

'And were you joking when you told me to follow the adage carpe diem, a fish a day!'

'Yes and no,' she giggled.

'What!' I said with palpable disgust. 'Was your mothering just a form of entertainment to you, because the really funny thing is that I took it seriously.'

'Maybe that explains why your life's gone down the toilet.'

'What do you mean? How can you say that?! What else was I supposed to do, ignore you?'

'Yes, you were supposed to ignore me, Nora, the same way every other daughter ignores her mother. You were supposed to realise that I didn't have a clue what I was talking about. No mother does. We're just making it up as we go, and essentially trying to do the polar opposite of what our own mothers did so that our kids turn out better than us.'

'But you gave the advice so confidently …'

'Did I, Nora? Did I really? Or were you just blindly absorbing my every word like a little knock-kneed pigeon-toed sponge?'

'What?' I choked, as I subconsciously yet arduously began to clad myself in layer upon layer of my tailor-made emotional armour. 'I don't have knock knees or pigeon toes, Mum.'

'In my eyes you do.'

'What! What do you mean? Why would you want to see me as less than perfect?' I asked, angry and trembling as our whispered voices echoed around the ward and threatened to wake those who weren't sufficiently drugged.

'I didn't *want* to see you as less than perfect, Nora. You were born perfect. But you diminished yourself. Maybe it was your father being fatally hit by a car in the process of abandoning you. Maybe it was having too many brothers, maybe it was the death of your sister, my favourite daughter. I don't know but somehow you didn't believe that I loved you and so you tried hard to be even more perfect in order to win my love. And it really gave me the shits! I wanted to toughen you up, Nora. The people we all truly love are those who have the strength and guts and fucking courage to be who they are. Not those who are weak and directionless, desperately seeking approval. You shouldn't have wanted my love just because I'm your mother. You should have assumed my love because you deserve it! Real love isn't about adoring someone just because you share DNA. There should be an entirely different word for that familial love. I'm sure the Eskimos or Germans have one. Maybe they call it Geforcenfakenloven, the love you feel for people you wouldn't even like if they weren't related to you.'

'What the hell are you talking about?' I asked desperately as I leant toward Mum and then back again, urgently wanting to both stay and solve this crisis and walk away from it forever. 'I don't love you unconditionally, I barely even like you.'

'That's what unconditional love is, Nora. Loving someone even when you don't like them.'

'Really? *Really?*' I said. 'And what the hell do you know about love, Mum? You're so scared of love you try to make your loved ones hate you.'

'Name one example.'

'Me.'

'One example other than you.'

'There are none, Mum. There are no other examples of people who love you.'

'Really, Nora? What about Joy and Hope?'

'Joy and Hope are mine, Mum, get your claws off them.'

'No one is ever yours, Nora. Surely if motherhood has taught you anything at all it's that no one is ever yours.'

'Maybe you're right, Mum,' I replied. 'And if so then maybe I neither like nor love you.'

'Well, that's OK, because my sons love me.'

'Do they, Mum? Because I can't see them here. I can't see them looking after you, sitting up through the night listening to your rubbish. I am the only one here. And I am the only one who has *ever* been here. When Dad left you and died in the process, when we lost the house, when you feigned having breast cancer on that now memorable Mother's Day – were they by your side, Mum, or was I? *I* was Mum. *They* were nowhere to be seen. So let me ask you, do they love you?'

'Sons love differently to daughters, Nora.'

'Really?'

'Yes, the boys all pitched in and sent me flowers. You've never given me flowers.'

'Would you prefer flowers, Mum? Would you prefer I gave you a bunch of mixed gerberas that die in a week or that I kept vigil by your side for the rest of your life?'

'I'm just saying that you've never given me flowers and the boys do, and then everyone at Happy Days comments on how beautiful they are and I can say my sons sent them to me. And everyone comments on what loving sons I have. What proof have I got that *you* love me, Nora?'

'I'm here, for God's sake! I'm here.'

'Well, maybe you should think about sending me flowers too. So that I have proof of your love when you're not actually here.'

'Do you know who organises the flowers the boys send you, Mum? Do you know who comes up with the idea, pays for them, goes to the florist to personally select them and then writes the boys' names on the card?'

'I imagine Micky does, or Harry or Phillip or Charlie or Miles or Rob or Peter.'

'No, Mum.'

'Well, one of their wives then. Probably the youngest one, Mickey's wife, or Violet, the one that we'd all be proud to have as a daughter.'

'No, Mum, it's neither of them.'

'Well then one of their secretaries or assistants or some girl in their office.'

'No, Mum. The person who organises the flowers every single time is me. In fact your sons don't even know that they've sent them to you.'

'Well, Nora, you should tell them, because keeping them in the dark about their own acts of kindness is really very selfish.'

I didn't know what to say. Mum has always been great at winning arguments with me but appalling at confronting what we're actually arguing about. I can't blame her, I'm guilty of this too. I obfuscate and pussyfoot and hedge around the subject, for fear in fact of exactly what happened just now, an argument that leaves Mum feeling victorious and me feeling violated.

Or maybe Mum feels violated and thinks I feel victorious. I don't know!

One thing's for sure, neither of us will apologise. But if Mum apologised first then I'd apologise too.

2.47 PM

Dear Diary,

In the four hours and forty-two minutes that have passed since I last wrote in you, the woman from the bed by the window has said goodbye, left the ward with her wheelie bag and been returned with a nurse at least forty-seven times.

And the woman across from Mum has had some kind of attack. She was on the brink of death but an army of nurses and doctors resuscitated her and brought her back to life. Back to her miserable life. After they succeeded, one of the nurses picked up the woman's file as it hung from the bed end. She was preparing to record the incident and as she did she read the notation, 'Not for resuscitation'. I wonder who made that decision. I wonder if it was the woman herself. I wonder if she would have been relieved to die. I wonder how pissed off she must be now.

5.05 PM

Mum's dinner has just arrived, wheeled in by a mute man wearing something that looks like a light blue karate uniform accessorised with blue rubber gloves. The meal has come with a label, and I'm glad, because otherwise you couldn't know what it is. It's apparently *Beef with mashed potato and cauliflower*. I thought it was popcorn ice-cream.

The meals also come with a little cup of tablets to alleviate any pain.

I wonder if I could take one.

I have to stop writing and help Mum eat her dinner. She suddenly seems to have forgotten how to use a knife and fork. She's also forgotten how to chew.

5.23 PM

Mum has just finished eating. Her appetite still seems to be hearty. She ate pretty much everything on her tray, including the paper napkin which she described as her 'favourite part of the meal'.

Oh, and Soula and Thilma just tried to call again. They've been ringing my phone since we got here, but I haven't spoken to them yet because you're not allowed to speak on mobile phones in this ward and I don't want to leave the ward to ring them back in case Mum chooses that moment to die – you know, during the one minute I'm not by her side. That's exactly the kind of thing Mum would do, out of a deep sense of privacy, but also out of spite.

6.17 PM

OK, Dear Diary. In the half-hour that's passed since I last wrote, Joy and Hope came back to the ward but now they've left again. While they were here they spent their time unconstructively attempting to deconstruct the wedding plans.

'Can we talk about the wedding?' Hope said as she plonked herself on the arm of the lounge chair I was seated in and the chair toppled and tipped us both onto the floor.

'There might be a better time and place,' I replied as we repositioned.

'Oh, Mummy,' said Joy as she patted me on the head, 'Hope was asking a rhetorical question.'

Of all the things mothers endure, I wonder if being treated like you're an aged idiot is one of the worst. Being yelled at, being ignored; yes, they hurt. But it also hurts, perhaps even more, to be treated like you have the mind of a damp dishcloth. What it implies is that every lesson you've learnt in life, every bit of suffering you've endured, every pang of disappointment, every morsel of courage summoned, every obstacle overcome, every single action you've taken to survive this thing called life – which not one single person throughout history has actually definitively understood the purpose of – has been an utter waste. And deep down inside, isn't a wasted life everyone's ultimate fear?

'We should probably get down to the business at hand,' said Joy, as she took the biro from my grasp, sat on the bed next to Mum and banged her bedpan like a judge with a gavel, or a guest with a spoon and a champagne glass. 'I think we probably all agree that there is a chance that Grandma's near-death experience may affect the wedding plans. All those in agreement say "aye".'

'Excuse me,' I said as Hope, Joy and Mum all called 'aye'. 'Excuse me, but are you saying "aye" because you think Grandma's near-death experience *has* affected the wedding plans or because you think it *may*?'

'Why?' asked my mother. 'Why does it matter? And why do you always make things so difficult? The best thing to do here is the exact opposite of what you're doing and that is to simply fit in.'

'What?'

'Stop trying to be different, Nora!' said Mum.

'I'm not *trying* to be different,' I said.

'Well then start *trying* to fit in. You're far too old to learn that life is a hell of a lot easier if you simply swim with the herd.'

'The saying is actually run with the herd, Mum,' I mumbled.

'Oh my God!' said Mum, Hope, Joy and the man in the bed next to Mum. 'Stop nit-picking!'

'Maybe you've got a mental problem,' said Joy. 'Maybe that's why you can't control this urge and simply run with the flow?'

'But what's the point,' I asked, 'of running with the flow?' (Yes, I did cringe as I said that.) 'What's the point of living your life if you're not being your true unique self?'

'And what, my dear, is the point of going through the hardship of being your unique self,' said my mother solemnly, 'and then just dying?'

'Mum, we're all going to die anyway, whether we try to be ourselves or not,' I said.

'Thank you, Nora.' My mother smiled. 'That is precisely my point.'

Has this been the issue between me and my mother for all these years? Was it really just as simple as the fact we have diametrically opposing views on the purpose of life and the meaning of existence? Surely that's nothing a couple of drinks or a round of golf won't fix. Men prove that method to be effective all the time.

Joy resumed her banging of the pen on the bedpan. 'Let's get on to the issue *du jour*, which is how Mum didn't notice Grandma's decay and how that has completely the-f-worded up Hope's life.'

'Joy, sorry to interrupt,' said Hope, 'but to be honest it hasn't completely fucked up my life.'

'I get your point, and now it's my turn to say sorry. Of course Mum's negligence and Grandma's current bout with near death haven't completely the-f-worded up your *entire* life. It's just completely the-f-worded up your marriage and your relationship.'

'Well, *I* don't mean to be a nit-picker,' Hope said, 'but I don't think that Grandma taking a minor tumble in a bathroom will fuck up my relationship with Aspen.'

'That may be true,' said Joy, 'but it will the-f-word up your wedding schedule?'

'I don't know,' said Hope, suddenly looking helpless.

'Well, I think I can help sort this out,' said Joy. 'I've been keeping a digital diary of our progress, or whatever the opposite of the word progress is; regress, digress, wedding dress, I don't know. Perhaps you'd like to see and like and maybe even share my digital diary, otherwise known as my social media posts, which clearly show a somewhat reverse acceleration in the hitherto forward movement of the wedding plans.'

'Joy, darling,' interrupted my mother, seizing the biro and poking Joy in the tummy with it, 'you know that I've recently been hit on the head, so forgive me for asking, but what language are you speaking?'

'Let me translate for you,' said Hope as she patted Mum's hand, 'Joy is saying that she has some photos of all the wedding planning we've done so far and wants to show them to us.'

'Oh fabulous,' said my mother, easing her head back once again into the crispy thin pillows. 'But don't we have to send them off to the chemist first to get the films developed?'

I remember those days. I remember it like yesterday. Mum remembers it like it was today.

My reminiscing was interrupted by Hope.

'Mum, have you seen Joy's posts on social media?'

'I can't,' I said, 'I'm not on social media.'

'Honestly, Mum, no wonder you have no idea of what's going on in the world.'

'Sorry, Hope, but I read the papers, watch the news and actively seek diverse expert opinions on global current affairs.'

'Yes, Mum, that's all well and good,' said Joy, 'but I mean the things that matter!'

So right then and there, Hope signed me up to some form of social media and had me 'following' Joy. And no sooner had she done this than a message came through on my phone saying that I had a 'new follower'.

'Oh my God,' squealed Joy. 'Mum's got a follower!'

'It's probably a robot,' said Hope.

'Why would it be a robot?' I asked.

'Because no one in their right mind would follow you. You're not a style icon, you're not a fitness guru and you're not an inspirational leader.'

'Well,' I said, 'not everyone is looking for those things. Clearly some people, like this person, want to follow someone who knows nothing about life, dresses badly and is just a little bit tubby.'

'Just a little bit?' said Mum with genuine disbelief.

'Then,' Hope persevered, 'he's probably one of those men who gets turned on by wearing a bonnet and breastfeeding.'

'Actually,' said Joy, after grabbing my phone and analysing my 'follower', 'I can confirm that the follower's handle is Shycop56 and he is Officer Wittle from the police station! I signed him up to follow me when we were in jail, so he must have seen Mum follow me just then and now he's following Mum!'

'Oh God,' I said. 'Is that legal? Do I report him to himself?'

'Follow him back!' yelped Hope and Joy.

'Don't you dare,' said my mother as she tried to seize my phone. 'A woman should play hard to get!'

So I followed him just to spite Mum.

Moving on, we used my phone to look at every photo that Joy had posted since the wedding planning began two days ago. There were 2325 photos. None showed anything other than Joy making a duck face.

'What are you talking about?' defended Joy. 'These are a documentation of more than just me. In a lot of photos you can clearly see Hope reflected in my iris.'

It was at this point that Hope said, 'I think the wedding notes that Mum's been making might give us a better idea of how the plans are going. Let's look at them.' And Hope grabbed you, Dear Diary.

I grabbed you back of course, but Hope seized you again, so I grabbed you once more and then, with you clutched by both of us we tussled like baby penguins in a boxing ring. I'm sorry, but the process tore the tired old sticky tape from your spine and you split in half, into two separate exercise books. The rear book, the empty one, was in Hope's right hand. The front book, the only part I had written in so far, was in mine.

Hope and I froze, still and silent, as though the tearing of you Dear Diary was a symbol of the final devastating severing of our relationship. My hands shook, Hope's lip quivered. Joy's eyes darted from Hope to me to Hope. Joy was showing all the anxiety of someone who knew the time had finally come to pick a side. The man in the bed next to Mum's started to chant 'Fight! Fight! Fight!' The recently revived woman in the bed opposite joined his chorus, clearly thrilled to at last have a reason to still be alive. And the frustrated Wheelie Suitcase Woman roared, 'Follow me, now's the time to escape!' then lay on her bed and either died or fell asleep.

And Mum? Well, Mum waited quietly until the uproar had peaked, then gracefully held out both her hands, palms up before us. It was like she was about to part the seas.

Mesmerised, Hope and I stopped tussling. And in response I then solemnly tucked my half of you under my arm, Dear Diary, and reached out to accept Mum's surprisingly gracious gesture by taking her hands in my own. It was a special moment, for less than a moment, until Mum flicked my hands away and said, 'For God's sake, Nora, what the hell are you doing? Just give me the flipping book.' And then she took you.

I closed my eyes, tightly; tightly like I used to when I was little and scared of monsters and believed that if I couldn't see them, then they couldn't see me either.

I said nothing, but my heart beat loudly. I feared its thunderous thumping could be heard through my nose, mouth and ears.

'We haven't got much time,' Mum said, speaking with all the gravitas of Mufasa in *The Lion King*. 'Hope's wedding is in a matter of days and I could be dead any second. So I will read Nora's notes and assess which of the wedding plans have been ruined and which, if any, can be reset.'

I desperately muttered, 'These notes aren't about the wedding. I lied! The truth is they're a diary of my bowel movements.'

The room became pin-drop silent, save for the gentle sound of the man in the bed next to Mum pissing into his bedpan. An anxious Hope trembled as she struggled to breathe while Joy, aroused by the catastrophic drama, glowed like a recipient of a Lifetime Achievement Award. And me? Well I prayed to the gods to help me, in whichever way they chose, as long as the method was covered by both my personal liability policy and my life insurance.

But the gods did not act right away. The gods allowed my mother to hold you in her mocking hands, to agonisingly flick her thumb down the corner of your pages, to ask for her reading glasses and to hear us tell her she was already wearing them. Then the gods allowed Mum to say, 'Right,' perch her glasses on her nose, open you, Dear Diary, look down upon you and begin to read.

I thought Mum would read from you out loud, Dear Diary. But instead she read silently, mouthing words as she went. I leant forward to hear her, to perhaps interpret a breath as it brushed past her lips, but I heard nothing. And finally, after more page turning and apparent circumspection, she closed you, took a deep breath, nodded and looked up.

'Well,' Mum said as she took the glasses from her nose and delicately popped them in to the glass of water on her bedside table.

'Yes,' I mumbled.

'Well,' she said.

'Yes,' I sobbed.

'Well,' she said, 'having surveyed the entire document and processed many a word within it …'

'YES?!' screamed Hope and Joy.

'It is my pleasure to announce that according to this all seems to be on track for the wedding. It is, I can pronounce, slightly in the shitter, but nothing our esteemed leader Joy cannot fix.'

And now I'll stop writing for a moment because I need to consider what I promised to each god in order to get this result – and whether 'negotiation under duress' could be a legitimate legal argument for reneging.

Dear Diary,

I'm sitting in the tea room provided for visitors to Ward 3. I've just left the bathroom. I came here to sit on the loo to do some thinking – because that's what Rodin's *The Thinker* looks like he's doing.

But there was blood on the floor of the bathroom and pooh in the toilet and hair in the basin and signs on all four walls about the importance of washing your hands, but not one single sign to tell you how to get water out of the new non-touch hi-tech taps.

So now I'm in the tea room. In one corner a weary young mum is breastfeeding her new baby while her two-year-old and four-year-old sons try to sit on her head. In another corner an elderly husband and wife are fighting about how many biscuits he should have with his cup of tea. I'm standing by the fridge, it's a bar fridge. It's not very tall, so I can lean over it and collate my thoughts as I doodle with my finger in the fridge top's dust and grime.

I've taken my mind back to Mum's assessment of your pages, Dear Diary, because I'm baffled by her behaviour. She's always loved prying into other people's business, and she's particularly loved humiliating *me*, especially in front of an audience. This means she could have just won that trifecta. So why didn't she read you out loud, Dear Diary? Did she *intentionally* save me from that shame?

The notion that she may have been protecting my back is not only surprising – it's also disturbing, because the last time Mum surprised me was on my fifth birthday, when she said she'd arranged a surprise birthday party for me and the surprise was that she didn't.

8.05 PM

Dear Diary,

I'm back in the ward with Mum again.

The man in the bed next to Mum joined you together, Dear Diary, using some pieces of surgical tape from the side of his head. And now his ear is kind of falling off.

The girls are not here. When they left I asked if they were OK about Mum's assessment of the wedding plans and Hope said, 'We're fine, Mum, everything is under control. You just relax and leave it all to us.' And I said, 'Fantastic,' but in my mind I said a different f-word because the first half of that comment, 'relax' and the second half, 'leave it all to us' completely negated each other.

The nurses have changed shift and our new nurse just entered the ward. She's not a tall girl. She is very thin. She's got nice happy eyes, but I wonder if she is happy. I don't wonder this because she's very thin. I wonder it because she's doing the evening shift in a geriatric ward, full of nightmarish cries emitted by the wide awake. So I doubt she thinks she's living the dream.

When the nurse entered the ward she touched my arm and told me visiting hours were over. My eyes welled with tears. It wasn't the fact that I had to leave Mum; it was the fact that no one's brushed against me so intimately since 2007 when I was targeted by a pickpocket in Rome.

'I understand this is difficult,' the nurse said, assuming I was crying at the thought of leaving Mum. 'Your mother has reached an age where she's begun to depart this mortal coil. I wish for you that this could be a time of fond reminiscence,' she continued comfortingly, 'full of laughter and love; indeed a time of peaceful closure for you in which all the natural conflict between a mother and her daughter can be resolved and released.' (I confess I felt calmed by the nurse's words, but unfortunately she continued.) 'I fantasise that this could be a time in which all the agony of misunderstanding, presumed betrayal, suspected emotional desertion and outright manipulative competition and coercion would be quelled and forgiven with the simple phrase "I love you my darling …"' (At this point the nurse looked at me and said, 'What is your name?' and I said, 'Nora,' and she picked up where she left off, but now with an added head nod.) 'It could be a time in which all the agony of misunderstanding, presumed betrayal, suspected emotional desertion and outright manipulative competition and coercion that exists between a mother and daughter would be quelled and forgiven with the simple phrase "I love you my darling Nora." But unfortunately this will not be the case.'

I think I responded with the single syllable 'Oh' and yet the nurse ploughed on. 'From here on your mother will begin to fade from life on earth, not only physically, but mentally and emotionally, as well to the point where she will try to say, "I love you my darling …"' (I interjected at this point, familiar with the routine now and said, 'Nora', and this clearly annoyed the nurse.) 'No,' she said, 'your mother will not say your name. And that is precisely my point. Your mother will not say, "I love you darling, Nora," she will say instead something like, "Do I know you, did we go to school together?" or "Get the fuck out of my room I'm calling the police." Therefore seize this time, Nora. Seize it!' I nodded as the nurse continued, 'And, in conclusion, let me add that you are welcome to stay and pat your mum to sleep or maybe tell her a story. Or we could both sing her a lullaby.'

I recalled the bedtime lullaby Mum used to sing to us as children: 'Once upon a time there was a fairy godmother, and then she died, now go to sleep.' So I sang that and after a moment the nurse stood up and then danced backwards out of the ward, I think assuming that if she did it backwards, I wouldn't notice that she was leaving.

8.45 PM

I can't leave Mum yet. I just can't. And so I'll write.

The girls, as I said, also left a long time ago. They didn't want to leave. I told them to go home and rest. They're both sad and terrified for their grandma and completely exhausted.

Joy is particularly tired, presumably not only because of the debilitating impact of constantly repressing her emotions for the past twenty-nine years but because she also spent much of today telling anyone within earshot that her grandmother and her two friends, Vera and Babs, raised both herself and her sister. One hospital porter asked where Vera and Babs were now. So Joy had to explain they died in a car crash and then Joy felt compelled to comfort the porter.

I'm hurt that Joy's description of her childhood with Hope doesn't include me – yet I gave birth to them. I financially supported them. I barely slept for twenty years in order to look after them – feed them, bathe them, help with their homework, drive them everywhere, cuddle them, negotiate their fights, take them to school, cook their dinner, arrange their play dates, fearfully give them freedom, reluctantly discipline them, clean up after them, dance with them, sing with them, read them to sleep, dream with them, inspire and protect them.

Once when Hope and Joy were fast asleep in my bed, a deadly spider crawled onto the pillow and I smashed that spider with a hammer. So what did my mother and her gals pals do? They just filled gaps when I was held back at work. All they did was feed my children, bathe them, help with their homework, drive them everywhere, cuddle them, negotiate their fights, walk them to school, cook their dinner, arrange their play dates, fearfully give them freedom, reluctantly discipline them, clean up after them, dance with them, sing with them, read them to sleep, dream with them, inspire and protect them.

Oh.

Maybe my daughters will suddenly discover *my* value when I'm old and have some sort of minor, apparently insignificant, fall in the bathroom that makes me think one of them is a pony.

Anyway, today has been much harder for my girls than for me, as this is the first time they've been so close to the suffering of ageing and the complete and utter futility of it.

And today's not only been emotionally hard it's been physically hard as well. Hospitals wear you down; there's no privacy, no sleep, and there's constant noise and shit food that screams, with every bite, 'This is all you are worth!' Basically a hospital is the last place you should be when you need to be in a hospital.

Yet my wanderings around the corridors have made me realise that some wards do make an effort to cheer. Ward 4B for example is festooned with Christmas decorations. The fact that they're festooning in mid-March, with the decorations either 'still up' or 'up early', is potentially depressing but this depends entirely on perspective.

And I've been told that Mum's hospital has a clown who sashays through the wards to bring cheer to the patients. But I've also been told that, try as he might, the patients here in Ward 3 find him less funny than their desserts.

So, well, now the girls have gone home and I'm here with Mum and Mum's just told me she wishes the girls were still here – and that I'd gone home instead.

'That's a mean thing to say,' I said, instinctively withdrawing from Mum. 'Did you say it because of what you read in my diary?'

'What diary?' said Mum.

'You know, the exercise book that I wrote in and you read.'

'Oh for heaven's sake, Nora, I didn't read that. I couldn't!'

'Do you mean "couldn't" in the moral sense or couldn't as in physically couldn't because of your eyesight?'

'Well, that's difficult. But if I had to choose one of those lies, I would go with the second and then elaborate by saying that the writing was too messy and small.'

'What? Even with your glasses?'

'Yes, Nora, my eyesight is fading fast. I just never told you because I was afraid that blindness might be the last straw and you'd have me put down.'

'So you living sightless, and choosing not to get better glasses, is my fault?'

'Um, yes,' my mother said. 'So does that make us even, after all that you wrote?'

'So you did read my diary?' I said.

'Of course I did,' my mother replied. 'It would be irresponsible of me as a mother if I hadn't.'

'So you lied when you said that the writing was too small and messy.'

'Oh for heaven's sake, Nora, I've been reading your diaries since you were a child. I'm very used to deciphering your scrawl.'

'So are you going to tell everyone what I wrote?'

'Of course I'm not. I'm your mother. I would never betray you.'

'You would also never support me,' I said as I picked up my handbag and pretended to prepare to leave.

'You might regret saying that one day, Nors, because it is not true,' said my mum, tugging on her too tightly tucked sheet. 'And before you go,' she continued, 'before you leave, carrying your handbag full of misery and resentment, may I offer you a word of advice? Turn around, Nora. Turn around! You are staring at the past and not the future. You'll never get anywhere in your life if you keep facing in the wrong direction.'

8.58 PM

With everyone asleep, and the nurse absent, I just went to the bathroom and sneakily rang Thilma and Soula to give them an update. And I also rang my brothers to tell them about the flowers they sent Mum.

9.17 PM

I'm still sitting in a chair next to Mum's bed as she snores. I'm pretty sure this is the longest time I've been with Mum without fighting since I was in utero. She looks so sweet and soft and pretty.

She also looks small and vulnerable, like a lost worm you might spot on the footpath. She suddenly seems precious to me. Like she's the last worm on earth.

A little while ago I decided to take this moment to hold Mum's hand as she slept, in the hope that she would subconsciously feel my warmth and love and know that she's not alone. I reached my right hand out and gently touched hers. Her skin felt thin, and unnaturally cool. I decided to warm her right hand by cradling it in mine. And like a guillotine, her left hand smacked my hand away.

9.39 PM

I nodded off too, but I'm awake again now. Wide awake. Wide awake and waiting. I've been waiting for someone to tell me what to do; to tell me to leave or to stay or prepare for the worst or prepare to come back here day after day or prepare for Mum to die in her sleep. I feel like I need a grown-up to take control. I feel I'm too young to be this adult.

I wonder where that nice nurse is. I wonder what the nurses here think of old age and death. If they're anything like my family, they don't think about it at all. My mother's mother didn't think about 'life after death' even when she was actually dying. But then she was emotionally constipated. I remember as she lay in the old people's home, diagnosed and fading, I said, 'I love you,' and she replied, 'Yes, yes, enough of that moosh. Could you please just clip my toenails.'

I think about death all the time. Not necessarily mine, just death in general, because I reckon if we knew the meaning of life then we'd know the meaning of death, and then we'd know whether to be sad or happy about the process of dying, and we'd know whether or not to cling to life.

Once, when I was ten and we were both drunk on cheap plonk after I skolled the contents of Mum's fifth glass when she left the room to wee, I asked Mum what she thought the meaning of life is and she said, 'Honestly, Nora, I haven't a clue what the meaning of life is, but as someone who's spent the majority of their adult life working three jobs, cooking rissoles, vacuuming the house and plucking my pubic hair, I can categorically confess that I'm pretty sure that none of those are it.'

Mum doesn't seem to be suffering now though. She's dozing and smiling. Those pills must be strong.

I think I'll sneak out now, while things are relatively fantastic.

9.45 PM
In the hallway
Outside Ward 3

Dear Diary,

Before leaving I kissed Mum's forehead. It woke her up and when she realised what I'd done she pressed her panic button.

So now I'm out in the hallway. I'm planning to leave the hospital before the panic button staff arrive. But I've taken a moment to prop myself against the hand rail and write in you, Dear Diary, because there may be too much bedlam when I get home. And, judging by the recent observations I've made regarding staff response times, I think I've got at least one and a half hours to walk the fifteen metres to the exit.

6 AM
The hospital car park
It's March 26!

Dear Diary,

I just woke up in Eduardo's sports car in the hospital car park. I must have fallen asleep when I sat down to drive. I was woken by a call from the hospital.

All the test results are back and apparently Mum's perfectly fine. 'You can come and take your mother home because we can find no reason whatsoever for the cause of her fall,' said the nurse over the phone.

'Well, isn't that a good reason to keep her in hospital? You know, until you find the cause?'

'In theory, yes.'

'But …?'

'But in practicality, no. Because we may not know what that reason is until she has another fall.'

'So you're anticipating another one?'

'Yes.'

'Well, shouldn't that be the precise reason why you'd keep her in the hospital?'

'If you follow that theory to its logical conclusion we'd have the entire population of the world in hospital at all times under constant surveillance twenty-four hours a day so that we could be on hand whenever something untoward occurred. Or in an even more perfect world, we'd have the entire global population attached to a monitoring device so that we could ascertain when something untoward was *about* to happen and therefore prevent it occurring. But you may be surprised to know that isn't economically feasible, so what we will actually do is send your mother home and wait for her to have another fall.'

'And then what?' I asked.

'And then hopefully that incident will cause enough damage to your mother to warrant a longer stay and more tests so that we can finally see what caused the first incident and the second incident, and therefore be prepared for when she has a third.'

'What do you mean "be prepared"?'

'Oh, you know.'

'No, I don't.'

'Well, there you go, neither do I, so we're finally on the same page. So could you please come and get your mum straight away because we desperately need the bed for a poor elderly woman who's just had a fall.'

6.15 AM

The hospital just rang again. I'm still sitting in the car. They sound pretty desperate for me to come and get Mum. They're probably fed up with having her around; complaining about the thread count of the hospital sheets.

They said that I have to come and pick Mum up or they're going to fine me for the cost of her accommodation. The conversation with the hospital was uncannily similar to the one I had with the local council when we dumped a fridge outside our building a day earlier than the designated day for hard rubbish collection.

6.32 AM

Dear Diary,

I'm now back in the hospital waiting for the paperwork for Mum to be discharged. The good news is that Mum's acting like her usual self. The bad news is that Mum's acting exactly like her usual self – whingeing to strangers about me behind my back, right in front of my face.

There seems to be an enormous amount of paperwork to complete considering nothing appears to have actually been achieved during Mum's stay here. I hate paperwork. I find the mere sight of it overwhelmingly depressing. I suspect this is because it reminds me of paperwork.

Anyway, I did read through it all, or to be fair, I kind of mimed reading through it all, with my mother peering over my shoulder. Having pretended to finish, I applied my signature. And then my mother took the pen and wrote a big letter 'F' for 'failed' on the front page, drew a circle around it and added a handwritten note that said 'could do better'.

BACK IN MY APARTMENT

9.30 AM
Still March 26

Dear Diary,

OK, I successfully collected Mum and dropped her back at Happy Days and am now considering getting a second job to pay for the hospital parking. Unlike the airport parking where the rate gets cheaper the longer you stay there, the hospital car park gets more expensive with every millisecond that passes.

As I paid I said to Mum, 'Oh my God, how can any organisation possibly consider making a profit out of other people's suffering!' And Mum yawned, took a deep breath and said, 'Oh my God, get over it Nora, that's the way the whole world works!' I then asked about her experience with the common people in the public hospital system and she said she thinks she's caught the plague. And I finally asked if she'd like to come to my place and Mum retorted, 'Why the hell would I want to do that, Nora? It's far too early to have a drink.'

I'm now back in my apartment. I'm writing at the dining table. Hope is in her room still fast asleep and Joy is sitting at the table writing next to me. Joy is perfectly happy, thinking that I'm writing more notes for the wedding. Joy has been writing a eulogy for my mother. When I realised this was what she was doing I said, 'I always thought I'd be writing the eulogy.'

'No, Grandma asked me because you can't be trusted.'

'Oh,' I said, hiding my hurt. 'May I see what you've written?' Then I read it and said, 'Why have you described Grandma like this when you know that no one at her funeral will know who you're talking about? I mean, really, your grandmother is your Rock of Gibraltar, your Sword of Damocles and Sir Walter Raleigh's cape?'

'Yes.'

'But that doesn't make sense?'

'Honestly, Mum, you really don't get the modern world. These words are just to fill the air. The important message will be the photo we send out on social media.'

'And what will the photo be of? Burning flames in hell?'

'No, it'll be a selfie of me and Hope with Grandma in the coffin.'

'You're all going to be in the coffin?'

'No, Grandma will be in the coffin and Hope and I are going to bend down and put our heads next to hers. We practised last night using a watermelon.'

'Are you going to do a similar thing when I die?'

'We haven't really thought about it. But if I have to give my answer now I'd say that we'll probably hire actors as our body doubles for your funeral.'

'Why? Because you'll be too sad to speak?'

'No, because you wrote our scripts for your eulogy years ago ...'

'Yes ...?'

'... and it will be too hard for us to present them without laughing.'

'Well, I felt I needed to highlight several of my qualities and achievements as you two seem ignorant of all of the amazing things that I've done with my life.'

'Mum, your eulogy has quotes in it, allegedly about you, from people you not only have never met but who actually died before you were born. And the photos you've included don't even look like you.'

'I thought you'd think that was a good thing,' I said. 'But, don't worry, I'll just ask Soula and Thilma to read my eulogy.'

'I hate to tell you this, Mum,' said Joy, before sighing, 'but assuming that you'll die of old age, like Great-Grandma and Grandpa did then, Thilma and Soula aren't likely to still be alive.'

'Oh,' I mumbled, as I imagined my dotage without my two best pals and realised this must be how Mum's felt for the fifteen years since Babs and Vera passed.

'But you never know,' persisted Joy, now embracing an optimistic cheerleader persona, 'you might make some new pals in your nursing home.'

'I'd rather be dead than go to one of those,' I replied, secretly hoping that Joy would offer to care for me in her own home in my dotage. But instead she said, 'Sounds like you should sign up to an assisted dying program. If you like I could get you the forms.'

4 minutes later

Oh, Soula just walked into my apartment. She's dressed in a full-length evening gown, heels and feather boa. For most people this kind of outfit would signify the advent of a significant celebratory occasion, but in Soula's case it signifies all her other clothes are in the wash.

'Oh my God,' she said as she sashayed in, choking briefly as her feather boa got caught in the little menopause fan that I'd rested on the dining room table. 'How is your mother?'

'Mum's fine, thank you,' I said. 'She just hit her head. She has signs of dementia and currently thinks I'm her pony, but I'm proud to say it was the great love of her childhood.'

'Mum,' interrupted Joy, charmingly, 'Grandma didn't confuse you with the great love of her childhood; she genuinely thought you were a medium-sized horse.'

'Oh well,' said Soula, 'I take back everything I said. Sounds to me like your mother might not have dementia at all, because confusing you with a horse could just be a lighting issue.'

'Mu-u-um?' asked Joy in that ingratiating voice my daughters usually use when they're about to say something really mean or ask for cash. 'What will we do if her dementia gets too bad? Should we euthanise her?'

I was surprised by the question, it didn't seem cash related at all. 'Well first,' I said, leaning back on my chair somewhat professorially, 'how will we know when it's "too bad"?'

'The same way that we'll know with you,' said Joy simply. 'When you're too unhappy.'

'But how will you know when I'm too unhappy?'

'God, Mum, I think Hope and I can tell when you're unhappy.'

'Really?' I said.

There was a long silence.

'Joy, darling,' said Soula, sweetly trying to be kind, 'you can kill *me* if you want.'

9.47 AM

Miss Binsa from Happy Days just rang. She was recently 'promoted' from casual chef at Happy Days to working as the receptionist too. This double workload means that she's either a wizard of multi-tasking or not doing either job very well.

The update from Miss Binsa is that Mum is still alive, but the bad news is that Mum's asked if she can play 'skipping rope' at recess. Her muddle-headedness is apparently getting worse so Happy Days wants to have Mum's cognitive capacity tested again and they've asked me to come in and help. They want to decide if this is a temporary situation as a result of the fall and the concomitant shock or if Mum needs to be considered for the dementia ward. This sounds so ominous that I find I'm already planning to tell elaborate lies on Mum's behalf in order to prevent her being sent there.

Miss Binsa is still talking but I've stopped listening. I'm aware this is the second time my mind's wandered in two days. I wonder if this is one of those things I do that gives Hope the shits. I'm going to write that down. I'm going to write all the things I do wrong and start a *How to Be A Better Mum* list: I don't listen, I think I know everything, I love the wrong way, I don't love enough, I love too much, I think everything is about me. OK, that's a start, now back to Miss Binsa. Oh, she's hung up the phone.

I'm thinking about Mum. I'm wondering if Mum is scared; I'm wondering if she knows she's lost the plot; I'm wondering if I should help Mum cheat or if I should lie to Mum instead. If it were happening to me in old age, and according to Joy it undoubtedly will, I wouldn't want to be told the truth. I wouldn't want to be told, 'You're an old lady living in a place that is called a home but is not a home at all. Your housemates are drugged, the staff are depressed, the hall smells like wee, and the air you breathe day in day out is shared with all the other residents – and so the air is sad.'

Yes, I'd like to be told a fabulous lie because surely there comes an age in life when it's too late to face ugly realities.

And surely I should listen to myself as I write this. Because those ugly realities can include the hurt we've caused each other. Surely there must come a time when we recognise that our parents did their best in raising us, and we call a truce and say all is forgiven.

If I were to draw my mother when I was a child I would have drawn a witch. But that wicked woman is fading with age. She's softening, or maybe I am.

9.51 AM

I told Soula and Joy that I had to go to Happy Days to fight for Mum's sanity and our conversation woke Hope. As I neared the front door to leave she pulled me into her bedroom where her unpacked clothes had bred and hurled themselves all over the floor.

'Mother?' she said with a previously unused inflection that could imply either devotion or danger.

'Um, yes?' I replied, terrified I was to be scolded for another parental crime I'd unwittingly committed.

'There's a problem with you visiting Grandma now because Aspen's family is meeting us for lunch today.'

'Today?!'

'Yes.'

'But we're not prepared. I mean, I don't know a single thing about Aspen or his family.'

'Well, that's why we're having lunch.'

'But surely you're going to tell me something about them before then.'

'No, I'm not.'

'But why?'

'Because I don't want you to prejudge Aspen with your misconceptions. And also because I don't know anything about his family either.'

'But when was this arranged?'

'Joy organised it last night while you were out gallivanting.'

'I wasn't gallivanting, I was at the hospital, caring for your grandmother.'

'Please don't be a martyr, Mum. This is not about you. It's about my wedding and the fact that Aspen's family is meeting us for lunch.'

'Oh, OK. Well, maybe Joy could book a restaurant too.'

'No need. Joy thought it would be more hospitable for us to invite them over to lunch here, at your place.'

'Really?' I asked, waiting for a punchline that didn't come. Pause. Pause. Pause. So then I said, 'Well, yay and yay. And is there anything else you need to tell me? You know like, how many of them are coming, what they do for a living, allergies, whether they're gluten free and, um, well, their names?'

It was the perfect question save for that tentacle 'what they do for a living'. Hope honed in on it immediately.

'What difference does an occupation make?' she quipped as she folded her arms.

'I didn't ask what their occupations are,' I replied. 'I asked what they do.'

'Same thing.'

'Not at all. I might be referring to their hobbies or their spirituality or their drug preferences.'

'Nice try, Mum,' said Hope. 'But it's obvious that you're being a bit of a snob and are asking 'what they do' so you can determine their incomes. Are you worried their rank in the capitalistic hierarchy isn't as high as assistant to a raving no talent narcissist?'

'Out of all due respect, Eduardo does pay my wage and that does pay the bills, so you probably shouldn't refer to him as a raving no talent narcissist.'

'I was talking about Dad.'

I confess I was both confused and shocked to hear Hope refer to her father in this way. And I felt an unfamiliar urge to protect him. Is this whole wedding thing making me go mad?

'And speaking of Dad,' Hope continued, 'Joy invited him to lunch today too.'

'Why?' I said. 'Are you going to eat him?'

Apparently that wasn't a punchline either and so I continued, 'Hope, while it's important for us to meet your fiancé's family, wouldn't bite-sized meetings be a better idea, with a series of smaller introductions of selected groups?'

'Joy said it would be good for Aspen's family to meet us warts and all.'

'Why?'

'Because that way they won't feel threatened or intimidated.'

'What are you talking about?'

'I've already told you, Mum, Aspen never talks about his family and I think it's due to embarrassment. I suspect they have no jobs, no assets and no prospects.'

'Well, other than the no job bit,' I fake laughed, 'they sound very similar to us. Aha aha. A ha a ha.'

'Jesus, Mum, this is serious. You work for a famous artist and some people see that as success.'

'Eduardo's fame has nothing to do with me.' I genuinely laughed. 'In fact, it barely has anything to do with him!'

'It doesn't matter who caused the fame. It matters who benefits from it. And you benefit from Eduardo's fame.'

'Well, if I do, Hope, then you do too.'

'I haven't benefitted from it, Mum, I've suffered because of it.'

'Sorry, what?' I asked so genuinely shocked that I sat on the clothes-covered unmade bed and risked totally disappearing. 'I didn't know that my job has caused you to suffer; I just thought it had provided the money for your food, clothing, shelter and education, not to mention also providing you with stability, connections, job opportunities and an insight into another world that most would only dream of.'

'Yes, that's the superficial analysis of the situation, but the essence of it is that Eduardo has been the centre of your attention ever since you started working for him, i.e. for my entire life.'

'Oh my God, surely you're not jealous of Eduardo?'

'Of course I'm not jealous of Eduardo. Absolutely no one is. I'm just disappointed in you. You are the artist, Mum! You could have managed your own artistic career. But you chose to manage a moron.'

'He offered good money, an immediate start and flexible work hours. I made that decision after your dad left. And I made it for you!'

'Oh yes, here we go, of course it's all my fault,' said Hope. 'But enough about Signor Eduardo because Eduardo is not the problem.'

'What is?' I finally blurted after bottling it up for four years. 'Tell me, Hope, what is the problem?'

'I don't know Mum, I don't know,' said Hope, now bursting into tears. 'The problem is everything. The problem is nothing. The problem is you!'

'But why? What have I done or not done? Tell me, Hope, I really don't know. There was a time when I considered my mothering of you girls to be the greatest achievement of my life.'

'Well maybe you tried too hard, Mum. Maybe you should have just been a mother.'

'What does that even mean, Hope, just be your mother? Who are we holding up as a role model here? Mother Teresa, Mother Mary, Mother Fucker, my mother?'

'What are you talking about?' Hope roared. 'Grandma saved your life after Dad left. She stepped in with Vera and Babs and carried the load. They were a brilliant mother to you.'

'No, Hope, they were a brilliant *grandmother* to you.'

'Oh my God, when will you get over your unwitnessed childhood suffering?'

'When will you get over yours, Hope?' I said, with immediate regret. 'Hope!' I whispered, standing and reaching out my arms to comfort her. But Hope pushed me away and my hip hit the silver handle that never really suited that door and sometimes doesn't even close properly.

Down the hall, in the living room, I caught a glimpse of Joy and Soula oblivious to my argument with Hope as they struggled to open a child-proof lid.

'I've protected you from everything bad so that your life would be different to mine,' I continued, 'But the one thing that I couldn't protect you from is yourself.'

'I wouldn't need to be protected from myself if you hadn't loved me the way that you did!'

'What?'

'You smothered me, Mum! *You smothered me!*' Hope yelled, her cheeks growing red with frustration, tears welling in her eyes.

'I was protecting you, Hope! Your health makes you vulnerable.'

'You were suffocating me.'

'I'm sorry, I'm sorry, I just wanted to make sure that nothing else bad happened to you. I was scared of losing you. Like I lost my dad and, um, other people, but in my efforts not to lose you, I lost you.'

'I went away to escape you, Mum. You and your needy desperation disguised as motherly love. Instead of giving birth to Joy and me you really should have just bought a poodle.'

I know, Dear Diary, that one might imagine that Hope and I were screaming at each other by now. Well, Hope *was* screaming. But I wasn't. I am not a screamer, nor a yeller, and I never have been. My mother yelled when I was growing up. But she'd storm from the room if *I* ever even slightly raised my voice at her. And then she'd disappear for hours. And no one wants their mum to disappear. Or their daughter. So that's why I'm not a yeller.

I don't know what facial expression I maintained during this exchange. I don't know if I looked shocked or sad or blank. But I know that inside, my heart had been punched. I imagined the referee in a boxing ring, banging the floor next to my heart as it lay fallen on the canvas, encouraging my heart to rise, defend itself and then attack. And I realised what the problem was with this battle. My heart would never fight against Hope, because it will always be on her side.

Ah, motherhood. Why didn't anyone tell me it's an extreme sport? It's an Olympic event played by absolute beginners; it's synchronised swimming meets weightlifting, meets marathon running. It's a little bit of whatever that sport is where you run through obstacles and shoot at a target. Except the target is yourself.

Anyway, at that moment, Soula called out. 'Sorry to interrupt the fun,' she said, 'but I haven't a clue what to wear for the lunch. I'll have to ask Thilma to bring something over because I heard you want us all to look unintimidating but at the moment I look strikingly fabulous. And also, Nora, shouldn't you get a wriggle on, if you have to go to Happy Days *and* clean up your apartment.'

'Actually, I'm thinking we might entertain in Eduardo's apartment instead,' said Hope.

'I live in a two-bedroom apartment that's littered with out-of-focus photos and faded finger paintings like a shrine to my children and it has a view of apartments that have actual views and in an effort not to be intimidating you want to transfer us all from my comparative pantry-sized apartment to Eduardo's twenty million dollar apartment and its views of the city and harbour?'

'I thought we could cover the windows.'

'But the obscene and overt wealth isn't just the view, the walls are covered in priceless art!'

'Yes,' said Hope, 'but it's contemporary art so if you didn't know the price you'd just think it was shit.'

'Darling,' I said, after taking a deep breath that to the canny ear signified a conversational gear change, 'we've just had a huge fight, your grandma isn't well and we're perhaps all not thinking clearly. Do you think it's wise for us to meet your fiancé's family today?'

'That is so typical,' roared Hope. 'You're always trying to avoid the real issues.' (I made a mental note to add this to my *How to Be A Better Mum* list.)

And that's when Thilma walked in and said, 'Oh my God, I have never seen a room full of people more in need of a hug. Everyone form an orderly queue and I'll embrace you one by one for five bucks a pop.'

AT HAPPY DAYS NURSING HOME

In the car park
10.37 AM
Still March 26

Dear Diary,

Thilma, Soula and I have just driven to Happy Days and I've successfully parked by hitting the car behind us and 'nudging' the car in front. None of us was surprised by this result; it was a very small parking space and fairly obvious that I needed to hit at least one car in order for Eduardo's car to fit.

Thilma and Soula insisted on coming with me to Happy Days. In a perfect world I would have asked Soula and Thilma to stay in the car and wait while I went in to check on Mum. As I sat with Mum in the hospital yesterday and surveyed the feebleness around me, it became apparent that with old age not only comes hearing loss, eyesight failure, falls and forgetfulness, but myriad problems that are both enfeebling and humiliating. And I didn't want Thilma and Soula to see Mum like this and laugh.

Actually, as the three of us compose ourselves in the car after our bingle, with Soula and Thilma trying to move the windscreen wipers with their minds and me writing in *you*, Dear Diary, I realise

Thilma won't laugh, she'll do the complete opposite. She'll take one look at Mum in her bewildered state and without doubt burst into tears. Thilma is a softy, way beyond practicality. The term a therapist might use to describe her is 'empath', someone who is so attuned to the emotions and moods of others that it renders them overwhelmed and often non-functional. At the moment she can barely speak because she's feeling sorry for the bumper bar.

Soula calls Thilma 'a bleeding fucking heart' and in defiant contrast Soula proudly calls herself 'a nasty bitch'. But Soula isn't nasty at all. Soula laughs at the misfortune of others because that's simply how she processes traumatic information – by completely bypassing the trauma of it. She doesn't have the mind nor the inclination for complex, quick witticisms, nuances or subtle, layered humour. She'd give you her last dollar, the shirt off her back, her life for yours; she loves with strength but simply. And she also loves a pie in the face or a slip on a banana, and many times I've seen her doubled up with laughter, clasping her stomach, gasping for breath, her eyes wet with tears of joy just hearing someone speak with a lisp.

So I told Soula and Thilma to wait in the car. But they've both refused, on the grounds that I needed their support – which is true, and ironically, why I'd asked them to stay in the car.

10.42 AM
Inside Happy Days

Um …

Actually I don't think I can write at the moment.

Back in the Car
11.07 AM

Dear Diary,

We've now exited Happy Days and are back in the car.

We're just sitting here for the moment. Gathering our thoughts. Thilma and Soula are talking about what aliens might look like. I'm taking this opportunity to write in you and share what just happened in Happy Days.

The entrance door to the foyer was locked. You have to press the intercom to be let in, and as I pushed the buzzer and waited for a response I could see Soula was already getting the giggles. 'I'm sorry, I'm sorry, it's just this buzzer shit is so freaking funny. I'm sorry, I'm sorry. I'll stop. You watch, I'll stop.' And sure enough, once we entered the foyer, and passed our first resident curled up like a foetus in front of a hallway TV which was playing a DVD of some cravat-wearing white English bloke on a train trip through India, Soula did stop giggling.

I have, of course, been to Happy Days many times before. But Thilma and Soula had never been to an aged care facility. Thilma's wealthy mum and dad died the old-fashioned way, you know, they just suddenly dropped dead one after the other, he of a heart attack and she of an undiagnosed gynaecological cancer that must have been eating away at her for years yet she never even mentioned it. Her dad died first, just like that, leaving her mum to live alone and lonely for several years, faking happiness and denying ill health even up to the day she collapsed at bingo and died shortly after her companions diagnosed her as simply being over-excited at winning the meat hamper.

Soula's parents died in a war in the Middle East. That's why she came to this country alone as a non-English-speaking teenager. She lived with relatives, then was betrothed to a third cousin who ran off with her best friend, and also with all her money.

Anyway, none of us was laughing as we walked to Mum's private room, led by a woman who'd quietly joined us. She had both a security pass draped around her neck *and* a shiny stethoscope so she was either in a position of authority or a kleptomaniacal resident. Her name tag said, Dr Geeta, but this name tag could also have been stolen.

'We're worried your mother may have had another stroke shortly after you brought her in this morning. But, then again, it may just be her medication. So we want you to help us measure her cognitive capacity,' said Dr Geeta. 'We can't know for sure unless she has more tests, but to be honest what would be the point?'

'Um,' I said, unsure if this too was a rhetorical, actual or trick question. 'Well, I guess one point would be that more tests could determine if she's deteriorating, and another would be that we could work out "if so, why", and the third point would be that we could then ascertain how we can cure it.'

'Bzzzzz! Wrong!' Yes, Geeta made a sound like we were playing a round of Beat The Buzzer. 'Age is causing it, my dear,' she said. 'And for that there is absolutely no cure.'

Thilma's right eye started to twitch. This twitch only appears when she's really annoyed about something or has accidentally stabbed herself with her crochet needle. I suspect Thilma was annoyed that the alleged Dr Geeta called me 'my dear' because, well, I am not three years old. Thilma believes that if women of our age and life experience deserve to be called anything other than our actual names we can damn well be called 'Fucking Legends'.

'Excuse me, Doctor,' said Soula, ignoring both the comment and the twitch, 'but why exactly have you invited us here?'

'I would like you to help me determine if the patient's current vagueness and disorientation are in fact medication induced. So I need you to just be with her as the medication wears off, then help her mentally relocate who and where she is.'

So we went into Mum's room and Geeta left us alone for a few minutes. We found Mum trying to stand on her ensuite loo while dressed in the tracksuit she'd stolen from the woman in the room next door who wore it as a volunteer for the Commonwealth Games in 1982.

'Here, let me help you,' I said gently to Mum.

'Oh, fuck off,' she replied.

I've been overwhelmed by a desire to help others many times in my life. And usually my actions are met with a smile and some level of gratitude. The only other time they weren't was when I laboriously helped an old lady cross the road, only to then discover she hadn't wanted to cross the road at all.

Anyway, my desire to help is why we stole Mum and why she's currently also squished in the car with us, thinking that she's telling us a Knock Knock Joke.

'Knock knock,' said Mum.

'Who's there?' said Soula.

There was a long pause. Then Mum said, 'Is someone going to get the door?'

Soula found this hilarious and as she roared with laughter she embraced Mum, who roared with laughter too.

'Do you know any other jokes?' asked Soula.

'Yes,' my mother replied. 'Why did the shopping trolley slash all the tyres of the cars in the shopping centre car park?'

'I don't know, why?' chorused Thilma and Soula.

'Because it was so angry and frustrated.'

And Soula laughed and Mum laughed and Thilma laughed as well and, much to my surprise, I found myself laughing too.

And then my phone rang.

11.14 and a half AM

Without answering or even looking at my phone I knew the caller was Joy because when we were incarcerated Hope programmed Joy's number with a special ringtone. It's the theme track from *Jaws*. Personally I think it's a completely wrong choice because Joy isn't predatory at all. If anything, she'd volunteer to be eaten by a shark so the rest of us would survive. In fact, she'd paint herself in lard and gizzards and hurl herself into the shark pack if she thought it would be helpful in any way.

Nonetheless I put Joy on speaker in case the call needed witnesses.

'Mum, I don't mean to ruin the fun time you're having, but I wanted to remind you that Hope's in-laws will be here in one hour and nine minutes and you only get one chance to make a first impression. So you should come home now and get dressed while I'm forced to get everything ready.'

'Joy, you're not being forced to do it. You've chosen to.'

'That is so typical!' Joy groaned. 'I've interrupted my morning, my day, my life to help make your life better and all you can do is treat me like I'm somehow intensely annoying when I'm actually unbelievably thoughtful and generous.'

'Oh my God,' Soula whispered to me, 'are you on the phone to you?'

IN THE BUFFER ZONE

11.43 AM
Still March 26

Dear Diary,

I'm currently in the Buffer Zone, the apartment that sits between Eduardo's North West Wing and my pantry-sized apartment.

We're going to hold the luncheon here. We did briefly consider holding it in Eduardo's North West Wing until we realised there was no way in the world that even if we hid the view and strew the place with garbage and bubonic rats we could not make Eduardo's actual apartment look unintimidating. While we could certainly cover the diamond sparkling views with sheets it was impossible to cover all the little things, like the solid gold toilet.

I'm actually currently sitting on a non-gold leopard-skin toilet in the Buffer Zone right now. I'm not using the toilet per se. I'm here because I want to sit and write in *you*, Dear Diary, and Eduardo is only letting select people sit on the furniture in the living room 'because the fabric is delicate and can only survive a certain number of sits'.

'Shits?' Mum said.

'Yes,' laughed Soula. 'You can only do a certain number of shits on these chairs.'

'How many?' asked my mother.

'Don't encourage her,' I reprimanded.

'While we're on the subject of Grandma's mental state,' asked Thilma, 'have we thought what we're going to do if her medication makes her go gaga while the guests are here?'

I was floored by how matter-of-fact Thilma was about this horrific possibility. She spoke of Mum's 'mental state' with no negative judgement whatsoever, and clearly saw it as a natural part of life, neither good nor bad, just life. I suspect, on the other hand, I see it as a failure. And as a result I find myself ashamed to have others see Mum like this; ashamed that her muddled mind presents my mother as lazy or weak or slovenly or careless. And I don't want strangers to think this meandering woman *is* my mum because I know that she is and was so much more.

'Well?' said Thilma.

The best option, I thought, would be to simply not include Mum in the gathering by dropping her back at Happy Days and not telling her the event was occurring. But I couldn't say this in front of Mum so I waited for her to turn around and then mouthed the words at Thilma. Unfortunately I forgot that, like all mothers, my mum has eyes in the back of her head.

'Why don't you want me to be here?' said Mum. 'Are you ashamed of me, Nora?'

'Of course not, Mum. You've only just come out of hospital and I'm worried that entertaining a multitude of strangers will be too much for you.'

'Too much for me, Nora? Or too much for you?'

I wanted to yell, 'Yes, it's too much for me!' But I decided to be silent and strong. And then I wondered if being silent can actually be defined as strong, or if not speaking your mind is just plain piss-weak. So I distracted us all by pointing out a completely different elephant in the room. 'By the way, may I ask how many guests we're expecting?'

'Yes,' said Joy, lighting up at the mere thought of adding the kind of value to the conversation that could be demonstrated by a spreadsheet. 'We've asked every one of Aspen's hundreds of friends and relatives on social media but unfortunately only five replied so I have no idea how many will actually turn up.'

'Um,' interrupted Soula dramatically, before pronouncing one of the most incredulous statements she's uttered in the forty-odd years I've known her. 'Perhaps I may be of assistance here?'

The chances of this were highly low. The last time Soula was potentially any assistance at all was when she had her hair cut in a mullet and Thilma used her as inspiration for a home-made floor mop brush.

'I can help,' continued Soula, 'by simply saying we need more than five guests because that is an unlucky guest number. So Joy, do you honestly think that out of the hundreds of guests you invited, it's possible that only five will arrive?'

'Oh, completely,' said Joy, somewhat peeved. 'People are relentlessly disappointing nowadays. They'll ignore an invitation, or accept and not turn up. I wish I'd been born in a more polite time. Like the 1950s or the Middle Ages. Having said that,' she continued at a suddenly rapid rate, 'outside of our little gang and the in-laws, I've also invited Booby and Dad and Eduardo so that will exceed five guests.'

'And speaking of brothers …' Mum blurted.

Oh God, no, I thought, *please don't say that you've invited them.*

'… I've invited your sister,' said Mum.

'The dead one?' I asked.

'Yes, the dead one.'

'Fantastic,' I replied with manufactured glee. 'She'll be the life of the party!'

12.12 PM

Dear Diary,

I'm back in the main room of the Buffer Zone. We're all here, waiting to start waiting for the guests. Everything appears to be pretty well done. Joy has finished preparing lunch and laid it out on the Eduardo-designed dining table that looks like a scrotum. Joy's prepared the meal with whatever the opposite of assistance is from Mum and the meal itself is an homage to what my mother would have made had she remembered how: French onion dip (made with packet soup and a tub of sour cream), cocktail frankfurts (because they're always hilarious), some 'prune and shrivelled un-defrosted bacon things' and 'some other stuff' Joy found in my freezer.

'Is this as good as we can do?' I asked.

'Mum,' said Joy, 'your tone is superior and rude.'

'Yes, please try not to speak like that when the guests are here,' said Hope.

'But I didn't say anything bad?'

'You didn't actually have to say it. I could tell what you were thinking,' said Hope.

To which I obediently replied, 'Oh sorry,' because having my daughters like me is more important than me actually liking myself. 'I guess I just want to make sure we present the best possible day for our guests.'

'Well, why didn't you just say that?' said Hope, sighing with tired exasperation. 'If you had then I wouldn't have just got upset.'

But, Dear Diary, I think she would have. I'm beginning to suspect that Hope *wants* to be angry with me. It seems to give her strength.

In the movie *Sophie's Choice*, Meryl Streep must choose between saving the life of her son or her daughter. To be honest I didn't actually watch the movie, but from what I understand, albeit via my mother so therefore this plotline may or may not have occurred, Meryl chooses her son because he has a better chance of survival. But in *Nora's Choice*, my low budget version of the movie, so probably just presented as a PowerPoint rather than a feature film, the mother would choose to save the weaker child in the belief that the stronger child could take care of themself. In *Nora's Choice* the nurturing of the weaker child would allow that child to grow strong and maybe one day change the world with an understanding of frailty, love and power. That's why Nora calls this daughter Hope.

And that's why I want her to marry someone exceptional. Not someone ordinary like us. And I don't mean ordinary by occupation or social status or class, I mean ordinary by aspiration, by impact! Someone who's better than *us*.

12.30 PM

Dear Diary,

Joy, Soula, Thilma, Mum, Eduardo and I are now all officially waiting for the guests to arrive. Hope meanwhile is presumably getting dressed in my apartment and finding something appropriate to don from her emotional baggage.

We're in the living room of the Buffer Zone. Eduardo's own actual apartment, The North West Wing, is massive with seven bedrooms, five bathrooms, three balconies and an indoor garden. It is imperious with blanket whiteness and minimalist furniture, all designed to make Eduardo's art 'pop'. The Buffer Zone, in stark contrast, is a nowhere place, undecorated since it was purchased from a deceased estate. The Zone is full of discarded 'Eduardos' and the carpet, the wallpaper and the skirtings are all pretty much the original owner's 1970s mission brown.

In the hour or so since first arriving, Thilma's designed 'common people' outfits for both herself and Soula and she's called them 'Inactive Wear'. Superficially their Inactive Wear looks like modern active wear, but they've added padding in all the places where a non-active person would need extra support when they're sitting or lying down for extended periods of time; for example, eating chips while watching the shopping channel.

Mum is here, too; she's still dressed in that tracksuit but now also holding a shoe. She's actually looking really well, particularly now that Eduardo has allowed Mum to perch her bum on the arm of his least favourite chair as a special nod to her recent difficult health challenges (*healtho challengo difficato*).

Eduardo himself is pooncing about in a smoking jacket and gold kilt. I told him he has to dress down and change into something that makes him look like less of a smug snob. 'What are you talking about,' he replied, 'this *is* me dressing down.'

Unlike Eduardo, Joy has followed the rules and dressed to unimpress. Joy, who normally errs on 'conservatively styled with a dash of Queen Elizabeth II fox-hunting' is wearing a crop top with high-waisted leggings designed to look like denim. She smells like she's added cooking oil to her hair. It looks lank and lifeless. And in the footwear department she's wearing Crocs and socks.

I've dressed to fit in too. After my daughters told me not to use my own clothes because 'they're gross but not fun-gross, more kind of loser', I've dressed using items I found in Eduardo's wardrobe: a shimmering pink zip-up disco jacket with accompanying leggings that clearly reveal not only my visible pantyline, but a camel toe that's so massive I look like I actually have a penis. I've topped off my look with one of Eduardo's many bumbags and, to my creative credit, I've also added the Ugg boots Thilma made for Eduardo in order to cure his gout. She made them by stapling four large chamois to some flip flops, so, even if they don't cure your gout, they're guaranteed to clean and buff the floorboards.

12.51 PM

Leonard and Booby just arrived. Apparently Joy requested they bring some festive decorations to brighten the Buffer Zone. So they've brought a Christmas tree, even though it's March.

'Why are you so negative about the tree, Mother?' Joy asked as she patted its plastic fronds. 'Why do you immediately assume that Dad stole it from Ward 4B at the hospital?'

'Because the tree's planted in a bedpan.'

'Isn't it possible they bought the tree from someone who stole it?'

'How do you do that when the tree has a swing tag that says "Property of City Central Hospital"?'

'Because Booby doesn't speak English very well, and Dad can't be bothered to read.'

'Good point. Except for one other simple thing, the star on the top of the tree is an inflated disposable hospital glove.'

'Oh, for God's sake, Mum, can't you ever look on the bright side? Can't you just be grateful that your ex-husband and his new wife went to visit *your* mother in the hospital? Even if it was after she'd been discharged?'

I'm briefly reminded of Soula's mantra. 'Be grateful. Surrender.'

12.53 PM

Hope has just come in. She's wearing a dressing-gown and curlers. It seems a strange choice of outfit for meeting the in-laws, even if you are trying to be common. But I said, 'Oh, Hope, don't you look fabulous,' because I've decided to be supportive no matter what and to express this with an attitude of effusive enthusiasm.

'Seriously, Mum?' Hope replied. 'Is this seriously as fabulous as you think I can look?'

I honestly didn't know what to say, so I ate two prunes wrapped in un-defrosted bacon from 'the nibblies table'.

'Oh my God, Mum,' squealed Joy, 'I can't believe you ate those. Now there won't be enough food for all the guests.'

'Yes, return them,' said my mother, giving me the Heimlich manoeuvre until I coughed up the prunes, which she then placed back in the bowl. And then my phone pinged. And Joy grabbed it and said, 'Oh my God, it's a notification! The police officer has posted a pic on social media.'

'He's holding a sign that says "Hi Nors".'

'Nora and the officer sitting in a tree,' sang my mother, 'K, I, S, S, I, N, G.'

'I told Mum she should go on Tinder,' said Joy.

'I knew someone who went on a Tinder date and accidentally got pregnant,' said Soula. 'And then gave birth to a Tinder Surprise.'

Soula's love-life breaks her heart. I don't want that to happen to me. That's why I'm not going to look at Wittle's photo. What if he looks fabulous? What if I want him in my life and he ends up not wanting me? So much better to be the rejector than the rejectee. So much better just to close and lock the door of my heart because the last thing I want to be is a woman whose self-esteem is entirely dependent on being liked by men. So much better to have low self-esteem that is entirely and solely dependent on me.

12.57 PM

Someone just rang the doorbell. Bloody hell, here we go. I'll probably have to stop writing now.

1.04 PM

Oh hello, me again, I can continue writing for a bit longer. The guest at the door was a guy called Leon Damon Francis Foual. He was hot, young, intelligent, kind and hilarious, and unfortunately at the wrong address. He's gone now to Apartment 703 to visit the guy who was having sex or a gallstone. Oh, there goes the doorbell again.

1.13 PM

There were ten people at the door. They appeared to be nine ladies of the night and their pimp. They looked quite successful, if breast size is the measure, and they also looked like they'd be great fun, so they obviously were also meant for Apartment 703.

42 minutes later
In the bathroom again

Dear Diary,

Yes, I'm in the bathroom again, sitting and writing – again. I know it seems like I'm becoming obsessed with you, Dear Diary, but I'm actually in here to get away from my loved ones.

Anyway, where was I? Oh yes, so the guests haven't arrived yet, but my loved ones and I have already drunk all the alcohol so I've just returned from our corner bottle shop where I bought more grog.

And it was while in the queue at the corner shop that I saw a man with skin so tanned that he looked like a raisin. He was wearing flared high-waisted faded denim jeans with a tucked-in T-shirt that read 'Yeah, nah … yeah.'

He was with a skinny woman wearing thongs and a kaftan who had blonded grey hair that was so firmly secured and shaped with hair spray that it could be mistaken for a motorbike helmet. From a slight distance she looked like the mastermind of an underworld gang of backyard meth manufacturers who got dressed up especially because the mayor is paying a visit.

Together they were buying up the store's supply of lo-cal cola. 'I accept that this experience will make us depressed,' said the meth mastermind lady, 'but I refuse to let it make us fat.'

While they waited in the queue to pay, they discussed how to behave when they got to their destination, which I assumed was Apartment 703.

'Apparently the mother is a bit of a cow,' smiled the man, revealing teeth so perfect they looked expensively capped, but I suspect were just painted over with Tipex.

'Who told you she's a cow?' said the woman.

'The daughter. Not our one, the sister. She sent me a warning message with the invitation on Facebook.'

'The single older sister? Well her opinion doesn't count,' said the woman.

'That's a bit sexist, isn't it?' said the man.

'Au contraire,' said the woman. 'Accepting the unpartnered older sister's opinion of her middle-aged mother is like a tabloid journalist asking a man for a character reference for his ex-wife who's been accused of murdering the bloke she left him for.'

At that moment all three of us, plus Wei, the shop owner, and some dude buying 'rollie papers', took a moment to get our heads around this concept. I rummaged in the gold bumbag I'd borrowed from Eduardo for something to draw a flow chart on and found a box of Viagra and a pen with 'Stolen From Dali' printed on its side. I drew the flow chart on the Viagra box; the tabloid journalist, the ex-husband, the wife, the lover, the murder, etc., and when I'd finished I totally agreed with the crime-boss-meth-lady.

'Well, no matter who said it or why,' continued the tanned man, 'I want us both to do exactly as we planned. Watch what we say and watch what we do. Our behaviour must be exemplary and beyond reproach, we must behave like perfect utter bogans.'

I noticed their posh accents and vocabulary didn't suit their outfits. Clearly these two were making a massive effort to appear to be something they're not.

'Yes, I agree,' said the helmet-head-crime-boss-meth-lady, 'the last thing we want to do is cause any kind of discomfort or consternation.'

What? First the use of the word 'exemplary' and now the word 'consternation'? I certainly didn't expect these words to be part of her parlance. Maybe she learnt them on one of those TV game-shows where you have to buy a vowel and you can win a house.

'You mean shit-fight,' said the man.

'Yeah, shit-fight, that's what I meant,' continued the woman reverting to a more suitable accent, 'The last thing we wanna do is cause a shit-fight that might fuck up this mission. We've come this close with him so many times before and then he does something stupid and ruins it.'

'Oh my God,' I thought, from behind the shelf that carried the two-for-one specials on 'cheap but drinkable' plonks, all of which I planned on purchasing. 'I need to contact the guy in Apartment 703 and let him know to expect two visitors who are either mobsters or really plainclothes cops.'

And then I quietly wished that our little gathering could look forward to exciting guests like these – people planning to extort, bribe or pinch our money, as opposed to the guests we're actually expecting: people who miss the toilet when they wee. I then briefly worried if our in-laws-to-be were planning on using the marital union to get access to our money. Until I realised the joke would be on them, because we haven't got any!

But of course the joke would also be on me because I've been working for thirty-six years so why haven't I got any money? Thilma says I should have married better. Soula says I should have divorced better. Leonard says I should have married a minimal-English-speaking Eastern European who has mysterious sources of undeclared income. Mum says I should have worked harder, saved more and eaten less. I think I should have hired a better accountant; one who didn't skim my accounts and move to the Bahamas. Booby says I shouldn't have been so tidy with my financial records because I made it 'so easy for accountant to them skim'. Eduardo says I should have followed Eduardo's advice. But the fact is I unfortunately did and it was Eduardo who recommended the accountant.

I paid for the grog and raced out, determined to beat the odd couple to the apartment building and therefore not have to share the elevator with them. I hurried home in a middle-aged kind of skippity-limp manner that on recollection possibly looked a little like I'd just received an enema and they'd accidentally left the hose in.

At the front door to the Buffer Zone I bumped into two more people. They seemed quite normal in a middle-aged unmemorable way. So unmemorable in fact that, despite the fact I saw them only moments ago, I can recall only their dowdy matching home-knitted cardigans, toy earpieces and toy guns. Of course I found their outfits odd but my mother is currently wearing a lampshade on her head, and we all told her she looks lovely.

The Cardigan Couple flashed Joy's Facebook invites. We had no choice but to let them enter.

Oh, the doorbell just rang again.

1.57 PM

I've opened the fridge door and am leaning inside the fridge to secretly write. A man just arrived. He's dressed in a conservative lawyer-look ensemble, which I personally find very suspicious. His dark suit is pin-striped, his shoes shine like the sun, his black toupee looks almost real and the skin on his face is so chemically exfoliated it looks exactly like a peeled grape.

He doesn't look at all like he belongs here. I think he'll be leaving any minute so I'm not stopping my writing and I'm not saying 'hi'. I've only got a limited number of 'hi's' in me today and I don't want to waste one on him when he's so obviously going to be leaving.

1.59 PM

He has a Facebook invite! Joy's let him in! Who is he? His well-dressed presence makes no sense at all. As an act of defiance I'm still writing and not greeting him.

Super empath Thilma must have sensed I was upset by these arrivals. 'Don't take it all so seriously,' she whispered as the guests followed me into the living room. 'It can be good to have a lawyer-looking person in the family. And I'm sure lots of people carry guns to engagement parties, and they all live happily ever after. Even if it's not for very long. Now calm down and take a sec while I give you a massage.'

'Oh, no thanks, Thilma,' I replied. 'Having a massage in the middle of this gathering might be seen as a bit attention-seeking.'

'No one will notice, I promise,' said Thilma, 'because I'll be massaging you with my mind.'

2.07 PM

Dear Diary,

Oh my God! I'm in the bathroom. The couple from the corner store arrived! Joy greeted them at the door and let them in after they announced they're Aspen's parents. I was tempted to ask for proof. But how do you prove that you're someone's parent? With your DNA map, the scars on your soul or the emptiness of your wallet?

Obviously I had to say 'hi' to them, because these outlaws are going to be my in-laws.

I decided to treat this situation like needing to wee in the middle of the night – you know, when you really don't want to get up and do it, but you feel so much better when you have.

Anyway, I walked toward them, and as I got closer I heard the man say to the woman, 'No, the plural of you is youse, but youse is also the singular. So the phrase "Are youse coming with me to the pub" can be said to an individual or a group.' Taking this as a cue I greeted them with 'G'day, I'm Nora, how are youse?'

And the woman replied, 'Yeah, g'day. I'm Bunny.' And then the man said, 'G'day, me name's Baldwin. I mean, oh shit, what's me name, youse can call me …'

'Balls?' I winced.

'No, you can call me Baldwin,' he replied as he moved to kiss me on both cheeks, stopped himself, punched me in the arm instead and said, 'So how's your bum for grubs?' I didn't know how to answer this question so, after a brief moment of contemplation I replied, 'Fine and how's your bum?'

A polite silence followed. 'We're lookin' forward to eyeballing your sprog,' said Baldwin. Then I said, 'Yeah, sounds grouse, yeah nah.' And then Bunny said, 'Yeah, Aspen's a beaut bloke,' so I said, 'Oh so Aspen's a bloke?' and then we shared an awkward silence during which I topped up our glasses with cheap plonk and we all skolled them in unison and then skolled five more. Then Bunny said, 'Yes, Aspen's a beaut son,' And Baldwin nodded like a wobble doll, 'We couldna arsed for a better sperm.'

To be honest I found their happiness very depressing because I was hoping to feel a tremendous sense of parental superiority over these people. But it turns out, while they may not have dress sense, money or a good grasp of the benefits of turmeric, they have everything that I've always wanted: a happy cohesive family.

I didn't say anything. I didn't need to. Trusty Mum said it for me as she whispered loudly in my ear, 'How did these ne'er-do-well fringe dwellers end up with a perfect family when you've not only worked every day of your life but, at the very same time, constructed sentences with compound prepositions?'

3 PM approximately

Hi, Dear Diary, I'm sitting on a loo again. I'm writing and I'm hiding. We're still waiting for Aspen to turn up and I've run out of subjects to discuss with his guests. We've basically talked about the weather since they arrived and our conversations have become so unutterably boring it's made me feel quite carsick.

Where the hell is this alleged golden son?

3.07 PM

I'm on my way to the toilet now, Dear Diary – lurking around the corner from the living room. I don't think I've ever actually 'lurked' before, so I'm not sure I'm doing it right.

I am sure however, and I say it with resolute conviction, this is probably the most repressed gathering of humans that I've ever been witness to. No one is talking and hardly anyone is eating. Only Booby who comes from a land where ear wax is the national dish seems to be finding the food at all tempting.

My friends and family have given up on trying to connect with the guests. Normally at least Soula and Thilma would be chatting to them, grilling them with a million questions and inviting them to 'relax, nude-up and dance'. But the only communication I've had from Thilma is a suggestion whispered in my ear that we sit on the floor and form a prayer group.

Soula seems a little lost, too. Normally she'd gee up a gathering with annoying games like charades. But the only suggestion she's made so far is 'Anyone want to play Statues?' I thought this was the best idea that Soula's ever had because the game of Statues gives the illusion of social interaction while disallowing talk or movement. But the gun-toting Cardigan Couple said, 'There is no way that we can be statues when our job requires that we keep moving.'

'Like sharks,' nodded Booby.

So then *I* suggested we play 'Hide and Seek' which I thought would be fabulous because I wouldn't seek out anyone. But the Cardigan Couple said no, that wouldn't work either, because they need us all to stay in one room in case they have to shoot someone.

And it was at this point that I started to wonder if the Cardigan Couple have dementia like Mum and so, in an act of Affection Deferral, I spontaneously hugged them.

3.11 PM

Hello Dear Diary,

I'm in the living room of the Buffer Zone. Due to the waiting time Eduardo has eased his restrictions and allowed the future in-laws to rest one bum-cheek each on the seating. As the official Mother of the Bride I've been invited to squat on a footstool. I've put a tray of 'nibblies' on my lap and am sneakily writing underneath it while staring straight ahead.

Aspen's parents are looking agitated but that may be because of the one bum-cheek thing. Aspen still isn't here yet. And neither is Hope. Maybe he's arrived already and they're in my apartment having a private smooch before making their grand entrance.

Mum's just suggested she entertain us with a slide show so that the guests can get to know our family. We actually don't have a slide projector nor any slides so Joy has suggested we pass our phones around and scroll through each other's family albums. I don't have a 'family album' on my phone, neither do Mum nor Thilma. Soula is currently busy frantically deleting all the dick pics on her phone. So we're just going to pass Joy's phone around.

3.17 PM

It's weird to see how many photos there are of us all together, particularly considering Joy usually only keeps photos in which she looks perfect. There are so many shots in so many different places, and in such a wide array of circumstances. I never imagined we spent so much time with each other, or that we looked like such a normal family. In fact, I asked Joy if she'd applied 'a happy filter' and she said, 'No, that's what we really look like.'

But you know what, Dear Diary? It isn't really what we look like, because every single photo taken over the past four years has been photoshopped by Joy to include Hope.

3.51 PM

Dear Diary,

Aspen is still nowhere to be seen but Hope has just arrived, dressed in the bridesmaid dress Joy 'stole' from Vietnamese Gloria. She looks somewhat like Cinderella during her scullery maid stage because Hope has crushed the fabric and added more stains – presumably to adhere to the dress code de jour which has become 'dress to depress'.

Hope looks so happy though it took a moment for me to recognise her! As she laughed and smiled and hugged everyone I realised I haven't seen her this ecstatic since she was eleven and singing the 'Circle of Life' in the living room dressed in a sleeping bag and a yellow shower cap that she thought made her look like a lion.

I'm ashamed to say that I can still remember wanting Hope to hurry up on that day, to hurry up with her singing, to hurry up with her distracting happiness and eat dinner, finish her homework, have a bath and go to bed. But now, I would wish for nothing more than for her happiness to last forever.

3.59 PM

OK, the last eight minutes have been quite busy. On arrival Hope approached her in-laws with an enthusiasm and gusto that I haven't seen her display since she was twelve and discovered neapolitan ice-cream was available in single serves. Unfortunately in reciprocating her energy level Baldwin and Bunny took a pissed stumble (pumble) and landed on top of her. So then the suspicious guy in the suit reached out to assist Hope with an extended hand

and the non-comforting words, 'Hello, I'm Dick Alcoq, the family's lawyer.' And in response Soula, for some inexplicable reason, begin to cheer.

'On behalf of the family,' Alcoq continued, after nodding his head in acknowledgement of the applause that he somehow thought he deserved. 'Please let me say that it's a pleasure to meet and congratulate you Hope on your meteoric rise from life's gutter. I hope you don't mind but Aspen told us that you grew up very poor with only one parent who was never around and you were forced to raise yourself and your sister and take care of your deranged grandmother.'

To which I thought to myself, 'Don't be ridiculous,' and Hope said to Alcoq, 'Yes, that's true.'

And then there was a long silence during which some of us would have wondered what to say next, some of us would have wondered whether to top up everyone's drinks, and some of us would have wondered if it were possible to casually run and jump out the window of the Buffer Zone without being accused of ruining the gathering and in the process making it all about them.

EDUARDO'S SEX ROOM

(It's inside the Buffer Zone)
It's still March 26
It's 4.07 PM

Dear Diary,

I guess that now would be a good time to get a few things back on track. First, I am currently in a small room in the Buffer Zone that Eduardo always imagined he'd use for sexual bondage but is currently being used as a storage area for bulk-bought toilet paper.

I exited the living room about ten minutes ago and implied by my walk that I was heading for the loo. I apologised effusively for needing to leave the room but actually everyone nodded with polite understanding and some even looked a bit jealous.

The truth, however, is I never planned to actually go to the toilet. I'd always planned to come straight to this room, but I felt it was a little early in our in-law relationship to publicly announce I was 'heading to the sex room'.

Interestingly, on the walk here I chanced to spy on Hope. She'd left the living room gathering shortly before me. I saw her sneak a look at the time on her phone, send a text, wait a moment, dial a number, listen for an answer, hang up, look at the time, send another text, wait a moment, dial a number, listen for an answer, hang up, look at the time and send another text.

I watched her anxiety grow, her stoic composure betrayed by her slightly heaving chest and shallow breaths barely discernible to anyone save a mother who'd counted those 'inhale exhales' for almost half of her own life.

She then took four puffs of her asthma inhaler, twice as many as prescribed, and went back to the living room. And that's when I came in here so I could write in private and sort out my thoughts. But I'm going to have to stop writing now because I can hear knocking on the Sex Room door. And I suspect it may be my pride.

One hour later
5.11 PM?
Still in the Sex Room

Dear Diary,

Since last writing I was joined in the sex room by my posse of family and friends who, as it turns out, are as confused as me. Thilma, Mum and Soula joined me first. When Thilma entered the room, she announced, 'There's something odd about these guests and we can't work out what it is.'

'Here, let me try using my unreliable psychic powers,' said Soula and because I was desperate and still a bit drunk, I agreed. So then Mum, Thilma and I waited patiently while Soula sat on a ninety-six roll pack and closed her eyes to 'receive visuals'. We were pretty well behaved, Thilma, Mum and I; we were quiet and respectful and gave Soula her time and space. And after about five or six minutes Soula started to snore.

'Sleeping is a sign you're very stressed,' said Thilma.

'What?' I asked (rhetorically).

'Well don't wake her,' said my mum, ignoring me. 'If you wake someone when they're asleep they can die.'

'That's only if they're sleep-*walking*,' said Thilma.

'Oh my God, don't be ridiculous,' I said. 'Why on earth would sleep-walkers die if they're woken? I think that's just a rumour spread by people who sleep-walk and don't want to be woken up.'

'I've always wanted to sleep-walk,' said Mum. 'But the problem is it's terribly dangerous, so I've been trying to teach myself how to sleep-drive instead.'

'I can hear you,' said Soula, 'and I was not asleep, I was thinking – which I understand may have been confusing to you three, because none of you has ever seen me think before.'

It was becoming abundantly clear that we were *all* showing signs of diminished thinking. It occurred to me that our thinking was possibly being dangerously affected by the rapidly decreasing oxygen available within the tiny Sex Room. So, it was a great relief when Joy suddenly opened the door and let air in. It was less of a relief when she entered the Sex Room and closed the door behind her.

'I think,' whispered Joy urgently, 'that this family is not what they seem. I think Hope is marrying a destitute orphan who's hired actors to pretend to be his loving extended family.'

'I agree,' said my ex-husband, who is so lacking in charisma that no one had actually realised, prior to him speaking, that he was in the sex room with us. 'Their accents are all wrong.'

And right then Eduardo burst through the doorway holding one of his artworks, saying, '*Scuzi, squigaro, molto importante sayo.*' (I have an important squeezed lemon?) To which Booby replied, 'For the sake of God's, English speak so we all overstand can.' (What! When did she enter the room?)

'I have proof this family is not what they seem,' whispered Eduardo, in such a heightened state of trauma he suddenly couldn't be fucked to pretend to speak Italian. 'I just heard that Bunny woman comment on my art. She was whispering to her husband Baldick.'

'Baldwin,' Joy corrected prudishly, despite the fact I suspect we all felt that the name Baldick suited him much better.

'She said it's infantile, lacklustre and intellectually dull with a leaning toward sheer imbecility.'

'So?' I said. 'Everyone thinks that about your art.'

'No, no, no they don't,' said Eduardo. 'Most people just say it's shit. But Bunny actually repeated the quote of the famous art critic, Invisiblo.'

'Ah,' said my mother. 'So you think that woman is that man?'

'No! I think this family must be art collectors. And that means they must be rich!'

'Don't ridiculous be, they not rich!' said Booby. 'I knew rich people many where come I from and they not dress like sad pillows.'

'Excuse me for interrupting this cultural exchange,' Soula blurted, 'and I mean this with all due respect,' (a phrase always used as a thinly veiled term implying not much respect is due at all), 'but what the fuck?'

'Oh Soula, please,' said Eduardo, in a timbre that perhaps only the son of a globally lauded professional opera singer could master because it is at the same time, condescending, conciliatory and yet creepy. 'I would have expected more support from you at this time. I mean you've actually said hello to my penis.'

Has everybody?

Why didn't Soula tell me she'd seen Eduardo's penis? I wonder why she would feel the need to hide such a thing from me. Is she ashamed? If so, then why do it? Does she think I'd be jealous? Does she think I'd be judgemental? Both are a very sad indictment, because the truth is, I'm suspecting I'd be both.

I wonder who else in my life isn't telling me the truth, for fear of my judgement. Is relentlessly single Joy secretly dating someone? Is Mum not really my mother? Actually, that thought is going way too far, because the intense confinement of the last few days is revealing we're too similar for her not to be.

'Eduardo,' interrupted Joy, 'I wouldn't normally say this 'cause it's a phrase I save for Mum …'

(Oh my God! Joy's going to tell Eduardo that she loves him!)

'Yes?' asked Eduardo.

'Today,' she said softly before standing on a twelve pack and raising her voice, 'today is not about you!'

'What do you mean?' Eduardo replied, unflustered and earnest. 'Of course today is about me. Every day of my life is about me. Just as every day of yours should be about you. But as someone who's chosen to spend her life as an extra, who are you to judge the relevance or necessity of my performance in life, Joy? My God, you are just like your mother!'

'What?' I said, stepping in to the ring to defend Joy like a rabid mother hen. 'How dare you compare perfect Joy to me. And, perhaps more to the point, who are you to judge any of us anyway?' And that's when the gloves came off.

'Oh *dio mio*, Nora. I have one word for you: hypocrite! Because you judge me all the time! I know that you believe I'm a fool swimming in a fool's gold. And yet, unlike you, I'm actually being brave every day, putting my heart, my mind, my soul out there to be judged as I perform my sacred role on this earth as … as … as …'

'As a douche-bag,' said my mother.

Spontaneously everyone in the sex/toilet-paper room broke into applause and at that moment Alcoq entered and assumed the applause was once again for him.

'Thank you, thank you,' he said as he took several bows, then did that thing where you run your hand up and down your face and turn your expression from a frown to a smile, and back to a frown and back to a smile again. At this point people normally stop this gimmick, but he continued to do the smile/frown/smile/frown thing fifteen more times and only finally stopped when he confused his expressions with his hand directions and Leonard began to boo.

'I'm sorry,' Alcoq said, though clearly not sorry at all, 'I've always been a bit of a thespian at heart, and indeed a public speaker, and it is for that reason I have joined you in this cupboard to give a small profound speech asking you to adjourn to the living room. Unfortunately we've just heard that Aspen is not able to attend today and it behoves me to announce to you that Baldwin would like to make an announcement.'

My thoughts turned to Hope of course. Where was she? Had she already heard this news? I hadn't seen Hope for a little while now. I prayed she hadn't disappeared again.

If she were still a little girl I would have known where Hope was. When I was the love of her life I used to know her every thought. I knew her favourite food, her favourite shoes, her favourite colours, her favourite sounds; I knew how to make her laugh and how to make her stop crying. I knew when she was tired, just by the way she rubbed her left ear; I knew when she was happy, I knew when she was scared. I knew, as I have said, the very rhythm of her breath. But now I fear I don't know her at all.

Should I add that to my *How to Be a Better Mum* list? Am I hopelessly comparing Hope to the little girl she used to be and disallowing the existence of the woman she's become?

Everyone's now exited the sex room and headed to the living room in anticipation of the forthcoming announcement. But I, Dear Diary, am going to search for Hope.

5.48 PM

Dear Diary,

I'm standing in the hallway outside my apartment. I'm resting you against the wall as I write so the pen is kind of upside down-sidewise. This means I have to stop and shake the pen every few seconds to get the ink flowing back to the tip. It's actually really quite annoying. I think I'll squat now and write resting on my knees.

OK, time for an update. So, I heard some yelling as I left the Buffer Zone and walked down the hall. (Oh, I've just realised that writing the words 'some yelling' makes it sound like several voices. But I only heard one person yelling.) The voice was high and muffled. I assumed a female. I assumed it was Hope. Who else would it be? The guy from Apartment 703? Or the old lady who lives next to him? She lives alone, she has no one to yell at. Could she be yelling at her self? (Actually that's not entirely impossible. I spend a lot of time nowadays yelling at my self. But I do it silently.)

The yelling got louder as I walked closer to my apartment. And the words became more distinct: 'I can't believe you had everyone here ready to love you and you let me down again.' It didn't sound exactly like Hope. It just sounded distinctly like an angry woman – deeply, deeply hurt but expressing it distressingly, alarmingly and uselessly as rage.

When we yell we yell to be heard – and seen. But the opposite happens.

I remember a woman who admonished her children in a whisper, because it was so much more scary.

The yelling was definitely coming from my apartment, so I assumed Hope must be in there with Aspen. The door to my apartment was closed. I fumbled with my keys while the tone of the yeller's muffled words grew more desperate, more hysterical, more sad. 'You promised me you wouldn't do this again. You promised me, you promised, you *promised* me!' I turned the key in the lock and entered the apartment. I saw Hope. She was embracing Bunny while Bunny screamed into her phone. I was both jealous and relieved.

'What are you smiling at?!' Hope snapped. 'What do you want, Mum?'

'I was wondering if you needed my help.'

'How the hell could *you* help, Mum?' Hope screamed as tears welled in her eyes. 'How could you possibly understand what's going on?!'

'Oh my God,' I thought. Here we go again. Another tunnel discovered in life's catacombs that I am presumed to be completely incapable of navigating. What do my children think I've done with my life for the past fifty years, other than not go to the gym? Does Hope honestly think that in my half century of existence on this planet I have never had my heart crushed?

I was on the precipice of telling Hope about Jack when Baldwin marched, yes, actually marched, into my apartment saying, 'A few words with Bunny if I may?'

I sent Hope from my apartment to freshen up in Eduardo's palazzo, and gave her the key to the very private secret bathroom that he keeps solely for pooing. And after Hope left, I left too, so now I'm hovering outside my apartment door positioned to enviously eavesdrop on the dulcet tones of a strong man comforting a devastated woman in the slang of the common people.

5.52 PM

I'm surprised there's more than an inflection and dialect change in the diatribe I'm overhearing.

'What the fuck are you doing, Bunny?' seethed Baldwin in an accent now crisp, posh and cold. 'You're going to ruin everything!'

'I'm sorry,' Bunny squeaked.

'Damn right you are,' Baldwin replied. 'You're a sorry excuse for a mother. Everything you do is wrong.'

'I'm sorry,' Bunny spluttered. 'I don't know what to do.'

'I'll tell you what you're going to do. You're going to try make things right by doing nothing at all!' roared Baldwin. 'We're going to head back to the gathering and I am going to give a small speech to the assembled crowd of carnies. You are going to say nothing. I am going to hold your arm, you will not recoil and you will not cry. We will present as a united front, we will fix the scandal you've inflamed with your theatrics and tears, and we will pull in the jib, tighten the mainsail and get this ship back on course. And together we will sail to the land of our son's future, a future of marital bliss with a woman who remains ignorant enough of his faults for at least a few more days, and therefore marries him before he turns thirty.'

'I really don't understand, the hurry,' said Bunny. ' I mean –'

'For God's sake, woman,' interrupted Baldwin, 'how fucking stupid are you? If I've told you once I've told you a million times IF ASPEN IS NOT MARRIED BY THE AGE OF THIRTY THEN THE EMPIRE THAT MY FATHER BEGAN WILL GO TO MY DELINQUENT BROTHER DICK'S MARRIED DAUGHTER. And that, my dear, will spell the end of our wealth because we all know what happens when a woman gets control – just take a look at today's mess!'

Oh God, I can hear them leaving my apartment. I'd better run, or at least perform a relatively close approximation of running that doesn't involve making my boobs bounce, and then sag so low, that I accidentally trip over them.

Perhaps a trot will do.

In LIMBO

6.17 PM
Back in the Buffer Zone

Dear Diary,

Hello. Well, that didn't go quite to plan either. The in-law posse has departed. My posse and I are still here in the Buffer Zone, but in shock. I can keep writing because no one is paying me any attention. They're all staring dumbly into the distance.

So here's what happened. When I returned to the Buffer Zone for Baldwin's announcement I found ten people in the living room. I tried to seem relaxed as I perched just a hint of my bum on the plastic-covered extreme tip of the arm of the sofa. Unfortunately this action caused the sofa to tip and catapulted me toward Alcoq. This caused the Cardigan Couple to draw their toy guns and the male Cardigan to shoot the couch, thus proving that the guns are real.

There was a little bit of bedlam, but not that much, considering. I mean no more than any normal family gathering that mixes alcohol with weaponry. But anyway, it was just after the shooting that Baldwin and Bunny appeared.

As they entered, my posse and I instinctively formed a standing huddle and Bunny grabbed a wine glass and tapped it with a spoon to get everyone's attention which, as you know, I find very annoying. Besides, and I don't mean to be a dobber, but wasn't Bunny ordered to do nothing at all at this point? Anyway, just saying.

Everyone was talking. Well we were. So Bunny ting, ting, tinged the spoon on the wine glass, but everyone ignored it, presumably because they're all annoyed by it too. So then Baldwin grabbed the glass and threw it and at the sound of the smash the Cardigans drew their guns and the woman fired and shot Eduardo's sculpture, which everyone thinks is a button mushroom but is actually modelled on his penis.

'Oh my God,' Eduardo responded in a state of utter emotional disarray, unsure as to whether the bullet increased or decreased the value of his work.

'Please, for the sake of our futures together as a family, let me buy the sculpture from you, Eduardo,' said Baldwin in an accent so British, clear and crisp it sounded like lettuce. Then he clicked his fingers like a magician and Alcoq instantly handed Baldwin cash which Baldwin gave to Eduardo who then said, 'Thank you, your Highness.'

'With that much cash they're definitely drug dealers,' whispered Soula. 'Or maybe hairdressers.'

'Now, let me begin again,' Baldwin continued. 'Thank you for your attention.'

'Oh my God,' said Thilma, 'is he Winston Churchill?'

'I dated Winston's best friend long ago,' Mum replied. 'He was an excellent huntsman, swordsman and gentleman, and also a marvellous root.'

'Hope, will you join Bunny and I please?' And Hope walked forward and stood beside them, and one couldn't help but notice that standing together they looked exactly like a real unphotoshopped family.

'It is with great sadness that I must inform you,' continued Baldwin, 'that our son Aspen is unfortunately unable to attend this wonderful function.'

The lawyer, Alcoq, clearly an appalling actor, feigned shock at hearing this news, even though he was the one who originally told us.

'Aspen's probably stoned on drugs or drunk somewhere,' whispered Soula conspiratorially while she hid her mouth with her hand in a gesture that made her look exactly like someone who was whispering conspiratorially.

'My better half and I,' persevered Baldwin, 'are of course deeply distressed by the inconvenience that this turn of events has brought to us all, but in particular to beautiful Hope who, with her intelligence, wit and strength is the daughter-in-law we've always wished for.'

'Seriously?' whispered Joy. 'I mean she's good, but she's not that great.'

'Yes,' Baldwin ploughed on despite his cynically inattentive audience, 'Hope is a truly extraordinary woman, particularly considering her background, upbringing and blood line.' Leonard, my ex-husband cheered at this (because his default persona is idiot).

'And so,' Baldwin persevered, 'by way of making amends for the wasting of the time you spent not only by, as it turns out fruitlessly waiting here all afternoon, but in preparing this sumptuous repast, which I thoroughly enjoyed eating – as a character-building challenge.'

'Not to mention the cost of the ingredients,' quipped Mum, 'which I had to import from 1970.'

'And so, by way of making everything right,' said Baldwin, unkindly ignoring my mum, 'I'd like to compensate your family for your time and financial loss.'

'Oh my God,' gasped Leonard, 'he's going to give us cash.'

'What do you mean "us"?' I admonished.

'So without further ado,' continued Baldwin, 'I would like to declare on behalf of myself and my wife Bunny that by way of making things up to you, in every way we can, we are going to take the wedding planning off your hands.'

'What?!' gasped Joy.

'Yay!' said Leonard. 'But what about the cash?'

'No,' replied Baldwin, 'I will not accept any cash from you at all. This deal is done. We are keeping everything as is except for the fact that we'll be changing the location, catering, clothing, security and guest list. Oh, and just to be safe, we're also bringing the wedding date forward to the day after tomorrow.'

'The day after tomorrow?' we all gasped (although to be totally truthful Booby actually said 'tomorrow after day' and Eduardo muttered, in his Italian, something that loosely translates to 'but the table is a fridge'.)

'This is not up for discussion,' continued Baldwin. 'And now we must away. *Bonsoir on se voit demain.*'

And in response Mum waved with exuberant vigour whilst mouthing the words, 'Fuck. Off!'

BACK IN MY APARTMENT

6.37 PM
Still March 26

Dear Diary,

Our gang is back in my apartment now but the others are in the living room and I'm in the laundry. Before absenting myself to come in here I explained that I was 'going to rescue the tablecloth'. It's splattered with bits of food, regurgitated by Booby when she asked, 'What delicacy this is?' and was told, 'It's a hot dog.'

I came in here just after Eduardo said, 'Well, that engagement party was both nail-biting and a little bit arousing. Would anyone like to have sex?' To which Mum and Leonard both said, 'No,' and Leonard added, 'but thank you for asking.'

The tablecloth isn't actually worth saving. It's plain and white and looks like an old bed sheet but Mum thinks it's her wedding veil so I'm making the effort. It's a bit gross. The regurgitations look kind of like stigmata mixed with snot balls, but I'm finding the scrubbing meditative and it gives me time alone to think.

For a brief moment this afternoon, when Aspen didn't turn up, I confess I prayed that the wedding would be called off. I prayed that his no-show would be a wake-up call to Hope or that Aspen's absence was a prelude to him totally cancelling the nuptials. I prayed that we would be free of this onerous family and their son. But instead, in a very bad deal, we've been acquired by them.

So I'm going to have to stop writing in you, Dear Diary, because now that my family isn't planning the wedding, I have no excuse to keep writing in front of everyone.

And there are only so many times you can excuse yourself from a room to write without looking like you keep leaving to fart.

6.39 PM

Oh, my family is calling me into the living room. 'Mu-um, Daughter, Nora Fawn!' I'd better go, it sounds like they all really want me back in there with them.

I'm both excited and terrified.

Farewell, Dear Diary.

Thanks for the companionship.

47 SECONDS LATER

OK, well, I'm in my living room now and I've just been ordered to continue writing in you. When I walked in everyone looked crestfallen, save for Hope who looked like a statue of self-control. She learnt to adopt that countenance as a child, when she couldn't breathe but didn't want me to fuss. Hope walked out of the room as soon as I entered.

'Nora,' said my mother 'we've decided you should continue to make your wedding notes just in case this wedding ends up shaped like your bottom.'

'Do you mean like a peach or a pear?' I asked.

'No, like a beetroot,' said Mum.

'What she means,' added Joy, 'is we think you should keep notes as evidence in case someone needs to sue someone.'

'Does Hope agree with this?' I asked.

'No,' Hope yelled from her bedroom.

'Don't listen to her,' whispered Joy, 'Hope's in love and has therefore lost all ability to think rationally.'

'I agree,' said Mum. She's absolutely besotted with Aspen. She's in no mental state to get married.'

'Yes,' added Soula. 'The best time to marry is when you've taken the rose-coloured glasses off completely. You know, after you divorce.'

'But the fact is they *are* getting married,' said Joy, simultaneously standing and waving her arms in her first ever display of unbridled passion. 'And Baldwin and Bunny are planning the wedding! How the hell can these people even begin to plan a wedding? Did you see the shoes they were wearing?'

'I know,' said Thilma, 'I could make better shoes out of old tyres and two eggs.'

'And can you imagine the wedding location?' said Joy. 'Can you imagine where they'll choose? A caravan park, a disused shipping container, a bog in a sewerage refinery? I mean if we'd wanted to have the wedding somewhere tasteless we could have just had it here at Mum's place.'

'Someone must stop them!' said Leonard as he spun himself around and around on my only swivel chair, boyishly enjoying the dizziness high, until he stopped with the words 'I'm gonna puke.'

'I feel a bit queasy too,' said Thilma. 'I think it might be the dip.'

'Maybe it also made of dogs,' nodded Booby.

'I agree, it tasted like it was,' Soula replied. 'But to be fair, maybe it was just off.'

'I'll have you know I made that dip,' said my mother, 'and it couldn't have been off because there was nothing fresh in it in the first place.'

'Well,' said Joy, straightening her crop top and high-waisted leggings while forcing herself to smile. 'The good news is that

Bunny and Baldy didn't take over the hen's party so that's all still going ahead as planned. So fuckem!!!!!!!!'

We all gasped at Joy's swearing. Her chest visibly puffed as she continued, 'I've booked the fucking clown from the fucking hospital to perform for us as our fucking stripper.'

'I'm sorry, I'm not really in the mood for a stripper,' said Thilma. 'And I haven't been since early menopause hit in 1973. Can't we have some sort of craft class instead?'

'Thilma,' said Joy, 'you're going to love this guy. He's a phallic craftsman, specialising in making sculptures with his penis.'

'Oh my God!' said Eduardo excitedly. 'Could he teach me how to make my penis look like the Sydney Opera House?'

'Maybe,' said Soula, 'he could start off by teaching you how to make your penis look like a penis.'

'Excuse me,' I interrupted. 'But when is this hen's party taking place?' And that's when the doorbell rang.

'Oh wonderful,' said Mum. 'Our entertainment is here. I'll bring out a snack for us all to enjoy. I found some cookies in the lower bowel of Nora's freezer. By the way, is everyone inoculated against tetanus?'

1.03 AM
And now it's March 27
and the wedding is Tomorrow!!

Dear Diary,

It's 1.03 am! We're still in my apartment. The hen's party went on longer than expected, not because we were having fun but because the clown/penis puppeteer turned out to be a nervous eater and the cookies 'from the freezer' turned out to be frozen by Hope during her wild youth and thus had hash inside them. So, after his performance, which was barely visible, the clown/penis puppeteer reported us to the police for trying to 'dope' him. And that's when Wittle arrived.

But all might have been OK if Wittle had not forewarned us of his arrival by buzzing on the intercom and saying, 'Hello, this is the police, just letting you know that I'm downstairs and about to barge into your apartment on allegations of drug use and dealing. Thank you.' And then buzzed again and said, 'Yes, just confirming it is I here, a police officer investigating an accusation of "doping".' And then buzzed again and said, 'Oh, I forgot to mention, I need to stop and do up my shoelaces, so I will be at your apartment in about seven minutes, I repeat seven minutes, which is just about the amount of time that anyone harbouring any kind of illicit drugs would need to dispose of them. But I am not in any way suggesting that you throw them out a window or flush them down the toilet though that is a common and effective means of disposal. OK, well I'll now tying my other shoelace so I'll be up in about six and a half minutes, I repeat, six and a half minutes.'

Yes, if Wittle hadn't forewarned us of his arrival then we would have been taken completely unawares. Thilma wouldn't have climbed out the fire escape screaming, 'Follow me girls, let your mother take the rap,' and my mother and I would not have hidden the remainder of the evidence in our digestive systems.

But then again if I hadn't been stoned when Wittle came to the door about half an hour later than forewarned then I might not have had the lack of inhibition to finally say, 'Ah Jack Wittle, what a surprise, the once great love of my life.'

'So you finally recognise me, Nors,' he said, leaning so casually against the doorframe he was almost seductive.

'Of course,' I replied as I mirrored his actions, leaning against the half-opened door and falling backwards. 'I recognised you the first moment I saw you, Jack, despite the weird hairy ferret thing you've got growing under your nose. But tell me,' I continued as I rose like a stick insect from the floor, 'would you like a cookie?'

'Thank you,' he obliged.

'Please take three,' said Mum.

'You seem different, Jack,' I said, as I watched, increasingly mesmerised by his munching.

'Well, it's been a long time. And besides that, I am different. We've all changed.'

'I haven't changed,' I replied. 'Well, I mean my hair, face, figure, mind and heart have changed, yet not enough it seems to forgive you for dumping me and marrying Dildra nearly thirty years ago,'

'I was trying to do the right and moral thing,' said Jack as he wiped crumbs from the ferret.

'The right thing!' I mimicked. 'You and I dated since Year 10 at Congregatta High. Our plan was to get married and run your family's vineyard. I was going to paint at night. I was going to be like Frida Kahlo but without all the sadness and pain. But instead, while I backpacked through Europe for just three bloody months, you slept with Dildra!'

'But you told me we were having a break. You said we should sleep with other people before we settled down.'

'And then you married her. How is that the right and moral thing?'

'She announced she was pregnant. I was being faithful to my unborn child.'

'And how is that child now, Jack?'

'Turns out there was no child.'

'And Dildra's dead?'

'No, she's living in Canberra.'

'Same thing,' said Mum.

'Mum might have dementia,' I explained.

'Yes,' said Mum, 'and I have piles! But Nora's *entire* life is a haemorrhoid and it's all your fault, Jack Wittle. You broke her heart so she married a budgie, and he left her with two children and now they treat her with absolutely no respect because she hasn't ever partnered up again which would suggest that no one wants her because she's a bit of a loser.'

'Really?' I said with the innocent curiosity of a baby's first taste of solids. 'That's why they treat me this way?'

'Well no, actually I don't know specifically about Joy and Hope. But everyone else in the world? Yes, of course. In my experience everyone thinks a single woman is a loser. That's why single people pay a "single loading" when they go on a cruise. Because no one wants them there.'

'Really?' I gasped incredulously.

'Yes, Nora. All living creatures are meant to be part of a couple. That's why the animals boarded the ark two by two. There were no single animals included at all, no matter how much fun they are to have around or how neatly they squeeze their toothpaste.'

'I'm sorry, Mum, but are you suggesting that Noah's ark was a cruise?'

'I'm sorry to interrupt,' Jack interrupted, presumably in an attempt to move the conversation on to lighter topics. 'I'm sorry, Nora, I didn't realise I ruined your life.'

'How could you not have realised?' said my mother. 'Nora *cried* in front of you. She cried in front of you for *weeks* if not *months*! How could you have missed that? You know how Nora cries. She doesn't look like a Disney princess, her face blows up and her eyes get all inflamed and red. She looks like a puffer fish with the plague. Trust me, a woman doesn't look like that if she has a choice. You knew perfectly well that Nora was hurting and you did nothing to stop it.'

'I wanted to, but I didn't know how,' mumbled Jack, as he hung his head and raised his eyes only to glance from Mum to me to Mum.

'Oh my God, Jack. None of us *knows* how to do these things,' said Mum. 'We work it out. We try, we fail, we think, we try again. None of us intrinsically knows!'

'But women instinctively know more than men,' Jack mumbled.

'Is that your excuse? That you're a man? Even if that does make you biologically behind the eight ball in terms of intuition and rudimentary life skills you could have *learnt* how to treat Nora. It was the early nineties, Jack. Chick-lit rom-com time! You could have just rented any video that starred Meg Ryan. But no, you did nothing. And so whose responsibility did the loving become? Mine and my pals Vera and Babs!'

Suddenly it was my turn to realise that I wasn't the only mother who'd made sacrifices and that maybe Mum did love me after all. And that realisation would have been a poetic and positive conclusion to the conversation if Mum hadn't decided to blab on for just a little bit longer.

'To be honest,' she continued relentlessly, 'loving Nora didn't come naturally to me at all. I would have preferred colonic irrigation.'

'Not everyone shows their love in the same way, Nora,' Jack blurted, presumably to stop Mum elaborating further.

'And how did you show yours, Jack?' I replied, 'By marrying Dildra Hip when she told you she was pregnant, crushing my heart, discovering she'd lied to you about her pregnancy and not leaving her to come back to me?'

'Yes.'

'Oh my God. Sorry, but how the fuck does that work?'

'I don't know.'

'But it was your responsibility to know, Jack. You did the damage. You were meant to fix it. Why didn't you leave her and come back to me?'

'How could I have gone back to you, Nora? I thought I was doing the right thing. How could I have asked you to stuff up your life with Leonard when I'd already stuffed up your life with me? I wanted you to get on with the new life that you'd chosen. That's how I showed you my love. And I'm showing it to you again, Nora, just by being here.'

'Are you kidding? You were called here to arrest me as part of your job, Jack.'

'Nora, I'm the boss. My rank is very high. Police in my position don't attend domestic drug disputes. I came to this situation personally because I knew it was you.'

'Well, Jack, that's all very impressive but why are you in the police force at all? What happened to the vineyard that had been in your family for five generations and we were going to run together with our brood of six kids and four cattle dogs and a fish called Frog?'

'Dildra took everything when we split.'

'No, you took everything, Jack – you took it and you threw it away. Why, Jack, why? Was I more in love with you than you were with me?'

'I told you why I didn't come back. I was trying to do the right thing.'

'Well it just shows, doesn't it, Jack, that sometimes trying to do the right thing is the fucking wrong thing to do.'

'Give me a break, Nors. I'm not a bad man. I'm just a stupid one. I became a policeman. I've moved up the ladder over the years and I've just been transferred to the city. I had no idea you were living around here. And I had no idea you were in such constant conflict with the law. That being the case, chances are that we'll be seeing a lot more of each other, so is there anything I can say to make this right?'

'Fuck off, Jack. Relationships are like buying a new a pair of shoes. Sometimes, no matter how much you want them – they just don't fit.'

The conversation just kind of floated away after that. Mum sang the national anthem in four part harmony. All by herself. Jack got the munchies and ate the remaining four cookies. And I realised that maybe all the big heartbreaks of my life are at least partly my fault.

Then we all got the giggles and laughed until we couldn't breathe and Mum said, 'At times like these, I find the best thing to do is kind of roll on your side and then just lie there, looking at the stars, until the nurses come to assist you.' And so that's what we did. We lay on our backs on my living room floor and, while the nurses never did arrive, Jack's arms did, and he held me tight as we lay on the floor and watched the stars appear.

And when I woke up just now Jack was gone and I was hugging Mum.

1.52 AM

Dear Diary,

Mum woke up and asked if I'd walk her to the loo. She didn't say why but the last time she went to my bathroom at night she fell and ended up in hospital. So I agreed of course and felt strangely close as I took her arm.

'This is nice, isn't it?' I said as we ambled.

'Is it?' my mother replied.

'I think getting stoned together helped us to bond. Is there anything you'd like to say?' I asked sweetly and Mum said, 'No.'

'Not anything at all about our relationship and where it's been, or where it is, or where it's going? You know, our relationship as mother and daughter. Is there anything at all you want to say about that?'

'No, thank you, Nora,' my mother replied, 'not everything needs to be put on the table and discussed. I know that's what your generation thinks, but mine finds it indulgent and egotistical. It's actions that prove emotions, Nora. And having said that, I will now say this. Thank you for walking me to the toilet.' And then we finished our walk in silence, because there was just too much to say.

Then as Mum sat on the loo I heard her say, 'You know not every conflict in relationships is all one person's fault. Most are the fault of both. But it's very rare for both to equally move forward and meet each other halfway to bridge the gap. So sometimes one person might have to walk twice as far as the other, way past what is actually the middle, just to make that initial reconnection.'

'Mum,' I called through the space at the side of the bathroom door. 'I think what you're saying is very wise but are you talking about you and I, Hope and I or myself and Jack?'

'I'm talking to the toilet brush, Nora.'

1.57 AM

I'm still waiting for Mum but not talking. I want to be alert to any sound of her falling.

To pass the time, I'm thinking about Jack. To my alarm I've got that 'heart a flutter' feeling. I'm nervous like the teenager I was when we first met, in fact even more insecure and more full of self-doubt. I'm a little surprised by this. I thought your fifties were meant to be the 'don't give a fuck' decade. Well you can stick that theory up your bum for grubs.

I wonder if Jack went home tonight because he felt snubbed that I fell asleep. I wonder if he feels like he was too boring. I wonder if he thinks he should have told some jokes. Maybe he did tell some jokes and I didn't realise. Maybe I should have laughed anyway.

But I remember I once laughed uproariously at a guy's joke, and it turned out it wasn't a joke. It was about his mother walking backwards every day of her life in order to keep fit and agile. Then one day, she walked backwards straight over a cliff.

Jack's mum died when a cow sat on her. Weirdly I have never found that funny at all.

2.04 AM

Dear Diary,

Mum came out of the bathroom and I tucked her in to my bed. She's fast asleep. I'm still thinking about Jack. I've got limerence – you know, obsessive romantic thoughts about him. I'm wondering if I should have asked him for his phone number. Oh well, no problem I guess, I could just dial Triple Zero and ask them to pass on a message.

Or Jack could easily ring me instead because Hope, Joy and I had to give our contact details when we were arrested, three days and a lifetime ago.

2.06 AM

I'm starting to feel a bit angry with Jack for the fact that I'm thinking of him. I really hate liking someone. I don't like how vulnerable it makes me feel.

So maybe I should just wait for him to contact me and stop all this chatter going round and round in my head, because one thing I can be absolutely sure of, based on the fact that Jack is a man and I am a woman, is there is no way in the world that he will be analysing this situation anywhere near as much as me, if in fact he's analysing it at all. He's probably just thinking, 'Went to Nora's, ate biscuits, went home.'

In THE DEPTHS OF HUMILIATION

4.47 PM
The wedding is still Tomorrow

Dear Diary,

I'm now waiting in the foyer of my building. I'm dressed as an alien. I'll explain.

I fell asleep after my last diary entry and woke again a few hours later at about 8 am when the doorbell rang at the same time as the phone. The phone call was from Miss Binsa at Happy Days. She sounded completely depressed as she said, 'Your mother's come back. She walked from your place at four o' clock this morning.'

The doorbell was the concierge delivering a huge bunch of flowers. The flowers had no card attached. So yes, I assumed they were from Jack. I was beyond ecstatic.

When I unwrapped the flowers and placed them in Mum's chamber pot I saw something white, the size of a tennis ball, float in the water then dissolve. As I watched it the phone rang again. It was Soula.

'Are you fucking joking me?' she said. 'Did you just get a freaking invitation?'

'No, but I just got some flowers,' I said smugly.

'I got flowers too,' Soula said.

'From Jack!'

'What? No, why? Mine had a white ball inside the bunch. The ball is the invitation.'

'What?'

'Yes!' said Soula. 'Look closely. It's soft and fragile, like a pure round egg, and it's got gorgeous gold handwriting on it. I haven't got my glasses on but I can read the stuff in the big font, and it says *You Are Cordially Invited*.'

'Put your glasses on!' I demanded.

'I can't, I can't see where they are without my glasses. But I can tell you the ball smells like meringue. I'll lick it and ... uh oh.' There was a pause.

'Did you just eat the invitation?' I asked.

Thilma rang on my landline at precisely that moment. It took me a while to find the landline because I didn't know I still had one. Then I held the mobile phone and the landline phone close to each other so that Soula, Thilma and I could hear each other and together thoroughly explore the boundaries of technology, forensic investigation and middle-aged patience.

'Oh my God,' said Thilma, 'I've just received the most beautiful bunch of flowers.'

'Was there an invitation inside?'

'No.'

'Are you sure? Did you look?'

'Of course I didn't look. How would I know to look for something that I didn't know was there in the first place?' said Thilma.

'Well, look now,' chorused Soula and I.

'I can't. I gave the flowers as a birthday present to the homeless man who lives in our alley.'

'You re-gifted?' gasped Soula.

'Yes, of course I did. I'm allergic to flowers.'

'But re-gifting is so wrong.'

'No, it's not,' said Thilma. 'What would you rather I do? Just throw them out? Re-gifting saves on resources and landfill and it doesn't do any living creature any harm.'

'You harmed me last year when you re-gifted to me the exact present that I'd gifted you,' said Soula.

'Well it's better than no-gifting, which is *your* current style.'

'Only since you started re-gifting my gifts!'

'The issue here is not whether to re-gift or otherwise,' I interrupted. 'The issue is whether or not Thilma can ask the homeless man to give the flowers back.'

'No, that's not possible,' Thilma cut me off. 'Just after I gave them to him, I saw him sell them to a passer-by. But maybe we could ring your mother, Daphne, to see if she also got flowers and get someone to read her invitation to us?'

'Oh good idea,' I said, 'but actually I can't ring her because you two are on both my phone lines.'

'Oh my God,' sighed Soula. 'You would be hopeless in a war. Show some initiative and borrow Hope's phone!'

So it was then that I obediently snuck into Hope's bedroom to borrow her phone and found a man in bed with her.

Sorry, I have to take a break because I'm still recovering.

4.53 PM

OK, I took the break, I'm back. A little wheezy but still able to continue writing.

So I saw the man in Hope's bed but I said nothing. I took the phone, snuck out of the bedroom, hyperventilated, took a swig of wine, took another one and dialled my mother.

'Mother,' I said, as I loitered outside Hope's bedroom door, juggling three phones while trying to peer through the door crack and ascertain the identity of the man and whether or not he might be a good excuse to call the police, or at least one policeman in particular. 'I'm just calling to ask if you received any flowers today Mum?'

'Yes,' she said, 'of course I did, I receive flowers every day. Sometimes from your brothers but usually from your dead father.'

'Oh, OK, and in the flowers that arrived this morning, did you happen to notice a note, or a message or an invitation?'

'No, I didn't. There may or may not have been one. I no longer seek out nor read the notes that come with the flowers because your father always addresses them to a different person and always signs them with a different name.'

'So,' I said, 'you're basically taking any flowers that arrive at Happy Days reception. Why do you think they're all for you?'

'Because a woman knows,' my mother replied.

'OK, fair enough,' I said. 'Can you have a look for a note in the flowers that arrived this morning?'

'No, I most certainly can't. I did what I always do and flushed them down the toilet. I can't have people knowing I receive flowers from a dead person. They'll think I'm completely mad.'

'Excuse me,' interrupted Thilma, 'but speaking of dead-to-me-ex-husbands, would you like me to ring Leonard, just to confirm he hasn't sent us all flowers?'

'Why would he be sending an invitation?'

'Maybe,' said my mother, 'he's finally realised he's a moron and wants to have an apology party.'

And so we waited on our phones while Thilma rang Leonard on her landline to see if he'd sent us each a bunch of flowers with an edible invitation. I quietly passed the waiting time by dusting the furniture, Mum sang the national anthem once more, and Soula did something that involved a mechanical buzzing, vibrating sound. It's possible that she was brushing her teeth, but whatever it was that she was doing, it sounded like she enjoyed it.

'OK,' said Thilma on return to our conference call. 'I rang Leonard and Booby answered. Apparently a bunch of flowers arrived there too and Leonard told Booby they were a gift from him "to say thank you for just being you". Booby thought this was so out of character she assumed Leonard has been cheating so she hit him with the flowers and in the process a "white ball fly through sky and on floor smash". Booby assumed it was either cocaine or anthrax so she tasted it and it was meringue, which coincidentally is her "thing favourite of capitalistic decadence".

It was at this point that the man emerged naked from Hope's room. I tried to act natural, but he was nude! I mean it couldn't be Aspen. Could it? Surely Hope wouldn't let him stay the night after his humiliating no-show at the engagement party. Would she? Maybe this guy was that hipster from Toscinos. I really, really hoped so. I couldn't tell. I couldn't look. To avoid eye contact, or any contact at all, I grabbed a broom and started sweeping the ceiling.

'I'm sorry, but could you keep the noise down a bit?' he said.

'I'm sorry, what?' I replied, still looking upwards.

'I said could you keep the noise down a bit?' he repeated with such self-confidence and utter ignorance of my mood that it suggested he was a bit thick.

'Are you serious?' I said aghast, but in a whisper to ensure I didn't wake Hope. 'You're naked in a stranger's house and you're telling *her* how to behave! I suggest the best way to avoid the noise is if you were to leave.'

And then Eduardo barged in unannounced wearing a version of his normal 'loafing at home' attire – handwoven silver slippers and a silver knitted sweatsuit, topped off with the draping of a shimmering violet cape that kept sliding from his rounded, drooping shoulders. He was carrying a huge bunch of flowers and an ugly grimace, which was actually just his normal facial expression. He took one look at the naked man, then a second look, removed his own cape, draped it around the stranger, bowed and said, 'Oh my God, it's you!'

Now that the nude guy was 'caped' and it was safe to look I could see that he was gobsmackingly good looking. His skin was golden, his hair was too. His eyes were blue, his teeth were white but I had a mum's intuition that his heart was black.

'Oh, where are my manners?' the naked man replied. 'Let me introduce myself. I'm Aspen Van den der Roth, Hope's fiancé.'

'Thank you,' said Eduardo as he thrust his bunch of flowers into Aspen's arms and said, 'I love you. I love your family. I love your wealth and that's why I've brought you these flowers.'

And Aspen slowly purred, 'Really.' Then he dipped his hand into the bunch, withdrew a round ball of meringue and read its golden writing, *You are cordially invited by The Van den der Roths to a pre-wedding soiree at our private residence to celebrate the impending nuptials of Aspen Van den der Roth and Hope Fawn. A car will collect you from your foyer at 5 pm March 27. Dress code: fancy.'*

With a white-toothed smile that brought light to the room, and possibly came with a tinkle sound, Aspen removed the cape and placed it like a knighthood upon Eduardo who remained kneeling on the floor. Then Aspen and his nudity returned to Hope's bedroom with a flourish of everything.

Eduardo seized all three phones and my left ear and whispered, 'Oh my God, it's Aspen Van den der Roth, son of the famous mega-rich mining family. I can't believe I didn't recognise them at our gathering, but then again they were wearing excellent disguises. And in return we must go all out to impress with our fancy dress at this party!'

'But what do you think fancy means?' I asked. 'Does that mean formal?'

'Of course it doesn't mean formal,' said Eduardo. 'I was born and raised in posh social circles and I can assure you that if they meant formal they'd refer to it as "Black Tie". The Van den der Roths are inviting us to have some fun. Let's embrace it and leave the outfits to Vietnamese Gloria,' said Eduardo. 'After all, she's a specialist.'

'I'll contact Vietnamese Gloria,' added Soula excitedly, 'and speak to her about helping us even though we're not speaking to her.'

So Gloria promised to find something brilliant for each of us to wear, something that would 'resonate and yet reflect our inner souls'. And as a result she turned up at my apartment at 4 pm today with her hand-picked selection of specific outfits that she traded for an Eduardo painting of a dog that looks like a coffee mug.

Vietnamese Gloria has dressed Hope as Cinderella, but this time it's the 'going to the ball' version, and she's supplemented the look with two wicked stepsisters played by Thilma and Soula. Sticking to the theme, my mother is dressed as the wicked stepmother, Leonard is Prince Charming's footman, Booby is the fairy godmother and Eduardo is the pumpkin carriage.

And me? Well, according to Vietnamese Gloria, I'm dressed in a 'special costume' because amongst the vast array of the thousands of outfits she keeps at *Glam on The Go* there wasn't one single one that suited my particular combination of traits.

'You are a mother, a daughter, a worker, a divorcee, but above all else you are, most importantly, someone who feels misunderstood, someone who feels like an outsider,' she said.

'Oh my God,' I thought, 'she's right.'

'And so I made an outfit specially for you, using my very own fat uncle's white ski suit for the body coverage, one of those papier-mâché balloon helmets to cover your head topped with an old TV antenna!'

And that's why I'm dressed as an alien.

Now the limo's arrived outside and I'm in my building's foyer just waiting for my gang. I'm planning to take a moment in the car trip to talk to Hope about her relationship with Aspen and the all important issue of self-pride. I think that will be very worthwhile and just hope she can hear me talk through my mouthpiece which is positioned to also function as a peephole because Gloria said 'aliens don't actually have eyes'.

AT THE VAN DEN DER ROTH MANSION

5.45 PM
It's still March 27
The wedding is still tomorrow!!!!!

Dear Diary,

So everyone else has gone into the mansion but turns out I can't get out of the limo because my antenna has pierced the limo's leather ceiling and I'm stuck.

To maintain my pride I'm trying to look brave. But to be honest I don't know why I'm bothering because my 'alien head hat helmet' is covering my face.

This is not how I imagined I'd make an impression on arrival at the Van den der Roths. I thought the car door would be opened by some sort of Lurch and my little tribe and I would be greeted warmly by our hosts, Baldwin and Bunny, who would themselves also be wearing excellent fancy dress; he dressed as a lion and she as some sort of prey he'd caught – or perhaps the mere ghost of her former self.

I didn't want to wear this alien outfit of course but the others convinced me.

'Honestly, Mum,' said Hope, dishonestly, 'if you looked any more fabulous you'd be drawing all the attention, and as you know *my* wedding … '

'… is not about you,' they all chorused.

'And,' continued Joy, ignoring me as if I were a nagging child, 'we really don't have time for you to get changed. Seriously, Mum, you can't make all of us late just because you're being a bit vain.' And then she came close and whispered only to me, 'I mean how can we possibly maintain the moral high ground against Aspen's rude no-show yesterday if we're *all* late today?'

That comment clinched it and I agreed to wear this outfit. And in doing that I fell for the oldest trick in the mother book – I took one for the team, known in Mum circles as 'eating the burnt chop'.

6.10 PM
I'm still stuck in the limo

I don't really mind sitting here. I've managed to keep writing because I took my white ski mittens off with my teeth after poking my mittens through Gloria's thoughtful mouth-eye hole. Plus I've worked out how to see out of my mouth and, although the limo's windows are tinted, I can clearly see the surrounds – the beautiful lawns that cascade to the magnificent harbourside and a mansion the size of a village.

To be fair, when we arrived, and discovered I was stuck, Joy did offer to stay with me and try to get me out but Hope, Thilma, Soula et al all kindly declined this offer on my behalf.

Interestingly however, keen as they all were to enter the mansion and join the soiree together, it would appear they've since been seated separately in the soiree room and have been forced to communicate via a group text, in which they've been gracious enough to include me.

The first text came from Soula: 'Shit, who decided that "dress fancy" meant fancy dress? All the women here are wearing evening gowns and the men are in tuxedos.'

The second text came from Thilma: 'This is like that movie where a whole family gets held for ransom.'

The third text came from Joy: ' Then what happens?'

The fourth was from my mother: 'They all die.'

The fifth came from Hope: 'Don't worry, Aspen will protect us.'

The sixth came from Booby: 'If up turns he.'

The seventh came from Hope: 'Aspen is a very important and busy man.'

The eighth came from me: 'Oh, really? And other than nudity, what is it he does?'

The ninth came from Hope: 'He's involved in finance.'

'We're all in finance, Hope,' I texted. 'We all need money, earn money, spend money.'

The flurry of texting suddenly stopped. Hope had obviously decided to employ the texting equivalent of 'the silent treatment'. I wondered if I should apologise for something like – oh, I don't know! Anything really.

6.14 PM

Everyone from the party is coming out to the front lawn! I presume they're coming to help free me. There must be about a hundred men and women. I hope Aspen is leading them; I'll forgive him everything if he gets me out of here.

I wonder how many of these people are going to help solve my problem. Some of the men have removed their jackets, but that may just be so they can feel part of the action. Watching them reminds me of a joke we used to say in the eighties – how many middle-aged heterosexual men does it take to change a light globe? Infinity. One to change the light globe and the rest to confirm it's being done correctly.

6.21 PM

No one is coming up to the car. They've all stopped on the lawn and are looking heavenward. Of course I can't see what they're looking at, but the growing chant of 'Aspen, Aspen' would suggest they're looking at him! I can hear exhalations of glee as one onlooker loudly proclaims, 'I for one am not at all surprised, you know his parents bought him a pilot's licence when he was only four.'

I wonder if Aspen is going to whisk Hope away in a helicopter, draw a simple skywritten 'I love you' or tie the knot right now in a hot air balloon. Truth is no matter what this gesture by Aspen turns out to be he will become a living love legend.

What a thoughtful romantic young man! Sure beats the guy who gave me a nose hair trimmer for my fiftieth birthday.

6.37 PM

Dear Diary,

Well, the bad news is, turns out, it was not a selfless romantic gesture. But the good news is that I will now never have to spend a moment of my life wondering what kind of attention-seeking loser would arrive at his own engagement soiree, late, drunk and all alone but for a jetpack emblazoned with the message, 'My Other Jetpack is a Private Jet'.

As Aspen approached, the crowd initially cheered, and then they gasped as he crash-landed on this limo. He's now being carried to the house, 'sedan style' while a servant jogs behind him with the jetpack.

Meanwhile I'm excited to exit the limo because the jolt of Aspen landing on the roof seems to have successfully dislodged my antenna. Now I just need someone to open the door for me and then tilt my head to the side. Just one of the one hundred or so guests who were gathered here could do the trick.

6.37 and a half PM

I'm still in the limo and no one has come to help yet, but Hope has just texted to say that Aspen's parents would like to meet with us in their Panic Room so my mother has called Emergency Services to get me out ASAP. So I should be heading inside any minute – assuming Mum did actually call Emergency Services, and not just Uber Eats.

'Actually,' Hope just texted again. 'To be honest his parents asked if they could meet with me alone, but I insisted that you come too.'

I have no idea why Hope would want me at the meeting. Maybe for some kind of prisoner exchange?

6.44 PM

Oh thank God. Emergency Services must be arriving. I can hear a siren approaching.

6.58 PM

Oh my God, it's Jack.

7.45 PM

Dear Diary,

I'm now inside the Van den der Roth mansion. I'm sitting on another loo. This one is made of diamonds.

I was first escorted by security into the mansion, then to the Panic Room. After that I came to this loo, which is in a bathroom just outside the Panic Room.

For the sake of transparency and also any shreds of my reputation that future grandchildren may find in scattered tatters floating in puddles of sewage in a slum, I would like to clarify that I wasn't escorted because I was reluctant to enter the mansion or couldn't be trusted. I was escorted because my helmet thing twisted when I was extricated from the limo and we couldn't get it off my head, and I couldn't see at all because the mouth hole slid to my left ear. Despite this limitation I've donned my cloak of motherhood and draped myself in an authentic upbeat and positive demeanour – which is totally artificial.

I'm sorry but in terms of scene setting, Dear Diary, I can't describe the walk here as anything other than 'dark'.

Once we arrived at the Panic Room there was some talk about 'removing my head' but it was agreed, by everyone but me, not to waste time because progressing the Panic Room meeting was apparently more important than the regaining of my sight and independent mobility.

The room felt cavernous. Our footsteps echoed. I was seated on a chair that I think was one of many occupied around a meeting table, but I have never felt more alone. No one was speaking. I could smell a combination of tinea cream and foot deodoriser so I knew that Eduardo was there. I could also smell Soula (hairspray), Thilma (lavender BO), my mother (mothballs), Joy (oven cleaner) and Booby (no smell at all, because 'they us taught in my country how to escape enemy by not having no smell, even breath with anus'). Sitting beside Booby I could sense a big black hole, which I presume was Leonard.

Finally someone else entered the room; it sounded like a man with small, slippery shoed feet. I assumed it was Alcoq the lawyer.

'Well, good evening, Evil Sisters, Fairy Godmother, Wicked Stepmother, Pumpkin, Footman ...' He was interrupted by someone else entering the room. The steps were strong and confident, the accompanying smell was warm and inviting. I imagined a freshly baked muffin wearing RM Williams riding boots. Surely this couldn't be Aspen.

'Ah,' said Alcoq, 'a new arrival in a police uniform! An excellent costume if I may say, though somewhat of a deviation from the Cinderella/Alien theme we have going on. But then again who am I to judge? I once went to a pirate party dressed as a carrot. Please take a seat at the table.' At this point I heard the shuffle of chairs as the gathering accommodated the new arrival. Ever desperate to please and also belong, I tried to shuffle along and help make some space but in the process tipped from my chair and fell onto the floor.

To be honest I did imagine dying there on the plush floor covering; like a turtle stuck on its back on the sand as the tide withdrew and climate change irrevocably baked the planet. But I was actually only on the carpet for a moment before I was retrieved by two strong hands and the warmly whispered words, 'Don't worry, Nors, I've got you.'

Yes, the guy in the police costume was Jack. Is he everywhere? Talk about not playing hard to get. I struggled to my feet alone, determined to prove what an easy partner I'd be because I have no need for anyone else. I retrieved my chair, sat in it, and unable to see that the chair had castors, slid across the room. I then walky-wheeled myself back to where I thought I'd been originally positioned. Joy, I think, tried to help me face the right way, but pride made me resist her assistance so I suspect I spent much of the meeting facing the wall.

Alcoq continued, 'As you all know, our Prince Charming is to marry your Cinderella. Now *I* know that up until now Hope was unaware of Aspen's lineage. Like many women throughout history she no doubt simply saw a guy who was almost perfect, and who with just a few tweaks and personality adjustments she could rescue and live with happily ever after. Am I right, Hope?' he asked.

'Well the first bit is true,' said Hope, not realising that Alcoq was delivering a monologue, not engaging in conversation. 'But it's not true that I wanted to change him because I think he's already perfect.'

'Really?' said absolutely everyone.

Ignoring us, Alcoq continued, 'By now I'm sure you'll have all ascertained that our Prince Charming is in fact Aspen Van den der Roth, the first, last and only child of the oldest living member of the Van den der Roth family and therefore heir to the extensive Van den der Roth family fortune. I won't disclose family ruptures, but I will reveal that fractious issues such as these are precisely what we're trying to avoid in the future here together now. So, where was I, ah yes. Obviously on first meeting his beloved Hope, Aspen tried to hide his heritage by not mentioning it at all. His parents similarly tried not to intimidate you by consciously disguising their abundant wealth at your gathering yesterday and compassionately dressing as your people dress, like you're auditioning for a role in a modern day *Les Misérables*.'

Some of us mumbled unhappily at this comparison. Others were thrilled to bits.

'But now,' continued Alcoq, 'the truth of their eye-watering wealth is out and so we must all act like bathed and well-washed grown-ups, even if some of us aren't, and proceed with open hearts and minds while at the same time making sure the Van den der Roth wealth is totally secure with all t's crossed and i's dotted. So if you will just sign here, Hope.'

I wanted to read the document but of course couldn't see it. I called out, 'Could someone read the document to me please,' but no one heard me speaking through my ear hole.

'Hope, your signature?' repeated Alcoq.

'Um,' said Hope, 'if you don't mind, I'd like to read it first.'

'Really, Hope,' said Alcoq, 'there is no point. If you want to marry Aspen, then this agreement is completely non-negotiable.'

'Yes, yes of course, I understand,' Hope replied, 'I'd just feel better if my adviser took a look.'

'And who might that be?' Alcoq asked.

''Tis I,' said my mother, who by the sound of the paper rustle, seized the agreement and then after a moment put it back on the table while loudly exclaiming, in a summary of her perusal, 'Mmm, nice font.'

'Can *my* mother read it?' Hope said.

'Obviously not,' said Alcoq, 'your mother currently has no eyes.'

'Then, if you don't mind I'd like to wait until Mum can see again.'

'I do mind,' said Alcoq, 'I mind very much. I'm under strict instructions for this to be signed before the wedding can go ahead tomorrow.'

'Well, maybe it can't go ahead,' said Jack.

'What about if I offer you fifty thousand dollars?' said Alcoq.

'No,' said Jack, 'that's not the –'

'A hundred grand?' snapped Alcoq.

'Well, the problem is –' said Jack.

'OK, you drive a hard bargain,' Alcoq roared. 'I offer you, on the table right now, a cash incentive of two million dollars per year for the rest of Hope's life and all she has to do is marry Aspen before midday tomorrow.'

'I'll marry him,' said Soula, Thilma, Mum, Eduardo, Booby and Leonard.

'We need a little time to think,' said Joy. 'Could you give us some privacy for a moment please?'

Alcoq obliged and left the room with his feet sounding like wet fish sulking across a linoleum floor.

'The first thing we have to do now he's gone,' said Hope, 'is get Mum seeing and able to read.'

'All hands on deck!' Jack ordered as he rallied the troops to assist with my helmet removal. 'All hands out of the way,' he said, as the hands proved to be no help at all.

Rescuing me took Jack a while. Well, longer than one would want, which would have been about no minutes. Anyway my helmet head hat finally came off and the first thing I saw was dear, kind sensitive Hope hovering two centimetres above my face saying, 'Mum, Mum, get your shit together, I really need you!'

What? Had I died and gone to heaven?

'Mum,' she said, 'Mum, I'm talking to you. What do you think we should do?'

I wondered if this was a trick question. I looked at Hope to detect her intention. Even accepting that up this close her face did look a bit like a pink dinner plate, it was clear that her expression was earnest and keen. She didn't look as if she were setting a trap for me, but I've fallen for that non-trap setting trap before. On this occasion, what were the rules? Was Hope's request for support a peace offering or a time bomb? My heart was palpitating as I said, 'I support you in whatever you choose to do.' And Hope looked at me and said, 'Mum, concentrate. Give me your actual opinion, I really, really need you now. Please help me like you always do.'

If only I could have captured that moment and had it converted into some sort of trinket to attach to a key ring because during that second my body was flooded with the overwhelming comfort I hadn't known I was seeking, recognition that I've done this mum job right. That I haven't completely failed after all.

'It's true, Mum,' Joy said in a remarkable combination of enthusiasm and reluctance. 'You do always help Hope. I mean you don't help *all* of us all the time.' And everyone nodded in agreement with this. 'But you do always help Hope, sometimes to the detriment of others who may actually have needed the help more legitimately and desperately and appreciatively, for example Soula ...'

'No, I have no complaints,' said Soula. 'You've always helped me, Nora. In particular I remember the time I accidentally married a gorilla.'

'That's a bit sexist,' said Hope.

'No, Hope,' I interjected, 'Soula really did once accidentally marry a gorilla.'

'OK, well maybe you have helped Soula,' continued Joy, 'but you haven't for example always been there for Thilma.'

'Yes, she has,' said Thilma. 'Your mum's always been there for me, even when my labia got caught in the photocopy machine.'

'OK then,' persevered Joy. 'Well, what about Grandma? Mum hasn't always been there for her.'

'Actually, I'm really sorry to have to say this, Joy, but your mother has always been there for me. Even when I desperately didn't want her to be.'

'She's been there for me too,' mumbled both Leonard and Eduardo with expressions that were hard to read, but possibly a combination of embarrassment, gratitude, shame and gas.

'Well, she hasn't been there for me,' sobbed Joy. 'I've had needs and wants and simple desires for attention as any child will from her mother. But every time that opportunity has come, Hope fell ill, or Hope disappeared, or Hope came back and announced she was getting married and all the attention was diverted from me and –'

'Yeah, yeah, enough about you, Joy,' said Hope. 'Mum! What do you think I should do?'

I confess I was torn. I was torn between helping Hope immediately or waiting for just a few extra moments in order to allow, what I understand in the theatre is called 'a beat', a moment in which to give those nice compliments time to linger. Unable to choose between the two options, I chose to hug my Joy.

'Mu-u-um!!!!' wailed Hope with dismay as Joy sighed with pure, well, joy.

'Hope, I want you to lead a passionate life,' I said, as I somewhat awkwardly kept one ski-mittened hand on Joy's shoulder and reached the other out to Hope. 'I want you to find your purpose by moving through life in rhythm with your heartbeat. But I am your mother and my job is to protect you, and I think that while marrying Aspen may well be an exciting short-term adventure I think that in the long-term it will be full of pain and pitfalls and the deep longing that comes from never being the most important person in your beloved's life.'

'How on earth can you know all that?' cried Alcoq from the hallway where he was not meant to be listening. 'How can you know he's a spoilt, self-centred, self-obsessed twat when you've never spent a day with him?'

I continued talking to Hope, ignoring the fact Alcoq was listening, 'So I say with all my heart and soul, do not marry this man! Let's leave now, let's all go home and watch *Chitty Chitty Bang Bang*!'

My decree was followed by a very long deafening silence.

'Thank you, Mum, in fact thank you all,' Hope finally said, as we all heaved a communal sigh of relief which, as it turns out, was some moments too early. 'Yes, thank you for being honest for once, Mum. I appreciate it must have been hard. And your perspective has totally convinced me to unhesitatingly say ... that I'm going to marry Aspen Van den der Roth.'

'Alcoq, you can come back in,' screamed my mother with disgust, 'our Hope has agreed to be sacrificed.'

And with that Alcoq reentered the Panic Room carrying the agreement, which Hope signed with a flourish. Alcoq then looked at the signature and looked at Hope and said, 'I'm sorry, you have to sign your own name.'

'Oh dear,' said Hope, apologetically, 'I've accidentally signed my mum's. Sorry, force of habit.'

UNCLE DICK'S PRIVATE JET

9.17 and a half PM
Still the day before the wedding

Dear Diary,

Yes, it's true. Hope, Joy, Thilma, Soula, Mum, Eduardo, Leonard, Booby and I are all now in a private jet. We're heading to the Van den der Roths' private tropical island for tomorrow's wedding.

Aspen and his family aren't with us because, according to marital traditions, and also spatial limitations, the young betrothed are being kept apart on their wedding eve. No one is saying, but it's glaringly obvious, that this separation of families is also because we've really got the shits with each other.

Aspen, his family and Alcoq are all flying in Baldwin's jet. In fact Aspen told Hope that he was actually flying it. That Aspen would be the pilot!

Their jet is named *Lion* and it is so big it wouldn't surprise me if the Van den der Roths are playing tennis inside it.

We, on the other hand, are in the jet that's used by Baldwin's inferior delinquent disinherited brother. That's not his official name. His official name is Dick. Apparently our jet is primarily used by Dick for weekends away 'with the boys'. Our jet's name is *Beaverlicious*.

I once saw photos of the interior of a female pop star's private jet. It was soft and pink and curved and velvet and looked like the intestines of a marshmallow. This jet doesn't look like that due to the addition of footy scarves draped around windows, nude female centrefolds cellotaped to the walls, and scattered breast-shaped comfort pillows which I just discovered double up as fart cushions.

The main cabin is carpeted with shag pile. When I was young in the seventies we had a 'real shag pile' toilet seat cover, which was considered to be so precious and posh Mum got it framed and hung it on the wall above the cistern.

Like a proper private jet, this plane has its own flight attendant, but she's wearing a bikini. Before take-off I attempted to override her objectification and validate her as an intelligent woman by enquiring if there was anywhere in particular she'd like to travel. 'Yes, I'd like to go to Albania,' she said, 'because I really like Albinos.'

Music is playing on the intercom; it's AC/DC on eleven. And despite the relative smallness of our jet, we have a spa on board. Soula found it in the master bathroom when she was looking for little bottles of shampoo and conditioner to steal. We didn't use the spa because Mum decided to make a bed in it but we've all changed into the fluffy white post-spa bathrobes provided by the flight attendant (who should also be covering up with one).

At this moment everyone is stretched out on their seats having dozed off one by one. They're sleeping in an assortment of positions, ranging from the traditional 'Foetal' to the more advanced and more exotic 'Human Fly Trap'. Leonard and

Eduardo, in their sleep, are snoring the banjo duet from the soundtrack of *Deliverance*.

I'm not asleep. Obviously. I'm not tired. I'm shattered, but I'm not tired. I'm thinking about wealth. I'm not necessarily thinking about wanting more myself. I'm thinking about the wealth of the Van den der Roths. I'm wondering what determines that those who have the money to live like gods invariably possess most ungodly qualities. The distribution of wealth appears to have nothing to do with one's value as a human. It also seems to make people miserable. So perhaps wealth is not a privilege after all. Perhaps it is a punishment.

I'm also thinking about Hope's marriage. I know this wedding is not meant to be about me but after tremendous analysis and contemplation I think it actually might be. In trying to understand what on earth possessed Hope to choose emotional servitude to Aspen over the independent feminist life that I've lived, I've realised that Hope must find my life totally non-aspirational, i.e. that my life looks like shit. A shit life that she fears is contagious.

And who am I to tell others who to marry when I married Leonard, who's like a broken Swiss Army knife, full of potential but actually useless. I wonder why nobody tried to stop *me* marrying. But maybe my marriage to Leonard was actually right at the time. Without it I wouldn't have Hope and Joy, the loves and bunions of my life.

Maybe Hope is marrying Aspen because she needs a father figure and this is all Leonard's fault. Maybe Aspen will become a better person with time. I mean that's what happened to … Actually I can't think of an example.

I could ask Soula for one of her psychic predictions for reassurance but I suspect I can already see the future. Aspen will consume Hope. And Aspen's family? They will without doubt subsume her. She will become theirs and I will lose her. And I'm struggling to accept she's chosen them over us. I mean I accept I've made enormous mistakes, but these guys lying around me sleeping like Munch's *The Scream*? They are absolutely fabulous.

4 hours later

Dear Diary,

It was night-time when we started this journey, and now, after four or so hours of flying, we seem to be heading toward the dawn. I'm alone in the cabin now. The others have retired to the bedrooms. Well, Mum is sleeping in the spa but I guess you could call the others 'bedrooms'. Why not? Each one has a bed in it where there's currently a sleeping person. Actually one of them has two sleeping people, despite the fact they're single beds Leonard and Booby are sharing theirs. When I first saw this I was shocked. The closeness of their faces made them look like battery hens, but the fact that they're sleeping while holding hands makes them look like they're in love.

Soula and Eduardo are also sharing a 'bedroom'. In all the spontaneity of us catching this flight, Eduardo didn't have a chance to bring his teddy, and Soula is now wearing a teddy, so he asked her to sleep with him and that all makes total sense (if you're Eduardo or Soula or on acid). I suspect Soula initially fell asleep resting on Eduardo's tummy, but she's since rolled off and is now lying on the floor. Exactly like a teddy.

Actually, I'm completely empathetic to the 'forgot my teddy' situation because in all the rush and spontaneity required to get on this flight I seem to have forgotten to pack everything except my anxiety – which, to be honest, I didn't know I suffered from until four days ago with the announcement of this wedding.

I've tried breathing into the air-sick bag. I've also tried to distract myself by thinking happy thoughts, but I actually couldn't think of any so that made me even more anxious. I'm now planning to take one of the fifty 'calming tablets' that the hospital gave me to give to Mum. I wouldn't take them if supply was short. And I wouldn't take them if I wasn't 100 per cent sure they're actually sugar placebos.

The others don't seem to be anxious at all. Perhaps they have better coping techniques than placebo popping with plonk. I do know that Thilma does yoga in her mind and Soula finds time in her busy life to listen to relaxation tapes by playing them on fast forward.

But, while we are the closest of friends, I'm not actually at all like Thilma and Soula. They don't seem to find life a burden the way I do and are constantly discovering new ways to enjoy it. Soula, for example, recently started a car with a safety pin and Thilma cooked a fish in her dishwasher.

Nonetheless *I* am anxious. I think perhaps reading would be a good distraction but the only reading matter on board is the safety card, which someone has desecrated by drawing breasts and genitalia all over it and writing the word 'Yippeeeeee' next to the mouth of the woman sliding down the exit to escape an on-board fire. The last time I saw this kind of silly safety card shenanigans was on a budget airline where our male flight attendant was wearing a badge that said, 'Hi, my name is Penelope'.

Oh my God, I have to go, someone's just howled.

10 minutes later

The howl came from Soula. I ran to her, as did Thilma and Mum – well, Mum didn't so much run as do a weird kind of space walk (but in fairness that might have been due to her falling asleep on the strangely located spa taps). Anyway when *I* reached Soula's side I asked if she'd had a terrible premonition, or just realised she was sleeping next to Eduardo.

'I looked out the window at the vast expanse of emptiness …' she said.

'Yes?' said ever-encouraging Thilma, in a tone that suggested she might later charge Soula for this interaction.

'I saw a plane crash at the airport,' continued Soula, oblivious to Thilma's ploy. 'The plane was filled with good-looking happy people.'

'Oh that's a relief,' said my mother, 'it obviously wasn't us then.'

This did not ease my anxiety. I popped another placebo and quietly prayed that the oxygen masks might spontaneously deliver some sort of gaseous anaesthetic.

'Nonetheless it is perfectly possible that *our* plane could crash too,' my mother quipped.

'Is it, Mum? I don't think you think so. If you did, you wouldn't have drawn penises and bosoms all over the safety card.'

'How did you know it was me?' she said. 'I tried to make the drawings so bad that you'd think Eduardo did them.'

'If I had done them,' said Eduardo, 'that safety card would be worth millions and we could have given it as a priceless wedding gift. After you'd all contributed financially of course.'

At this point I asked if we shouldn't perhaps give something more valuable or more useful.

'Really, Mum,' said Joy. 'Are you *really* asking that? Because for our entire lives you've given us cheap useless shit that we had no use nor desire for.'

'I didn't want to spoil you by giving you things you requested. I gave things to prepare you for life.'

'In what way?' said Hope. 'To let us know that life would be full of disappointments?'

'Yes,' I replied.

'Oh my God,' said my mother. 'Who taught you that?'

'You did,' I replied.

'I have no recollection whatsoever of doing that,' said my mother. 'Let's ring your brothers and ask them.'

'They don't know. You didn't treat them like you treated me. God, Mum, how many times do we have to talk about this? You taught me to aim low and expect defeat. You taught them that the world was their oyster. When I was five I asked for a doll for Christmas and you gave me a cricket ball in a frock.'

'Life is tougher for girls, Nora.'

'I think that is an absolute lie,' I hissed. 'You raised me like that to punish me for *not* being a boy.'

'I raised you the way I was raised. And the way I was raised made me who I am.'

'And are you happy with who you are?' I asked.

'My generation doesn't think about whether we're happy, Nora. That is another obsession of yours. My generation simply focuses on whether or not we got the job done. I raised you tough so you could survive. And you have. So job done! You have survived despite all life has thrown at you – Jack and sick Hope, and Leonard abandoning you, and raising your children as a single woman.'

'Well, maybe life has thrown that at me *because* of the way you raised me.'

I heard Soula and Thilma gasp at this point. A gasp that suggested they both thought I'd gone too far. And the three of us waited for Mum's response. But, after terrifying moments of silence, Mum just smiled, and said nothing. She refused to engage. Like a tennis player with a killer forehand, she just let my shot fly past, in the comfort of knowing she could slam me any time.

And this made things even worse. With fifty-odd years of anger bubbling inside me I wanted to remind my mother of all the suffering of my childhood. But I couldn't remember examples of what she'd done. So instead I reminded her of things she *didn't* do.

'You, you never once said, I love you!' I said to Mum.

'Of course I didn't!' Mum replied. 'No one said I love you in those days Nora, it would have been regarded as creepy.'

I went on and on. And my mother listened to me, looking increasingly agitated, and when I'd finished, with welling tears in my eyes, and I finally thought that she'd understood my pain, Mum said, 'I'm sorry, have we met?'

And that's when I took three more of Mum's placebos. Or maybe four. And returned to my seat.

But I couldn't settle. I tried to sleep but didn't succeed, and I still haven't managed to. Maybe I've taken too many pills and made myself completely sugar-wired. Sugar-wired and a little bit fatter.

My thoughts are random, undisciplined, disconnected. A little while ago I was thinking about the years I spent raising the girls; the hugs, the laughter, the purpose. Then I was thinking about the time we built a beautiful flowerbox to hang on our side of the neighbour's fence. And then I thought about how the weight of that flowerbox made the entire fence fall down. And then I thought about what an excellent metaphor that is – but I don't know what for.

Now I'm thinking about how shitty the world has become and when that shittiness began. Some people say it was the onset of social media. But I think it was when suitcases got wheels.

I'm thinking about how the snores being emitted by Eduardo and Leonard make the plane sound like a zoo. I'm thinking a bit about middle-aged sex. I'm remembering one guy I went out with a few years ago, who broke up with me because he said our sex was bad. I remembered how astounded I was to hear this, because I didn't know he was awake.

I'm thinking about what a failure I am.

As a daughter.

As a mother.

As a woman

As a human.

5 seconds later

Dear Diary,

Good news! I've found the controls to my seat's entertainment system and discovered *Chitty Chitty Bang Bang* buried in the menu.

15 minutes later

OK, so I clicked on an episode and as the film began the theme music must have roused Joy, because without a word she entered the cabin from her bedroom, sat in the seat on my left and snuggled up to me, to watch the screen. Moments later Hope appeared, plonked herself in the seat on my right and silently rested her head on my shoulder. I didn't open my eyes. I didn't dare move. I didn't speak. I pretended I was asleep. To feel their warm skin, have them so close, not fighting, not berating, not hating, just snuggling; well it was the happiest seventy-five seconds of my life. Even when I heard Joy take a selfie and discuss posting it with the hashtag #kidnapped. Yes, it was the happiest time of my life until they started talking.

'Do you think Mum's asleep?'

'Yes, she's dribbling.'

'I hope I don't dribble when I get old.'

'You probably will,' said Joy. 'You and Mum are very similar.'

'That's a mean thing to say.'

'I don't think it is,' said Joy. 'I've seen photos of Mum when she was young and she was really quite attractive.'

'Oh I thought you meant my personality is similar to hers.'

'You do have similar personalities. You're both smart and passionate. And you both have chips on your shoulders about your mothers.'

'But my chip is valid. And I don't want to be like Mum at all. She's wasted her own life and is suffocating mine. I don't want to be near her sphere of influence, because I don't want to end up all alone like she is.'

'But you might, Hope. In marrying Aspen you will be all alone. That's why Mum wants to stop you.'

'Well, to be honest, the best way for Mum to get me to do something is to encourage me to do the complete opposite.' I made a mental note.

They were both quiet for a bit after that. I heard Hope unwrap and chew a lolly. I heard Joy sit up and straighten her posture.

'Hope?' said Joy. 'Why did you disappear?'

'I just couldn't handle Mum anymore. I needed to get away.'

'But what couldn't you handle?'

'Honestly? I can't put my finger on it. It's like she couldn't see me. It's like I didn't exist. It's like I just couldn't be near her. It was like a physiological reaction. I really don't know what happened. But it's like, little by little, it grew and grew until finally I just felt like everything she said and did was complete and utter bullshit. And I couldn't be around it anymore.'

'Really?' whispered Joy.

'It's like I realised that our little family's leader actually has no idea where she's going. Haven't you ever found that with Mum?'

'You know what, I honestly haven't. I guess I see the same broken bird as you, but I want to nurture her.'

There was another pause. The comfortable pause that can exist perhaps only between siblings – those who spent years of Christmas holidays being driven to visit their grandma's country relatives and entertaining themselves along the way by counting road kill.

'But what was it that made you leave *that* day?' Joy asked.

'I guess I'd been wanting and waiting for a final straw – for an excuse to go.'

'And what was it, what did Mum say?' Joy asked gently, encouragingly.

'I don't know.' Hope sighed. 'Actually *she* didn't say anything.'

'What!'

'I remember that day I said something that was really important to me. It was about wanting to be an artist. And Mum just kind of shrugged.' There was another pause, then Hope continued, 'it felt like she was jealous or something and it outraged me at the time and was kind of good justification, you know, the proof I needed for myself, the final straw.'

Another pause.

'Proof of what?' Joy asked.

'Proof that she thinks she's me,' Hope said, awkwardly. 'It makes me feel lonely that you don't understand. I just kind of want the whole thing to go away.'

'Yet at the same time,' Joy said quietly, 'your anger with Mum is like your fuel – your purpose, your identity.'

'I knew you wouldn't understand.' Hope sighed. There was another pause till Joy spoke, kindly, desperately. 'Mum was always angry like that with Grandma, but I've watched Mum and seen her soften. Maybe the fire of Mum's outrage has died, maybe Grandma's ageing and dementia have made outrage seem ridiculous. Maybe Mum just knows more now. Maybe that will happen to you too – your anger will fade and pass.'

'Maybe,' said Hope. 'But first I'm marrying Aspen.'

I waited about a minute, but it felt much longer, and then I pretended to talk in my asleep and mumbled, 'Hope, I'm so happy that you're marrying Aspen. It's the best decision you could ever make.'

Unfortunately Hope seems to have seen through my ruse because she just stormed off. I find this very sad. But Soula would think it was really funny because on a jet this size you can only storm off for about five metres and then you reach the end of the plane and have to storm back again.

5.10 AM

Dear Diary,

Hope has returned and is once again sitting next to me and Joy. They're both asleep.

The flight attendant has just announced the 'time at our destination is 5.10 am.' The pilot followed this with his own announcement but it was impossible to understand because he was giggling when he said it.

But now he's making another announcement.

'This is the pilot speaking. I'd like to apologise for the somewhat unprofessional nature of my previous announcement – our flight attendant was tickling me. The good news is we do have our destination in sight. The bad news is I don't think we will reach it because we've lost the use of one of our engines.'

I may have to stop writing for a minute, Dear Diary. I'm going to take six more placebos.

5.12 and three quarters AM

The jet is now 'cruising' at what one might describe as an 'unnatural downward angle'.

The inflight screen's no longer showing *Chitty Chitty Bang Bang*. It's gone blue. I'm struggling to breathe. The girls have woken. I feel like going to sleep.

I try to tell the girls that I love them but Joy says, 'Ssssh! We're concentrating.' And Hope adds, 'Mum, this isn't about you.'

I nervously pop two more sugar pills.

In a perfect world, at a time like this … Actually, in a perfect world, a time like this wouldn't be happening, so in a perfectly unrealistic fantasy about a time like this, I'd be hugging my children. But a hug isn't possible at the moment because we're strapped into our seats.

Joy has, of course, obediently assumed the crouch position you're supposed to adopt when preparing for impact, but she's also taking a photo of herself at the same time and posting it on Instagram as #thelastpost? And Hope is just focused on struggling to breathe. I'm rubbing her back, the way I used to for all those years. I'm rubbing with my left hand and writing with my right.

I stopped to kiss the top of Joy's head and then, as it turns out, Hope's right ear. 'What are you doing, Mum!' Hope hissed.

'I'm kissing you because I want you to know that I love you.'

'Oh for God's sake, Mum, don't you think we know that?'

'And?' I asked Hope teasingly.

'And we love you too.'

5.15 AM

Dear Diary,

This may be my la s t

TO WHOM IT MAY CONCERN:

Joy is Writing This!

5.37 AM approximately.
(Please note: I don't normally use the word 'approximately' because I like precision, but I don't know the precise time because I don't know where the-f-word we are.)

Good afternoon, my name is Joy Fawn. I'm writing, very neatly, from the private jet of a man called Dick who is the uncle of my soon to be brother-in-law who is an f-word-wit. Grandma has asked that I document our current disaster in case we need the info when Mum's taken to hospital or 'we want to release it as an album'.

I'm with my mother Nora, my grandmother Daphne, my sister Hope, my self-appointed godmothers Soula and Thilma, my mum's boss Eduardo, my dad Leonard and his wife Booby, whom I prefer to respectfully call Bosom, out of basic politeness.

We've just survived a plane plummet that lasted a few seconds but is now over. As soon as it finished Mum passed out on the floor. She's still on the floor but Bosom, who apparently practised as an untrained doctor in Bognokistan, said that Mum is 'OK (ish)'. When I first noticed Mum collapse I thought she was dead. But I am very happy to write that she wasn't, and isn't, though she's still lying on the floor with her eyes closed. The pilot's turned the plane around, 'just to be safe' so we're heading back home instead of going to the Van den der Roths' tropical island. Apparently the Van den der Roths have also turned their jet around and are now heading back home too. I wish we could have ditched them.

When I first noticed that Mum had passed out I fearfully told Hope that Mum was blue. And, without looking up, Hope replied, 'Of course she is, I'm getting married.' So I responded in a loud but still polite shriek, 'No, look at her, she is actually blue!'

Now that I look back on the situation I understand that Mum's face was reflecting the blue of her entertainment screen. But at the time I panicked and said, 'We have to do CPR!' So Hope, who always has to be the centre of attention, said, 'I'll do it,' and started breathing into Mum's mouth like Mum was a party balloon.

After that I shoved Hope out of the way and I tried to do CPR, 'cause I really wanted to be the one who saved Mum's life as it's been an ambition of mine since I was about three. But I was sobbing too much to do it well. (So I'm pretty sure I'll beat myself up for that inadequacy for at least the rest of my life.)

Luckily though, it was at that nanosecond that Bosom found the remaining pills, counted them, held her nose, chewed a pill and said, 'Your mother in sleep deep after pill sugar high. Not die today. Hooray!'

'I think that we should not wake her up,' said my grandma with uncharacteristic gentleness. 'Nora's had a very tiring fifty-one years.' And then I started to sob.

'Oh for God's sake, Joy,' Hope just said, 'you really need to calm down.'

'I can calm you,' Thilma replied. 'All I need is a wand and a signed permission slip.'

Thank God, the flight attendant's just appeared.

5.48 AM

The flight attendant said, 'Good news, the Van den der Roths are close behind us and we'll be back home in a few hours.'

So I said, 'But why has it taken us hours and hours to get here but will only take a few hours to get back?'

'Well,' she replied, 'um, I don't know if you're smart enough to grasp this concept but the anticipated rapid speed of return is either because of the excessive tail wind or it could be due to something else.'

This made me more stressed. So Soula told me to calm down. 'Mothers can sense their daughter's stress,' she said. 'Even if they're unconscious. And stress makes toxins and toxins can kill so you should really stop stressing out because you're currently murdering your mother.'

'I don't mean to be rude,' said Hope, which even though we all love her we also know meant she was about to be rude, 'I have first-hand experience of being calmed by Mum and made to feel safe, loved and secure, so everyone move out of the way so that I can do it for her.'

'Would you like me to tell you our favourite story?' Hope whispered into Mum's ear.

'Oh God,' I moaned. 'This will be pathetic. I think it's best for everyone if I don't write this down.'

'Write it,' Grandma hissed and in so doing released a waft of denture wash. 'I suspect it will be a tale of love and your mother needs to know what really goes on when she thinks we're all plotting her downfall. She's been picking the scabs of her wounds for too long and become an emotional hypochondriac.'

'OK,' said Hope dismissively. 'Now everyone be quiet while I tell Mum an uplifting story about me living happily ever after with Aspen.'

To which I replied under my breath, 'Now who's murdering Mum?'

5.51 AM

Dear Diary, Hello! OMG!

Well we're all still alive but OMG, I've just been informed that you're a diary, Dear Diary, and that Mum has spent the past few days diarising in you! Prior to that I totally believed my mother when she said you were notes for the wedding!

When Grandma told us the truth just now, I wanted to read your pages for myself, because I like to be thorough but Grandma insisted that she'd give me the gist of what Mum has written in you. 'I've read the whole thing from woe to go,' she said. 'And the entire diary's filled with nothing more than boring observations about the wedding planning and a few bits about the weather.'

I didn't comply straight away with Grandma's documenting order. 'But why do I have to write it?' I asked. 'Why can't Hope? She never does anything for anyone else and I always do everything for everyone!'

'And that's why you should be the one who does this,' Grandma replied. 'Because you've had so much more practise.'

'And besides,' screamed Hope, 'I can't!! Don't you understand? My mother is ill!'

'Your mother is asleep. And besides she's my mother too,' I said.

'Yes, Joy,' said Hope, 'but this is so much worse for me. I might be about to lose a mother *and* a marriage because we're going to miss the midday deadline.'

'Darling,' said Thilma while practising yoga in her seat and standing on her head, 'I know all about the married by midday deadline. I read it in your mother's diary after the hen's party when I snuck back in through the window to check on your mother and found her sleeping with Jack.'

'What!' Hope and I yelped.

'Oh for heaven's sake, girls, stop making a fuss,' said Grandma. 'I slept with him too.'

'Um, getting back to the midday marriage deadline question, Hope,' I said. 'I really think you should ignore it. If you truly love each other then no "married by midday" time limitation will stop you being wed.'

'And besides,' said Soula, 'we're gaining extra hours by crossing time zones as we head back home. So basically we could land before we left.'

I suggested Hope call Aspen to confirm what time they planned to land back home.

'I can't ring Aspen!' said Hope in horror. 'It will look like I'm desperate!'

Then we had a quick discussion about whether or not this would look desperate and decided it would, because it is. So Hope didn't contact Aspen and now she's just a blubbering mess.

8.15 AM
I have no idea what day it is.
It might be yesterday.

Hello Diary,

We're still flying. The others have now returned to their seats and their sprawled positions. I'm still sitting upright on full alert and Mum is still sleeping on the floor.

Soula's just cried, 'Great news!' Her utterance has me totally fearful because she's the kind of person who thinks that 'two for the price of one' is great news even if you didn't want any in the first place.

'I've been receiving some psychic messages,' she said. 'The guides have shown me visions. The first was four doves flying out of a box. Two were merrily carrying a flowing evening gown between them in their beaks, and the other two, somewhat more cumbersomely, were each carrying a fancy shoe.'

'Oh God my,' whispered Bosom. 'This exactly is happened wedding my number three. The dress pink orgasma, which like organza but wipe it clean can you. And on my feet wore I work beets.'

'You mean work boots,' I said helpfully.

'No, beets, you know like beetroots, I wore them on my feet with fancy laces.'

'Oh what a brilliant idea,' said Thilma excitedly.

'My second vision,' roared Soula in a weird ghost voice, presumably in order to regain control. 'My second vision is a celebration. I see everyone on a roof garden, drinking bubbly liquid from glass wine balloons that have flowers floating joyfully inside them (mine also has a dead bee). I see Nora alive and recovered and revelling in the attention of the common people around her who seem to find her endlessly fascinating and hilarious.'

'Are you sure it's Nora?' asked Grandma as she lounged in her seat like a bloke.

'Yes, I'm sure. And now,' Soula is persevering. 'I can see Joy taking a selfie with Oprah Winfrey but she doesn't look very happy.'

'But I love Oprah,' I gasped.

'It has nothing to do with the selfie, Joy,' said Soula, 'nobody at the gathering is looking happy. They're all looking at the bride.'

'Oh my God,' Hope interrupted in a rather typical vain, self-obsessed way, which by the way it is OK for me to say because I am her sister and I love her (Hi Hope, if you ever read this). Now where was I? Oh yes …

'Oh my God,' said Hope. 'What am I wearing. Do I look terrible?'

'Um,' Soula said, 'well, if you imagined the traditional costume of *The Handmaid's Tale* and then added a veil.'

'Ah yes, a handmaid's veil?' said Thilma.

'Is it flattering?' Hope is asking.

'Well,' Soula is umming and ahing, 'To be honest, it is hiding your best features – like your neck, your arms, your legs, your body and your head. But if it makes you feel any better your mother looks like a serviette in a Chinese restaurant that's been folded to look like a dead swan.'

'That sounds about right,' said Hope.

'Hope,' I said, 'Ssssh. Mum might be able to hear you.'

'Good,' said Hope.

'Good?' I said. 'Do you really want Mum to be weakened by your words?'

'I say these things to make her stronger,' Hope replied.

'My God, Hope,' I said, 'you sound like Mum *and* Grandma.'

'And you,' Hope replied, 'sound like a doormat.'

8.35 AM

The plane's just landed back in our home city. Looking through the window I can see the ambulance arriving. The flight was incredibly quick, much faster than even anticipated. I asked the flight attendant if the tail wind was unusually strong and she replied, 'Yeah and nah, but this time the pilot also released the handbrake.'

IN THE AMBULANCE

Hope is writing this!
(which is totally wrong because it's supposed
to be my wedding day.)
March 28 (yes, my wedding day!)
8.55 AM

Dear Diary,

I'm in the ambulance with Mum, Joy and Grandma. Mum's in the ambulance because she's still passed out. Joy's in the ambulance because she's sucking up to Mum. I'm in here because I'm very kind. And Grandma's in here because she felt like a sleep.

My name is Hope. But there's probably no need to introduce myself. I am my mother's second favourite daughter.

Mum and I really should get along. We used to. I don't know what happened. Well I kind of do. But I definitely think that everything could start to be perfect once again if Mum just made one apology, just one dream apology for absolutely everything she's ever done in my life. I'm kind of hoping that this may occur here in the ambulance, while Mum recovers from her placebo overdose and has her defences down.

I don't know if Mum knows how much I'd love her to reach out to me. Sometimes I think I'm like a dog that growls when it really just wants to be patted.

I'm not really ready to say sorry 'cause while I know that I've hurt Mum over these years, I didn't know what else to do. Joy says I should say sorry if Mum says sorry because that would be polite.

But the thing is I can't be the first one to say sorry. My sorry is smaller than Mum's so I need Mum to say it first. I need her to spread it out before us like a big picnic rug of sorry, and then I can help smooth it out as it lies on the lawn, by saying 'I'm sorry too'. Actually I'll probably just say 'ditto'.

Mum will say, 'I'm sorry for absolutely everything,' and I will wait a bit, one, two, three and then I will say, 'Ditto.' And then Mum will learn and she will change and everything between us will be good again.

So, um, I think I'll be quite good at writing in you, Dear Diary. The writing might be a bit messy, but it'll be reliable, because I'm really used to keeping a diary. In a clichéd display of adolescent behaviour I kept a diary throughout my teenage years. The early years started with detailed descriptions of my teenage torment and the final years finished with somewhat excellent cartoon drawings of penises (not dissimilar to the ones Grandma draws, in fact I think it was her pals Vera and Babs who were the ones who taught us all how to draw them).

But enough about me, because Grandma and Joy have both told me, in a rather bullying way, that you, Ms Diary, are not about me (even though you are) and that I'm to write in you for Mum's sake. So let's talk about Mum.

First I should probably tell you how I feel about Mum's placebo-induced near-death experience/sleep. Rest assured, I do not feel frightened or worried. Mum has conquered far greater monsters in life than slumber.

So how do I feel? I feel angry. And, after years of watching Dr Phil, I know what he would say about this. He'd say I'm angry 'cause I'm scared that if she's not strong, she won't be there to look after me. And he's probably right.

I constantly want Mum near, yet far. So I'm going to think about Aspen instead and why I haven't heard from him.

Meanwhile Joy is sitting by Mum's feet and focusing on repelling the male paramedic. He seems to be adoring her, so he no doubt has some form of brain damage.

Only weirdos are attracted to Joy. I'd worry about her suitors but they never last long. I guess because she out weirds them. And also because she doesn't know how to have an equal relationship. If she's not running around doing everything for everyone, which is completely emasculating, even if you're not masculine in the first place, then she doesn't know what role to play. When we were young, and Mum was at work, Joy often used to run around doing everything for me. Everyone thinks that Grandma did it with Vera and Babs, and to be fair they did, until about 5 pm each afternoon when they'd open the cask wine and get into the drinking. So Joy picked up when they faded away, usually around 5.15 pm each day.

Joy never talks about this. But having to be so big when she was really so little must have been really hard and probably gave her all her issues, that are deep and hidden and way less obvious than just her terrible dress sense.

Sometimes I want to thank her for looking after me when I was little. But I'm worried that if I say thank you that will sound like a full stop. You know like 'thank you for your assistance, you are free to go now.' But I don't want her to stop looking after me. And I don't ever want her to go. And that's why I don't say thank you.

Just out of interest, and to prove my point, Joy is now checking Mum's ankle pulse with the paramedic's equipment. It's not that she thinks she knows better than everyone, or thinks she does things better or anything like that (and if she did she'd be deluded, because she doesn't) – it's just that she seems to think that if she's not making a fuss and looking after everyone then she serves no purpose, and has no use, and therefore will not be liked, or even wanted, so will be abandoned at the first opportunity.

She's currently checking the paramedic's pulse. I'll be surprised if this relationship lasts as long as the trip to the hospital.

I'm sure Mum will be OK, so maybe we should take Joy and the paramedic's relationship to the hospital instead. Mind you, people can be surprising. Maybe these two are the perfect fit. I know that Aspen and I are not. I mean, I pretend we are, 'cause I really want a family of my own.

Thilma reckons finding a partner has nothing to do with love at all. She says that it's like musical chairs and when the music stops you just grab whatever's free. Maybe that's why Aspen grabbed me.

Mum's just lying here. The paramedic says she's sleeping, but because I'm not sure if he's an idiot, I'm performing my own tests on Mum by squeezing her nose with my fingers. My intention is to wake her up but if this ambulance has CCTV, it'll look like I'm trying to kill her. But then again, anyone who is a daughter will know that our actions often belie our feelings for our mums because we don't know what our feelings really are.

I confess I don't know what my feelings are for my mum. I need to have space to discover who I am. But I like to know she's not far away.

The past few hours are probably the most confronting I've ever had in terms of considering life without Mum. I mean if she died right now the main thing I'd care about is that if she'd lived longer we might have rebuilt our relationship. I've been waiting for four years for Mum to stop seeing me as a baby, a child, a sickly daughter and to finally see me for who I am. I suspect she's starting to. So if Mum died right now it would be like watching a really magnificent butterfly die minutes after it emerged from its chrysallis cocoon thing.

Oh, Mum's just started to mumble. I hope she's saying 'sorry'. I wonder if she can sense what I've been thinking. When I was a child Mum always knew what I was thinking. And I used to know what she was thinking, too; by the way she tightened her mouth or swallowed food without chewing or rubbed her wedding ring finger where presumably her wedding ring used to be. But now it's like we're not tuned into the same radio station. It's like we're not tuned into each other at all. I'm so confused about life and me and Mum it's possible I'm interfering with our transmissions.

But maybe that's why I ran toward Aspen. We met in a village in Greece. I was there for a job on the island and had no idea that he was there to buy it – buy the island that is. He came into the bar where I was serving and made me laugh and made me dance and made me the centre of his world. I didn't realise at the time there was actually no one else in his world, other than his parents and their hired help.

But even if I had, I doubt I would have cared. When Aspen asked me to marry him I suddenly felt like I had purpose – a future, the chance to build my very own family, which I could invite my mother into, under my own terms and conditions. It didn't occur to me that, having known Aspen for only five weeks, I didn't know him well enough to get married. And as it turns out, I didn't know him at all. Soula says you never really know someone until you divorce them. I guess I thought traveller's diarrhoea could provide the same insights.

I'm a bit worried why Aspen hasn't answered my call. God, I hope he hasn't done something stupid and is too embarrassed to speak to me. The last text I got from him, sent from their jet, said that he loves me and that makes me totally fear the worst! Because Aspen only says, 'I love you,' when he's totally fucked something up.

9.08 AM

The paramedic has heard Mum mumbling and just told me to make myself useful and write down everything she says in case it helps with her diagnosis and recovery. I think he just wants to keep me occupied and distracted from his courting of my sister, Beelzebub.

It's too late anyway. We're pulling up to the hospital now. The staff are running toward us and racing to get Mum inside.

Joy is talking to her new boyfriend. 'Why is everyone running? Is Mum's case worse than you thought?' And her new boyfriend is soothingly replying, 'No, we've just heard word of a major crash and they want insignificant cases like your mum fixed up before the accident victims arrive.'

And I thought, 'Insignificant? That word won't fly with Joy. I give the relationship three more minutes maximum.'

9.12 AM

I bent down to kiss Mum, before she's taken away.

She smelt like home.

9.15 AM

Joy's just leapt out of the ambulance, run to Mum's trolley, shoved the porters out of the way and begun to push Mum toward the hospital entrance at lightning speed like they're in some weird new event at the Olympics.

I plan to walk Grandma into the hospital shortly after I wake her. But first I'm going to try and contact Aspen one more time, in case I lose reception when we're inside.

30 seconds later

I couldn't get through. His phone didn't even ring. Aspen never, ever turns his phone off. Oh my God, this is terrible. Maybe he's blocking my calls!

CITY CENTRAL HOSPITAL

Hellllooooooo
My nAMe is Daphne!!!
9.59 and a half AM
March 28

Hello Dear Diary, it's Daphne here. Nora's mum. I'm writing in you from the posh people's waiting room inside the hospital.

You and I met a long time ago Mr Diary. I was there on the day that Thilma gave you as a gift in the maternity ward – twenty-five years ago, just after little Hope was born. It was a truly terrible day full of fear and anguish. It was me who hid you from Nora. It was me who smuggled you home in a plastic bag, with just a smudge of transparent red mucus on your top right-hand corner. It was me who tucked you away for safe-keeping till Nora found you and put you in her Treasure Box.

We actually met a few days ago too, Dear Diary. You were with Nora, in a tussle between her and Hope, and I ended up with you in my hot little hands and digested your contents and yet pretended that I hadn't. I did a speed-reading course in the late seventies when they were all the rage, so I've read all the secrets you hold. And I know that Nora will read this diary entry, too.

So Nora, let me write here what I cannot say. I love you. I think you're funny and smart and brave and kind. And while I'm being completely honest, I also think you could lose two or three kilos from your bottom.

I've taken over writing in you because Hope had to stop.

Hope walked me from the ambulance and when we entered the hospital it was abuzz in preparation for receiving crash victims. A news flash on the TV announced Aspen's family jet had crashed into an airport hangar. There are many injured crew from the hangar and optimism remains for only one survivor from the jet, a man presumed to be the pilot. But we don't know if Aspen was flying the plane. He said he was going to, and apparently has a licence, but maybe he was lying and just trying to impress. I once dated a man who called himself a pilot but he was really just a massage therapist with a hat on.

After the news flash, and Hope's subsequent asthma attack, the hospital realised that we're associated with the Van den der Roths, so we've been moved to a private room. It's a bit more posh than the waiting room we were in a few days ago after my fall. This one has carpet and chairs with fabric on them and a big tinted glass wall to let you see the outside world, yet not let them see you.

Hope is lying down with her body draped over two chairs and her tussled-haired head resting on my lap. I understand her pain. As much as I think Aspen is an arse, my dead husband, Nora's father, was a total arse too so I know how alluring that can be – because even an arsehole is nice sometimes – and those times shine much brighter than they really are – when compared to the normal super shit bits in between.

Apparently Nora is OK. In fact the sleep has done her good. I must remember to invoice her for the 'calming tablets'.

Nora is presently in Recovery right now. This means it's my job to make Hope feel safe as she lies across my lap. I'm currently comforting her by patting her head with my right elbow because I'm using both my hands to write in you, Dear Diary.

I'm determined to write in you for two simple reasons. The first is that I need the distraction, because I'm the head of the family and with everything about us falling in disarray I cannot, cannot, cannot fall apart myself.

Of course I'm worried sick about Hope and Aspen. I'm worried for Hope that Aspen will die, and I'm worried that he'll survive.

As I write, I can see Joy is over by the door, wearing a hi-vis vest and supervising the manoeuvres of the Emergency Services. Soula and Thilma and the others haven't arrived yet. I'm not surprised. They all mean well but they're thick as bricks. Leonard's car was at the airport, and they planned to drive here in that, so they've either got caught in the traffic, or gone to the wrong hospital or got lost walking from the hospital car park to its foyer.

The second reason why I'm writing in you, Dear Diary, is because everyone else has had a go at writing in you and I want to have a go at writing too. It's not that I particularly like writing. I don't like it at all. It's just that I don't like to miss out and I feel like I always miss out. I missed out on having a loving husband and I missed out on having two loving daughters, and now I miss out on having a drink at Happy Days! I mean it's not my fault Santa's such a hottie.

I missed out on having a career too because women didn't have careers when I was young. They were meant to have babies instead. And I missed out on being a hands-on mum because my husband left me and I had to go out and work. I missed out on putting my children to sleep at night and I missed out on giving Nora a happy childhood because, even as the youngest child, she was my only surviving girl, so she mothered her brothers when I was at work. From the age of five she cooked and cleaned and washed their clothes. Not well, but nonetheless she did it.

I tried to make up for my lack of mothering by being a fantastic grandma when the girls were growing up. But the difference is that Vera and Babs and I had fun with the girls. We loved helping to raise them. In contrast, I am pretty sure that Nora hated every minute of raising her brothers.

I don't know why her brothers never show an appreciation for her efforts; indeed they seem to go out of their way not to acknowledge them. It's almost like they resent her. Maybe it's a boy thing. Maybe it's a brother thing. Maybe it's brothers treating their sister like she's their mother. But maybe it's my fault. Maybe I encouraged the boys to ignore Nora's input, because if they were to acknowledge *her* mothering then I would have to acknowledge it too and that would make me feel like an even bigger failure of a mother than I already do.

Sometimes I wish I could say sorry to her for that. But that's not really what my generation do. We toughen up our kids for their own good. That's why we never say sorry to them yet demand they say sorry to us.

I wish I could have comforted Nora sometimes. But I couldn't. I wasn't raised like that, to show emotion. I was raised to do exactly the opposite. Emotions in my day were seen as an indulgence. People who showed them were weak. Even to this day I don't show my excitement at popping in to Nora's place for a Whine and Wine. I mean, I show my excitement but I pretend it's about the wine. But really, it's Nora I'm excited to see.

I'm worried now that as I age I'll never be able to tell her this. Every day I feel words slipping away from me. And I'm losing memories too. The recent ones. Not the old ones. Sometimes I can't remember what we're talking about right now, but I remember what I wore on the first day of school when I was five years old and I can feel how my new shoes pressed against my toes. It's as though the past is calling me from so far away, like sirens luring a boat to the rocks. For a long time I fought it, like I had a choice; I could choose to be in the present or drawn to the past. I used to make a conscious effort to keep my mind in the here and now. But now I don't seem to have that control, so I no longer have the choice. And even if I did, I doubt I'd choose to face the here and now of my own decay when my mind can reside in a happier place with my mother and the beetroot jam we made and the milk being delivered in a cart and the first dance I went to in the church hall, when I was fifteen, and everyone said I looked so pretty and was the life of the party.

Oh, I have to stop writing now, I can see Nora approaching. She's with a nurse. She must be much better now. Nora looks strong. Just like me. And just like my mother who by the way was an absolute pain in the arse.

I don't know what to do with all the words I've just written.

Part of me wants them to be read by Nora. Part of me wants to eat them.

CITY CENTRAL HOSPITAL

9.47 AM
March 28

Dear Diary,

Hello, it's Nora here. I'm back. I'm in the posh waiting room with Mum and Hope. Mum just told me she's been writing in you, Dear Diary, but when I took a look at the page there was no writing at all – just a stick figure of a pony.

But I can see that Joy and Hope have written in you. I'm curious to know what they wrote, but terrified it will hurt. So, in a rather masculine style of dealing with things, I'm going to ignore it all and just keep focused on what's here and now which is a waiting room filled with still air and contained fear.

Anyway, my 'condition' has been assessed as a sugar high low. And as a result of ingesting so many placebos I've been diagnosed as 'a greedy little piglet'. The nurse who walked me here told me she eats lots of lollies but hers have artificial sweetener. She also told me about the plane crash. She told me while she was checking my pulse. It was a rather strange thing to do now I think about it, you know, tell me about a plane crash while I was recovering from an anxiety-induced situation on a plane. But apparently it didn't add any trauma to me at all. In fact, quite the opposite.

'My God,' she said, 'I thought the news would make you stressed but your pulse has lowered!'

Yes, the nurse was surprised that I calmed at the news of the crash. But I wasn't surprised. The crash gives me permission to mother Hope through this dreadful time. And being a mum is my happy place to be.

Thilma and Soula and the gang aren't in the posh waiting room with us yet but I can see them through the tinted window. They're trying to get inside. Like Mum, Hope, Joy and myself they're all still wearing their airplane bathrobes and matching fluffy slippers, except for Soula, who's still in her teddy.

In the melee of media, security and police who've gathered outside the hospital for news of the crash, one might mistake our bunch for either surgeons post scrub, or patients from the psych ward. There is no way on earth you'd assume they were the friends and family of anyone associated with the power and wealth of the Van den der Roths.

Even through the tinted glass wall I can hear the chaos of outside. The wail of the police and ambulance sirens, the pounding feet of nurses, doctors and orderlies as they push rattling trolleys draped with all the poor individuals whom the Van den der Roth jet ploughed into.

Through the tinted glass I can also see the police are stopping the media from entering this building. They're also stopping everyone who's not medical staff. I wonder if Jack is there with the police. I hope he is and I hope he isn't. I wish I had someone in the world to look after me. But I also wish I didn't wish this. It's not a good thing to become reliant on someone, because you're left too weak when they leave or die.

Anyway, through the tinted glass I can also see that hi-vis Joy has somehow acquired a 'stop and go' traffic sign. I wonder if she's going to try and smuggle our gang in here past the police. She must be in a bit of a quandary. Joy's always loved to abide by the rules, but she also abides by 'family'. I imagine making that choice could be the most confronting thing she's had to face since her beloved Harry and Meghan left her beloved Royal Family.

9.55 AM

We're all in the waiting room now. The gang was finally allowed to enter after telling the police they're the loved ones of the Van den der Roths' fiancée. This begged the question why they didn't mention their connection to the Van den der Roths earlier. 'We were too embarrassed,' said Thilma, 'because the Van den der Roths are such dicks.'

'Thilma!' Joy admonished. 'That's not a nice thing to say.'

'Oh, sorry,' Thilma replied solemnly. 'I should have said *were* such dicks.'

Together we feng shui'd all the chairs in the posh waiting room and now we're sitting and facing each other in two rows. We're waiting for news regarding the survivor. Though they've brought the pilot here to this hospital we still don't know if the pilot is Aspen.

Booby is crying. I've never seen her cry before. Leonard is kindly comforting her, which to be honest is even stranger. Hope is still lying across two seats with her head in my mum's lap. Joy is sitting on the floor in front of her and I'm seated next to Mum. All three of us are patting Hope. Like cookie-cut images of one another we're all patting and staring into space.

And I'm also writing. Thilma is hugging Soula, who is quietly mumbling a prayer. Or I think she's mumbling a prayer; she's not speaking English so for all I know she's muttering a curse. To comfort us, Eduardo has bought every single item from the vending machine. And now he's methodically unwrapping them and eating them all himself.

'Aren't you being a bit selfish eating all that?' Joy asked.

'No, I'm not,' Eduardo replied. 'I'm actually doing you all a favour by preventing you from getting fat.'

10.23 AM

A doctor came in a few minutes ago and said he hoped to have a pilot update very soon. He told us he heard that the jet crashed while attempting to land at the airport. Then he looked at Hope, worried about her condition, and asked a nurse to take her for some tests.

10.42 AM

Oh my God, Alcoq's arrived. He's both flushed and ashen at the same time and his toupee is covering the side of his head like one massive ear muff but, considering we all thought he died in the crash, he's looking relatively fantastic.

Despite the fact he's still wearing his parachute Alcoq's entered, said nothing, draped himself over Hope's vacated chairs and laid his head in my mother's lap. The rest of us watched aghast, waiting for him to speak.

'With the passing of Mr and Mrs Van den der Roth,' he finally whimpered to Mum, 'I now have no one. Will you please adopt me?'

'Don't you dare! Get off her lap,' I spat, lifting him by his parachute straps. 'My mother already has too many sons.'

'But Mr and Mrs Van den der Roth were like my family. Albeit I was an employee, working long hours for minimal pay, in the glorious tradition of many a rich empire but nonetheless,' he sobbed, 'I know, I'm pathetic, I need help. Would you consider adopting me, Nora?'

'I *can't* adopt you,' I said. 'You're legally an adult.'

'Actually,' he replied, 'as the only lawyer present at present it behoves me to tell you that I could argue the case that while *women* become adults at eighteen years of age, men mature much, much later. In fact some never mature at all.'

I said nothing.

'Maybe if Aspen's dead,' he continued like a dog with a bone, or a lawyer with a voice, 'maybe if Aspen's dead then I could marry Hope?' I didn't respond and instead signalled Mum to talk to me in the corner. As planned, in the process of Mum rising from her chair to stand, Alcoq fell off her lap and onto the floor.

'We need to talk about Hope,' I said to Mum, as she and I hovered in the strangely dusty corner of the posh waiting room that the cleaner obviously can't quite reach.

'As much as I didn't want Hope to marry Aspen,' I confided, 'I didn't want their relationship to end with a horrific plane crash!'

'I know,' said my mother. 'It's so much better for a relationship to end because one's realised their partner is a fuckwit. The very worst thing is for a relationship to end at full bloom, abruptly through disaster, because it gets snap frozen at its best. I think you know what I mean, Nora, 'cause that's what happened to you with Jack.'

11.42 AM

We're still all sitting here waiting and waiting. Nothing much at all has changed though Alcoq has recovered with remarkable speed and has now joined Eduardo in eating all the treats. They seem to have formed a bond. As they eat they're discussing their struggles with weight gain.

12.51 PM

Joy has come inside now and sat down with our group. She's taking photos of us but she isn't posting them. This is entirely unlike her. I realise as I notice this that, as usual, I haven't kept an eye on Joy at all and have focused my attentions on Hope. In my defence Joy has always been such a bossy-boots; it rarely occurs to me that she might need mothering.

'Joy,' I called out, across our group, 'I love you.'

And Joy stared at me and then began to giggle – with total and utter delight.

1.13 PM

Oh thank God! Hope's just come back.

'How did the tests go?' Joy asked Hope.

'Fine,' said Hope. And that lit our Joy's fuse.

'We're here,' Joy said with uncharacteristic outrage, 'stuck in a hospital amidst death and trauma, broke and broken waiting to hear if your meathead fiancé is going to live to haunt us forever after our lives have already been on pause for you for four whole years and your answer to my question regarding tests that removed you from this room for in excess of three and a half hours is FINE?'

'Yes, Joy, my answer is F-I-N-E fine,' spelt Hope. 'And just for the record nobody asked you to put your life on hold. If you suffered it was your choice.'

'What are you talking about?' said Joy. 'I'm your sister!'

'I have two things to say to that,' said Mum authoritatively. 'When you love someone it can both limit and expand you. And, well, there you go.'

'Actually, Hope, I'd like to say something,' interrupted Thilma. 'I forbid you to speak so horribly to Joy. I mean for Gods' sake, she's your sister, not your mother.'

'What?' I said.

'The role of sisters is not to fight with one another, but to band together and fight against their mother.'

'Why?' I peeped.

'It's to, well, it's to …' muttered Thilma.

'I'll tell you why,' interrupted Mum, reaching for a bag of Eduardo's chips and alternately dividing her 100 per cent attention between its contents and the speech she was about to deliver. 'Mothers and daughters are biologically programmed to fight in order to force separation and cut the bond,' she began, before being distracted by one of those chips that looks like it's kind of folded. 'This is because a mother's natural instinct is to sacrifice her life for her children.' She took another chip and stopped speaking in order to chew the chip unbelievably slowly. 'But there comes a time when her job is done, when her children are adults, and she must rebuild a life of her own.' Mum now lost interest in the packet, screwed it into a ball and threw it over her left shoulder, presumably for good luck. 'The adult children must also build a life of their own. So the children, logically, must find fault with their mother and in turn become as revolting as possible so that their mother has no choice but to abandon them, and in so doing discover her new self.' Mum's continuing to speak, increasingly like a sermonising preacher, but has now resumed rummaging through the other treats on the table, selecting one after the other, and throwing them over her left shoulder. 'And only then, when the mother has had the space to restructure herself as a strong and independent being, will she be allowed back in the fold, to be embraced as the truly extraordinary woman she is, with all the skills and confidence necessary to care for her grandchildren, for free.'

1.27PM

A news bulletin is flashing on the TV. It's being broadcast from the hospital car park. On the other side of our waiting room's glass wall the reporter has announced that all living victims, from both the plane and the airport, have been brought to this hospital and there are no more bodies to be accounted for. In contrast to his solemnity the assembled crowd of exuberant onlookers is photobombing the live broadcast.

'Mum, Mum!' Joy just blurted. 'Look at the TV, it's Jack!'

Oh my God he *is* here. He looks like he's intentionally in the shot. He's not in uniform. My God he dresses badly, like a fat shearer in a sack. Who knew I'd find that look alluring?

He's holding a sign. He's trying to get it on camera. He's actually being a bit of a public nuisance. If he doesn't behave he'll have to arrest himself. Problem is, for all his effort his sign is illegible, it's just a series of dashes and dots.

'Oh, that is so mortifying,' said Hope. 'Is he accidentally holding his sign backwards?'

'What a tool,' added Joy. 'Mum, you have to ditch him! Now the sign's creeping in front of the reporter's face!'

'No no, sign in code morse,' interrupted Booby, 'my national language! Translate I you for?'

'Oh, that's a good idea,' said Mum to Booby. 'Then we'll just need someone to translate you.'

'Sign say,' persevered Booby, '"I tried ringing you but no reception."'

Oh the reporter has furiously grabbed the sign and hurled it like a frisbee out of shot. Jack is still standing there.

'He's mouthing a message,' said Soula.

'I'll handle this.' said Leonard. 'I'm a man − I speak bloke.' There was a very long pause during which we all respectfully waited for Leonard to speak and prayed to God he didn't say something stupid. 'He's saying,' said Leonard with tremendous pride, '"I'm gonna fun ma weeny forya."'

'Actually,' said the nurse who's just entered the room and glanced at the TV, 'he's saying, "I'm going to find my way in for you."'

1.32 PM

Our doctor has just reappeared. He looks tired and earnest as he speaks. 'Well, I have good news and I have bad news. Which news would you like first?' None of us is replying. 'The good news is that I am now free to announce that the pilot has survived and his name is Aspen Van den der Roth.'

'Oh, thank God,' we all gasped and burst into tears, inconsolably for some minutes.

'And you can visit him in the Very Important Patient Suite.'

'Thank you, your Highness,' said Joy as she curtseyed and we all rose to find the Very Important Patient Suite.

'But before you go,' said the doctor, blocking our way, 'there is also some really bad news, which I would have mentioned a minute or so ago but you all seemed to deal with the good news so badly, that I was scared of telling you. Nonetheless the bad news is that while Aspen has survived the plane crash and is alive … we doubt he will make it through the night.'

And now we're all running, yes, all running to comfort Hope in the room with Aspen and I must say it's rather difficult to keep writing.

'I'm going to have to stop writing,' I wheezed as we ran.

'I forbid it,' my mother replied, 'we need it now more than ever!'

THE VERY IMPORTANT PATIENT SUITE

1.35 PM

Dear Diary,

This room is very different to the hospital room Mum shared at City Central. For a start it has no other occupants, and it has windows that open and seduce with the possibility of fresh air, even when they're closed, like they are now. It also has a lot of medical staff, doctors and nurses – and, and a man of indeterminate purpose who's wearing a hospital mask, a surgical hairnet and a white coat that's so small he looks like he's been shrink-wrapped in it. And over there, in the full kit of professional security guards, is that the Cardigan Couple?

Despite the stress, Mum's holding herself together. We all are. In fact we're behaving so well I think we look kind of suspicious. The majority of us, including me, has no clue what to do at a time like this. I've never been in this situation before and it's not the kind of thing you learn in Etiquette Class at Congregatta Primary School where we focused on 'not slagging in the street'.

So we initially took the lead from Joy. We did this because she ordered us to despite the fact her only leadership qualification is an online course she recently took to become a volunteer librarian and her only experience of maintaining a bedside vigil is from a recent viewing of *The Godfather*. So, under Joy's leadership, we entered the room, no longer running, in single file with our heads bowed. And when we'd gathered around Aspen's bed, we did that Catholic 'Father, Son and Holy Ghost cross yourself thing' which as non-Catholics we have no idea how to do, so half of us looked like we were shooing a fly and the other half like we were performing the opening of Madonna's 'Vogue' dance routine.

1.37 PM

Soula's just taken charge and whispered, 'Follow my lead,' and touched Aspen's hand. 'My mother and father died in a war. I'm unfortunately very familiar with what to do around dying people.'

And so now we're all touching Aspen. It's actually hard to find space to make contact on his skin because it's covered in splints, bandages, metal frames and strapping. And it's also quite hard to keep writing. But I'm touching his left hand with mine. His is a nice hand, I guess. But it has no character. Well, it does now because of the blood and the massive bruising, but it's the kind of perfect, never-done-a-day's-hard-work hand that could have belonged to a mannequin.

Looking at Aspen, lying there with his eyes closed, attached to machines like fridges on wheels, a brace on his neck, drips in his arms, Hope begins to cry. Tears flow silently from her eyes in rivulets. And as I watch her pain I cry silently too.

And now the dams have broken and my tears turn to sobs and my sobs turn to gasps as all the pain and loneliness and self-doubt and self-loathing spew from me in a furball of grief.

I cry for my life. I cry for us all. I cry for the human condition that is at once so full of self-importance and at the same time so fearful and weak. And as I cry I hear the sobs of others, of all those around me, the nurses, the Cardigan Couple, the doctors in scrubs, my friends, my relatives. Eduardo my boss is gasping so hysterically they've attached him to a ventilator machine. And I can still hear him sob.

We're all crumbling. All save for the guy in the very tight coat. He's stepped forward and yet is holding back. He looks like a sentinel, refusing to succumb to his emotions. Watching us unflinchingly, protecting us all, like a dad. Actually what the hell am I saying! He's protecting us like a mum.

1.42 PM

Soula just started to wail so loudly that it set the smoke alarm off. And that's caused Aspen to open his eyes.

He's looking at my mother and saying softly, slowly, 'Are you my wife?' And Mum just said, 'Yes I am'.

He's closed his eyes. Machines are beeping like birds at dawn. Nurses and doctors have rushed to his side. They're checking his vitals, recalibrating machines, they're injecting him with something

267

and then something else. We're waiting, we're waiting, we're waiting and now he's opened his eyes again.

'Aspen, Aspen,' Hope is saying, carefully, politely leaning toward him as though introducing herself for the very first time. 'I'm Hope and I'm here, holding your hand.'

'Oh my beautiful Hope. Hello. Nice dress.'

'Do you know what's happened?' Hope's asking gently.

'Are we married?' Aspen's whispered.

'No, not yet. There was a problem with my mum taking drugs.'

'Oh that's no reason not to marry. My mum takes drugs all the time.' And now Aspen's looking at the faces surrounding him and slowly, almost incomprehensibly, muttering, 'Where is my mother by the way?'

'Um,' faltered Hope.

'Um,' said Thilma, 'She's gone to be with the great gods in the sky.'

'Stoned again?' asked Aspen.

'No, dead,' said my mum.

A machine's started to beep.

Now it's stopped.

'Well, I guess it's OK she's dead,' Aspen's mumbling. 'She didn't seem to enjoy life anyway.'

'I'm so sorry,' says Hope. 'I wish I could make everything OK for you.'

'You can,' Aspen's saying in obvious pain, 'let's get married now.'

'We can't,' I've interjected, softly, stepping forward and putting my arm around Hope. 'You're in a hospital, Aspen, you've survived a terrible accident.'

'All the more reason to get married.' Aspen's smiling, his voice soft and weak. 'Don't you agree, my Hope?'

'Um,' Hope stumbled. 'Um,' and her uncertainty's making Aspen panic. His attached machines are beeping, buzzing, sounding sirens. The nurses and doctors are rushing to his side but they cannot calm him. So now Alcoq's cutting a swathe through them all and saying, 'As everyone's lawyer and a member of both families I suggest, in order to save this man's life, that Aspen and Hope get married.'

2.15 PM

I'm still in the Very Important Patient Suite. The wedding's done, my daughter is married. As the mother of the new bride I've been offered a seat. It was the only one they could find in a rush. It's one you can sit on and use as a toilet.

It was a simple wedding, obviously. The bride stayed attired in the bathrobe she first donned on the jet, coupled with towelling slip-ons and the groom wore bandages and a hospital gown, coupled with four drips, and three monitors. He lay on the bed. She stood beside him. It was an intimate affair, with only twenty witnesses, about ten of whom I couldn't identify. The entire ceremony only took a few moments. Thilma performed it with a white pillowcase on her head, for no real reason other than 'wearing white takes years off your face'. No one objected to the nuptials. Joy took photos and posted the lot; with all of us dressed in either bathrobes or scrubs smilingly surrounding a bandaged body in a bed. We look like the cast of a really odd porn movie.

Thilma announced Hope and Aspen to be 'husband and wife', and Hope somehow kissed Aspen amidst all that gauze. Then Aspen took a very, very long time to exhaustingly say, 'I'd like to make a small speech.'

He held pinky fingers with Hope, looked into her eyes and slowly, very slowly said, 'This has been without doubt the greatest moment of my life.'

Tears fell from his eyes. Mum unearthed her emergency mini cask of moselle from her handbag and took a swig. She passed it to Hope with the words, 'Take a chug, wifey,' and the nurse who'd performed Hope's tests only an hour before, stepped forward with gusto and knocked the cask from Hope's hand.

'You can't drink!' she bellowed. 'You're pregnant!'

'I'm pregnant!' said Grandma, 'now I really need a drink.'

Aspen smiled happily and his machines went off in a cacophony of beeps, and the doctors and nurses rushed to his aid, and the security guards tried to push us from the room. But Hope refused to go, and I stayed with her. I got knocked to the ground, and one of the men, the one in the white coat that was way too small, bent down and picked me up.

He's been standing over there as I write. And now I've finished for the moment he's just approached me and whispered, 'Come on, Nors, Aspen needs some rest. Let's get you and your Hope out of here.'

In HOPE AND ASPEN'S PENTHOUSE

About 20 weeks later
6.17 PM
August 12

Dear Diary,

We're in Hope and Aspen's apartment. Yes, they have a home. It's enormous. Hope bought it when we learnt that Aspen will be on life support forever. As his wife, and with Aspen's parents no longer with us, Hope became the sole executor of his inheritance.

Hope bought the penthouse on the top of my building. Its vastness was of course overwhelming at the time so Soula and Thilma offered to help make the penthouse more 'homey' and now it looks like a knitted airport lounge.

When the furnishing was complete Hope brought Aspen home from hospital to live here with her. She also hired a super strong, capable and grumpy female nurse called Miss Happy to reside in the penthouse and take care of Aspen. But then much to our, and indeed Hope's surprise, Hope discovered that she likes to care for Aspen herself so she moved Mum into the penthouse too and now Miss Happy helps look after Mum. Meanwhile Mum is convinced that Miss Happy is Dad so she alternately hates or tries to hit on her.

Joy lives in the penthouse too. The plan is she'll help Hope when the new baby arrives. As soon as the pregnancy was announced Joy designed a daily Baby Feeding and Bathing Schedule which they've now been rehearsing ever since.

Oh and Joy is dating Miss Happy.

And me? Well, I've also started painting again. I've just completed one in fact. When Thilma saw it she asked, 'Is it finished?' and Soula said, 'Oh I love puppy paintings!' I didn't have the heart to tell her it's actually a self-portrait.

I'm looking forward to the baby arriving. I'm hoping to be the world's greatest grandmother, along with my affiliates Thilma and Soula. Yes, we plan to feed all my grandchildren, bathe them, help with their homework, drive them everywhere, cuddle them, negotiate their fights, walk them to school, cook their dinner, discipline them, arrange their play dates, fearfully give them freedom, clean up after them, read them to sleep, dance with them, sing with them, dream with them, inspire and protect them. Basically we plan to do precisely what my mother and her pals did for Hope and Joy.

6.19 PM

We're in the living room. I'm looking at Aspen on his bed in the corner. He's attached to all his life support machines and he's attached to round-bellied Hope, who's holding his hand.

And I'm looking at Joy with Miss Happy, and Thilma teaching Mum how to knit a scarf for the neighbour's cat, and Leonard and

Booby and Eduardo and Soula all, actually what are they doing? Getting nits out of each other's hair?

For the first time in my life Mum looked at me today and said, 'I love you, Nora.' It made me happy and it made me sad. Because I suspect it's the dementia talking.

Anyway Hope is turning her head and now she's looking at me – with her green eyes and wonderful face framed by that wild sweet seaweed hair. And now she's staring. I can't read her expression. It's like she's waiting for me. She's ready for something. And so am I.

'I'm sorry,' I said, across the room to her, not actually speaking, just mouthing the words. 'I'm sorry for all the mistakes I made – the mistakes I made in mothering you. But my role as a mother is not over. It will last forever. I will do better. Starting now. So first let me say I'm sorry for the pain I caused you. I'm sorry for everything.'

And now Hope is smiling at me and mouthing her reply. She's saying. Actually I can't quite tell by the mouthing of the word. It begins with the letter 'd' I think. Is it 'dino,' 'diddo,' 'dit o'? Oh surely that's can't be right. Is Hope mouthing the word 'dildo'?

Now Hope's standing up and walking toward me. She's reaching for you Dear Diary and...

7 moments later

Hope held you and opened you and she found your last page and she took my pen and she wrote something, right there and then.

Now she's given you back to me, Dear Diary, and walking back to her seat. I'm nervous to see what she's written but curious of course, like a cat.

I moment later

Hope wrote, '**Thank you.**' And she signed it too – accidentally with my signature.

6.30 PM

Dear Diary,

I want to thank *you*. This is my final entry. I think I know now how to move forward.

The land of mother–daughter love is a diverse terrain. Replete with mountains and valleys and quicksand. It's a land where a strange language is spoken – where 'I love you so much' is often expressed as 'you look so much prettier when you tie your hair back'. It is at once a civil war, a financial relationship, a friendship and a romance.

And mother love? Well to me I guess it's like a tube of paint. The paint's pure inside the tube but the nozzle it flows through can make it blob, and spurt and splatter. And sometimes, if the tube is broken or torn, the paint also squishes out the sides. My love for my daughters is totally pure, but due to my own cracks and flaws it often splurts all over the place. I've decided not to just accept this. I've decided to try as hard as I can to fix those bits and make the love squirt purely. I'll no doubt still stuff up and make a mess – but I've got a better idea now of how to clean and plug it.

Motherhood is not what I expected. The mother myth would have you believe it's all about 'I love you, Mummy' but the truth is so much more. It's funny and sad and sometimes too hard and sometimes fills me with fear. But I would do it all again in a heart beat (though I might need a defibrillator).

My children are the loves of my life.

And now I must away, Dear Diary. Jack is taking me to a movie. It's our first date in thirty years.

We're going to see a Meg Ryan retrospective.

The End

THANK YOU

Thank you to my beautiful children, my sisters and mum, Albert, my dingbat friends, the ridiculously generous Tim Ferguson, the gifted Bert and Christa, my entire Hachette family – and my extraordinarily patient, hilarious and brilliant publisher, Vanessa Radnidge, without whom this novel would not exist (so it's all totally her fault). xx

Gretel Killeen is a best-selling author, artist, award-winning comedy writer and host of award-winning TV. She's appeared on stage, film and TV as a comedian and actress, worked as one of the nation's leading voice artists, written as a journalist for many of Australia's leading news publications, directed a documentary to raise awareness of AIDS orphans in Zambia and regularly appears on TV and radio as a social/political commentator.

If you would like to find out more about Hachette Australia, our authors, upcoming events and new releases you can visit our website or our social media channels:

hachette.com.au

HachetteAustralia

HachetteAus